BELOW THE MOUNTAIN

BELOW THE MOUNTAIN

NO EYE HAS SEEN BOOK 2

ROANNE L KING

Published by Roanne King
Boise, ID USA
https://roanneking.com/

ISBN-13: 9798594696464 (kdp print edition)

ISBN: 978-0-578-86217-0 (all other print)

ISBN: 9781393751182 (ebook)

DEDICATION

To my husband who has endured tragedy and triumph alongside me and is my partner for life.

PART 1

*"Remember ye not the former things, neither
consider the things of old.
Behold, I will do a new thing; now it shall spring
forth; shall ye not know it? I will even make a way
in the wilderness, and rivers in the desert."
Isaiah 43:18-19, KJV*

ONE

1906, February. Penn Valley, California

Dylan Prescot brought his horse, Bailey to a gallop. The exhilaration of cold air burning his lungs released the tension from a long day's work. Hooves crunched and thudded, sinking and rising in pits across a layer of frosty grass.

Upon spotting a figure walking along the road at the edge of the property, Dylan tightened the reins.

Could that be one of the new ranch hands arriving a day early? God knew he could use the help now. Hope tingled in his chest and he flipped the reins and knocked his heels into Bailey's side.

Dylan brought Bailey to a halt as they approached a man with a distinctly wide frame and steady gait. Pete Evan, one of the new hires, adjusted a satchel dwarfed over his broad shoulder before greeting Dylan and apologizing about his early arrival.

"Did you walk the whole way from Penn Valley?" A twinge of guilt settled. Dylan had not considered how Pete would make the journey from town. He should have thought to send a carriage.

Pete tipped his hat and nodded. He looked more than a weary traveler as he pulled a crumpled newspaper clipping from his vest and handed it to Dylan.

Dylan dismounted Bailey. He shook Pete's hand and then took the paper.

Pete removed his tattered bowler hat and hung his head. "I . . . I . . . come to work as promised, but I didn't feel right about waiting the extra day to bring word."

Dylan scanned the words on the paper and his hands began to shake.

```
    EMPIRE MINE ACCIDENT
    LEAVES ONE MAN DEAD


    1906, 13 February. Grass Val-
    ley. After nearly a year of ac-
    cident-free reports, a portion
    of wall caved in causing huge
    rocks to fall on working miners
    below. All crew members, except
    for supervising manager, Dan Lo-
    gan, survived without major in-
    jury...
```

No.

It couldn't be true. He read it again and shook his head as if doing so would cause the words to change. But they remained, the truth of them pressing so hard into Dylan's chest, he couldn't breathe.

Dan was dead?

Pete coughed violently into a soiled rag. "Excuse me." He cleared what sounded like pebbles from his throat. "Side-effect from ten years in the mines."

Dylan held back a grimace and swallowed hard. "I appreciate your effort to bring the news, Pete. I've known Dan since childhood." Lacking the strength to mount Bailey, Dylan grasped the reins and nodded toward the house. "I'll walk with you the rest of the way up to the house. My wife is dear friends with Hattie, Dan's wife. This news will be just as devastating to her. Do you know if a telegram was sent to French Corral yet?"

Pete shrugged. "I didn't wait to find out. Since you and Dan were friends and you likely wouldn't get word right away, I headed here as quickly as I could."

Pete's effort, though comforting, didn't do much to ease the shock of learning Dylan's lifelong friend was gone. If Lydia wasn't such close friends with Hattie, it would be easier to bear. Though he was uncertain about how she'd initially respond, his wife would insist on being a comfort to her friend in her time of mourning.

Lydia Prescot pulled the chicken and sweet potato casserole from the oven to cool. Moments later, a bitter breeze blew through the house between open windows, reminding her that winter wasn't finished yet. Sighing, Lydia raced through the house, closing windows before the heat from the stove escaped for the night.

She still wasn't used to the differences living in such a large house made with the changes of seasons. Yet, it was only one of many adjustments she'd learned to make in contrast to the simple life she'd lived alone with her mama in their small cabin in the Valley.

Glancing toward the barn through a kitchen window, the shadowed outline of a second man standing heads higher and twice the width of her husband caught her breath. She patted her chest to calm her beating heart as she realized the strange man must be one of the farmhands Dylan had hired the week prior.

Curious about why the farmhand had arrived early and why the two men walked ever so slowly as they seemed engrossed in a serious conversation, Lydia exited the side door to gather more firewood. Maybe she could catch a bit of their conversation as they approached the house.

Bark digging into the sleeves of her blouse, Lydia tiptoed to the corner of the wrap-around porch where side-by-side windows acted as both outer walls. She hid in the shadows and peered through glass walls to where the men stood near the kitchen door.

"This is too difficult to grasp. We never hear of accidents leading to injuries, let alone deaths." Dylan's voice strained between a whisper and a whine.

The other man loomed above Dylan by several inches. Broad shoulders and a wide stance took up the backside of the porch.

"I understand, Mr. Prescot. It's terrible news and unexpected."

When the deep voice echoed in the darkness, a twinge in Lydia's belly brought her back to the instant she'd first met Dylan in the forest.

Lydia stood as still as a post, trying not to let the porch boards squeak as she adjusted the logs in her arms. In the flicker of light from the kitchen window, Dylan's expression looked pained. His forehead wrinkled and his head hung as he spoke with his hat in his hands.

"Any word on contacting his family?" Dylan's voice rose.

The other man shook his head. "Sorry, Mr. Prescot . . . I didn't ask questions. I just made my way here as quickly as I could."

Dylan patted the man's back and looked up, a small, yet strained smile on his face. "Don't be sorry, Pete. I appreciate you making the effort. It will make it much easier for me to tell Lydia now—for her to hear it from me."

Tell me what?

Lydia braced herself and sucked in a shallow breath. What could this former miner possibly need her to know? They were speaking of a mine, of miners. The only miner she knew of any consequence was Dan Logan, her friend Hattie's husband.

A vision flashed in her mind of the last time she'd seen and interacted with Dan. He hadn't known she was behind the house, pulling laundry off the line for Hattie after reading and writing lessons with her mother-in-law, Jaina. When Lydia had heard Dan's booming voice from inside the cabin, her stomach turned. Coming to the window, she peered inside to glimpse Dan gripping Hattie by the hair at the back of her neck. Their daughter, Olive screamed in the corner, while their infant son, Brian, wailed in his baby buggy.

"How could you forget to order me coveralls? So long as you refuse to sew, I give ye plenty of allowance to ensure I'm properly clothed for work and whatever else ye aspire to do while I'm away."

"I-I didn't forget," Hattie hissed. "Orders only come through every other week now."

Dan released his grip on Hattie's hair and pushed her forward.

"This isn't going to work much longer, Hattie. I'm going to make arrangements to rent a house in town for us."

"No . . . Dan . . . you know my parents will insist we stay with them—"

"They'll have no say in it. We've no reason to keep wastin' money and time in this god-forsaken town soon to be occupied with more ghosts than people."

"But what about Lydia?"

"Lydia is not my concern. She's a married woman now. As far as a social life, leave her to Mrs. O'Shea and Clara for all I care. I need my family close by. And apparently, all your time alone is giving you too much freedom to pick and choose when to serve your husband."

Lydia had begun to shake at the mention of her name. She slunk down and squatted against the back wall below the window. It wasn't the first time she'd witnessed an argument and Dan getting rough with Hattie.

Finding courage to finally confront him, she'd left the laundry on the ground and stomped around to the front door. About to open it, Dan swung the door open from inside. His face firm, and eyes bloodshot, he blew a wave of alcohol-infused air directly into Lydia's face.

He shook his head and scoffed, then pushed his way past her.

Lydia couldn't speak over the pounding in her throat. She'd wished him dead in that moment—a split second thought she felt would bring Hattie relief . . .

Footsteps clamored on the men's side of the porch, bringing Lydia back to the present moment. The doorknob clanked and hinges squeaked, indicating the men were going inside. Lydia tried to breath, but the weight on her chest was too heavy. Willing her feet to move, which now felt like large stones in her boots, she made her way back through the side door, and dropped the logs in a heap in front of the fireplace.

Upon hearing the rumble of tumbling logs in the living room, Dylan realized Lydia was not in the kitchen. He closed his eyes briefly and took in a deep breath. If Lydia was just outside collecting logs, she could very well have heard the discussion between him and Pete. He made a gesture with his hand to tell Pete to stay in the kitchen and strode through the doorway and into the living room.

Lydia stood still, eyes wide, lips quivering, and a cloud of soot at her ankles.

The tears Dylan fought to hold back while in Pete's presence erupted and he ran to embrace his wife.

"So, it's true?" Lydia sobbed and pushed away from him, forcing him to look her in the eye.

"Dan . . . was in an accident at the mine . . . a cave in. He didn't survive." Her faced blurred before him. He tried to caress her cheek, but she swatted it away.

"No . . . no . . . it can't be . . ." She shook her head and turned away from him, drawing her arms around herself.

Why would she turn away? It wasn't his fault that Dan was dead.

Lydia's shoulder rose and fell. She wailed between uneven breaths. "You could have . . . should have . . ." her voice shook, and she formed fists, bringing her arms down to her sides before she turned to face him again.

What could he have done?

"Did it ever occur to you that we could have hired Dan first? That he could be here, helping you run the ranch . . ."

What was she talking about? Dan made a good wage working for the mines. It would take years before Dylan could afford to match it. So, no, it never occurred to him to hire out a miner who still had a job. Not even his closest friend.

"Lydia, that wasn't even an option. And frankly, that's not your concern."

Even though less than an hour had passed since Pete told him the news, Dylan had imagined this going differently. How could she turn this around to be his fault? Up to this moment, her ignorance had been innocent, attractive even. But now she dared to cross the line and disrespect him? And within earshot of their new hire?

Lydia's fists tightened, turning her knuckles white. Tears streamed down her cheeks. Her eyes narrowed and she clenched her teeth. "Not an option? Not my concern? I have allowed you to make the decisions for us . . . allowed you to dictate our future—"

In two strides, Dylan crossed the room and clamped his hand over her mouth. Pointing a finger into the air, he brought his face close enough to hers that he could smell her tears. "You do not *allow* me, Lydia. I am the husband, remember? It is my job and position to make the choices for us around here. I *allow* you. And when we are alone, I have permitted you to speak your mind and express your opinion. But if there are others present—especially those we call employees—you will practice some self-control."

With each word, he felt her body grow from stiff to soft. Her clenched jaw relaxed, and her shoulders fell. She dropped her head, closed her eyes, and leaned her forehead into his shoulder.

After a long moment, Lydia's gained control of her sobbing. "Give me a minute." Grabbing a handkerchief from her apron, she took the doorway on the other side of the living room and bounded up the stairs.

What just happened?

One moment she is grieving over the loss of her friend's husband—wondering if her thoughts could have caused such an event, and the next she is screaming at her husband as if it were his fault that Dan was dead? Her mind had scrambled for a reason why or a way it could have been prevented. Her reasoning was convoluted, but for a moment, she thought if Dan was closer and spent more time with

Dylan and less with miners then maybe he'd still be alive.

She pounded the pillow with her fists. She was not actually angry with Dylan. She was angry with herself. Dylan had never been forceful with her—or had ever raised his voice at her. On all accounts, she probably deserved it after humiliating and disrespecting him like she did. She didn't believe Dylan was like Dan in that way at all. Yet, even if he became that way, she would never wish him dead.

"Lord Jesus, help him to forgive me. Help me to practice self-control . . . especially now that there will be another set of ears and eyes watching me." Lydia recalled a Bible verse that mentioned self-control. There was more to it—something about fruit of the spirit, patience, gentleness—she would ask Dylan to read it to her later.

First, she needed to pull herself together. She was sure there was an appropriate way to display her grief in front of their company—she just needed to do it quietly.

TWO

Dylan initiated introductions as soon as Lydia returned to the kitchen.

"Lydia, this is Pete Evan, former miner and our new ranch hand."

Heat crept up Lydia's neck as she tried to take in a breath and appear relaxed. Between her mind whirling at the news of Dan's death, the shock of Dylan losing his temper, and this strange man before her, she could hardly keep her senses.

Pete reached out a wide hand and thick fingers. His extended arm, twice the thickness of Dylan's, looked as hard as river rocks. Deep blue eyes, crisper than the sky on a fall day, stared back at her. A wide, square jaw sprinkled in peach-colored whiskers held a firm, yet gentle grin. He stretched his fingers closer to her.

"Lydia?" Dylan whispered.

She shot out her hand at the sound of her husband's voice but could not break her gaze with Pete. Her fingers shook as Pete took her hand and squeezed ever so gently despite the massive strength he must have held back.

"It's my pleasure to meet you, Mrs. Prescot . . . I only wish I didn't have to bear such sad news upon my arrival." The deep tone in his voice seemed to vibrate her bones.

"The feeling is mutual." She prayed neither man could hear the quiver in her voice.

A log popped inside the stove and Lydia jumped.

"P-Please make yourself comfortable." She gestured toward the table.

Dylan scooted around her back and pulled out her chair. "Darling, you know it is customary for the lady to be seated first."

"Yes, I know. But I still need to bring the rolls around. I don't mind serving you both." Lydia curtsied and found her breath.

Pete and Dylan took their seats and made small talk while Lydia finished bringing the food to the table. When she went to sit, they both stood.

Dylan said a blessing over their meal and the three of them ate without speaking for most of the meal.

Pete's eyes met Lydia's after he cleaned the bones of two chicken legs. "I haven't had a home cooked meal for weeks. Thank you, Mrs. Prescot." He wiped the corners of his mouth. A flake of chicken seasoning caught in his mustache, but the napkin retrieved it.

His gaze stirred emotions Lydia could not explain. His eyes held a combination of emptiness and want even though they sparkled in the lamp light.

She tilted her head and offered a small smile. "It was my pleasure, Pete." She swallowed the lump emerging in her throat and took a deep breath. "Did you know Dan very well?"

Dylan cleared his throat.

For a moment, Lydia had forgotten he also sat at the table.

"Would you like another roll?" Lydia began to hand the basket of rolls to her husband. Something about the crinkle between his eyes caused her to flush.

"Yes, thank you." Dylan took the basket with both hands and then faced Pete. "If I recall, Dan said you two worked the mines together for about three years?"

Pete nodded, took a roll, and then scooped out enough green bean salad to fill half his plate. Offering the salad bowl to Dylan, he replied. "Yes, sir. Three years. And we shared quarters as well. A boarding house on Columbia Avenue."

More silence as the men devoured their second helpings. Lydia felt talking would ease the odd feelings Pete's presence ushered into her belly. She didn't have an appetite with the spectrum of emotions flooding through her. But she kept nibbling anyway.

Finally, she stood to begin clearing off the table.

Again, Dylan and Pete pushed back their chairs and stood. However, Pete's chair hit the stove. He flung his arm back and his knee up, knocking the platter of chicken from the table.

Pete dropped to the floor and began picking up shards of china. "Pardon me . . . I misjudged—"

"Don't fret about it, Pete." Lydia was around the table and at the foot of Pete's chair in an instant. She tucked invisible strands of hair behind her ear and bit the inside of her lip as the scent of cloves washed across her face.

He shouldn't smell so lovely after walking all day.

She held her breath and hoped the warmth on her face and neck was due to the heat of the stove.

Dylan fell into place beside her, grazing her shoulder with his own. He waved Pete away. "We've got this, Pete." He shook his head. "This table needs to turn the other way anyway now that we'll have more than two of us for meals."

Pete stood and pulled his chair out of the way.

Lydia could finally inhale deeply and helped her husband finish cleaning up the floor.

"Why don't you gentlemen finish your meal while I clean up? The news of Dan has left me without much of an appetite."

Something about Lydia's overt attention to Pete unsettled Dylan. He thought she might be acting a little too friendly toward the stranger. But could she know better?

"That was marvelous as usual." Dylan winked to ease the tension he saw masking his wife's demeanor.

Lydia only nodded in reply. She stood at the sink and wrung a damp towel in her hands, eyes darting between Dylan and Pete.

"I should show you to your sleeping area in the barn, Pete. The thought escaped me earlier. Lydia, we'll be back to go over Pete's morning duties by the heat of the fire before he'll turn in."

Lydia nodded, then shook her head and laughed. "Of course. I'll be finishing up in the kitchen here and preparing the upstairs bath."

Pete turned toward Lydia and bowed. "Thank you again, Mrs. Prescot, for the meal and hospitality."

Lydia smiled and lingered awkwardly at the end of the table.

"Well, Pete, I would offer you a drink, but we don't keep liquor in the house." Dylan clasped his hands. "I will show you where the firewood is around the back porch before we go."

Lydia seemed to shudder, and then collected the empty dishes from the table.

"Lead the way, Mr. Prescot."

Dylan felt like he had to make two strides for everyone one of Pete's. As they approached the barn, sheep bleats put a rock in Dylan's gut.

"Have you any experience in the sheep business, Pete?" Dylan chuckled, sure he knew the answer, but hoping, nonetheless.

"Not since I was a small lad, sir. I have a few faint memories of visiting a relative in Wales who had a small flock."

"You're about to get in shoulder deep with lambing season on its way."

"I am at your service, Mr. Prescot. Grateful to have the chance to work in the outdoors."

It felt odd being addressed in such a formal manner after the casual introductions when they had met briefly the week before. Dan had introduced them during an impromptu meeting at the Penn Valley Saloon. After Pete's wife and infant had died during childbirth the previous winter, he had quit work in the mines and taken on odd jobs from town to town. But now, he was eager for steady work with the approach of spring.

Pete had been quiet and let Dan do most of the talking. In the end, Dylan felt Pete's status as a widower would serve them both well. He couldn't imagine losing Lydia. He was happy to offer a steady living situation to this stranger. Without a family to provide for, Pete was willing to work through winter in trade for room and board, agreeing to a reasonable, yet small wage once the ranch turned a profit in the spring.

Pete listened with only a nod or a grunt in reply as Dylan explained the daily tasks he'd be responsible for across the ranch.

When the air grew frigid enough that white clouds followed the words coming from Dylan's mouth, he suggested they head back to the house.

"No need for you to face the cold longer than required for tonight's sleep. I'll have Lydia grab a couple of extra quilts for you as well."

"Only at your convenience, sir. I'm used to using my knapsack as a pillow and my coat as a blanket."

Pete stepped onto the porch and went in the direction of the stack of firewood. He drew up two logs at a time, easily filling the crook of one arm with over half a dozen. "Should I grab another armload, or will this suffice until morning?"

He doesn't wait to be told, does he?

"That's plenty, Pete. Allow me to get the door."

After adding two logs to the fire, Pete stood with his hands folded before the flames and looked to Dylan.

"Please, take a seat." Dylan gestured to one of two upholstered chairs facing the fireplace in the large, yet cozy living room.

With the door leading into the kitchen closed, the living room would get stifling enough that the heat would push out the other door and up the stairs into the bedrooms overnight. While Lydia was still out of earshot, Dylan felt he should warn Pete about her lack of experience around people.

"At the risk of sounding like a lousy husband and less than a man, I must apologize for the earlier interaction you overheard between my wife and me."

Pete swung his head side to side and wrinkled his brow. "The affairs between you and your wife are not my concern. No need to apologize."

"Normally, you'd be correct." Dylan cleared his throat. He'd need to choose his words carefully. "But my wife is not accustomed to . . . she hasn't had much . . ." Perhaps gossip was not such a bad thing after all. If he only knew what Dan had already told Pete, this might be easier.

Lydia tapped on the glass window of the kitchen door. She held a tray with a teakettle and two teacups. Dylan jumped up to get the door for her.

"Thank you, dear. Mm . . . hmm. Chamomile, perfect."

Lydia brought in the tray and set it down, glancing past Dylan and smiling at Pete. "Would you like a lump of sugar or cream for your tea, Pete?"

Lydia waited for Pete's reply, spoon at the ready to scoop a cube of sugar into his cup. Her back to Dylan, she inhaled the cloves this time.

"Sugar, thank you." His voice lingered over her limbs like a blanket.

Nothing about him was what she had expected. Firelight flickered in intense blue eyes set below thick, straw-toned eyebrows that matched an evenly trimmed beard. Smooth, yet firm shoulders sat like river rocks above arms thicker than the oak branches they cut for logs.

Dylan cleared his throat rather loudly. "We can take it from here. Thank you." He patted the small of her back and nudged her.

"Of course. Of course." She sighed, trying to think of another reason to stay in the room. But nothing came to her. She went back into the kitchen, not realizing how hot it was in the living room until she closed the door behind her and felt relief in the cool kitchen air.

Was she flustered or just warm from the fire? She shrugged it off, forcing her mind to focus. There were more important matters adhering to her attention. Her thoughts turned to Dan and she wondered if Hattie had received word yet. She would be devastated.

Lydia knew her friend already felt isolated in French Corral. Hattie had told her on more than one occasion that if it weren't for her disapproving parents, she'd move back to Grass Valley. Sadly, they'd probably be relieved to hear that her abusive, binge drinking husband had left her widowed. Lydia didn't know how these situations normally worked out, but she couldn't imagine Hattie staying in French Corral as a widow with two little ones when her parents had a home in Grass Valley.

To avoid interrupting the men's conversation, Lydia took the longer route from the kitchen and around the porch to a small foyer which opened to the maid's quarters and upstairs bedrooms. Though it took her several trips between buckets of boiled and pump water, she felt she had earned the duty of filling the bath alone and did not request help.

Dylan had left the living room door open—the only way to coax the hot fireplace air upstairs to their room. She half-expected one or both men to help, but they didn't seem to notice her beyond the crackling fire. She ignored what bits of their conversation that hit her ears. Instead, she repented of her stupidity and prayed hard for the Lord to hold her tongue in the future.

After bathing, she left two candles burning on the bureau and slipped on a clean nightgown before climbing into bed.

Lydia's mind escaped the turmoil of temporary marital strife. The reality of Dan's death and Hattie's isolation stirred up deep grief from her past. She had suffered her own loss when Mama died—but the thought of losing Dylan ripped through her like a scythe across a field of wild grass. A part of her would surely die if anything ever happened to him.

The cool fabric of the nightgown clung to her skin, still warm and damp from her bath. She could no longer resist the weight of the day. She sunk into the pillow and mattress. Heavy eyelids closed and darkness eased her into sleep.

A rustling in the hallway woke her.

Lydia's heartbeat quickened at the sight of Dylan standing at the doorway, stripped down to his underclothing. Her belly flipped, unsure of his intentions. When he closed the door, she thought she knew, but then he got on his knees.

"Forgive me," he whispered.

Forgive him? She was the one who needed to ask forgiveness.

The light from the moon revealed just enough in his expression to know he was serious. He was hurting too. Dan was his closest friend as far as she could tell. His loss was even greater than hers was. Yet, she had the gall to accuse him of somehow being responsible. How could she make up for it? Asking for forgiveness alone did not seem enough.

She crossed her ankles and slid her legs around the edge of the bed so that her knee leaned into

Dylan's ribcage. She grabbed both his hands and set them on her lap to pull him toward her.

She bit her lip to hold back tears and shook her head. "I am the one who needs to ask forgiveness. I was not thinking at all. I was disrespectful and inconsiderate. I am so—so sorry you have lost your friend . . ."

Her tears spilled anyway.

Dylan leaned in, wrapped his arms around her waist, and bawled in silence, soaking the waist of her nightgown with his tears. They both sobbed and held each other for several minutes. The clouds shifted again, leaving them in near darkness.

As if the darkness were a cue, Lydia pulled her husband's arms in a subtle, yet clear way—inviting him to climb into bed beside her.

THREE

The next morning, Lydia stretched an arm across the cooled bedsheets. Normally she could still feel the residual warmth from Dylan lingering. She cracked open an eye and turned her head toward the window expecting to see a periwinkle sky preparing for the sun's shimmering rays to chase away the darkness until evening. It wouldn't be the first time she'd overslept, exhaustion from managing the house and garden while her husband spent every minute of daylight tending sheep, horses, and cows. But a sliver of moonlight hung still between the shadows of clouds against a black sky.

Bracing herself for the cold, Lydia pushed back the quilt and sat up. "Lord, prepare me for whatever has my husband awake already this day."

With shawl across her shoulders and a lantern in hand, Lydia descended the stairs, her mind recalling the previous evening's events and their new guest.

The fireplace sat still dark and cold. Surely, he would have had Pete start a fire.

Lydia's heart accelerated. She couldn't recall a morning all winter that he had not prepared a fire before heading out to the barn.

Pinning her shawl beneath her chin with one hand, she tried to look out the window toward the barn. But the lantern light's reflection only spilled across the dark glass, revealing unkempt hair escaping from every direction beneath her bonnet.

She entered the kitchen and closed the door behind her. No sense in keeping it open without the heat from a fire to warm her as she started the stove. As she lifted the lantern to hang it on the wall, the light shimmered across the glass doors on the hutch, revealing one of the doors standing ajar.

Lydia secured the lantern and adjusted her shawl. It had been weeks since she'd opened those doors, months even. She pulled open the door all the way in search for anything missing or out of place.

Except for the line of farming manuals along the center shelf appearing disturbed, everything else was in its usual place. Dylan could have taken one of the books out to Pete the night before and failed to secure the cabinet door. It still didn't explain why he hadn't started a fire before beginning the workday.

Concern eased while Lydia contemplated the items on the remaining shelves.

The two crystal vases holding bunches of dried wildflowers from her and Mama's walks still sat nestled into the corners of the top shelf. Between them, mounted against the back, the wedding certificate and portrait of Lydia's mother and father as newlyweds hung undisturbed and quiet. Lydia's throat caught as she recalled the day she'd discovered both items in frames in the hidden hole beneath Mama's bed. The words from Mama's diary echoed in her thoughts. The bliss of marriage had also dissipated all too soon after Mama and her father, Charles, had taken on the work of their own farm in the Valley.

Yet, unlike Mama, Lydia was accustomed to the work from a lifetime of toil and knew nothing else. Her frustrations shifted when her gaze fell to the second shelf and the music box that held more questions than answers about Mama's life before and after she had come to the Valley.

In the first weeks after Lydia and Dylan had completed the move from the Valley to the ranch, they'd spent hours reviewing the items within the box each evening. Aside from the dairy Miss Hastings had given Lydia on the day of Mama's funeral, there was little else to explain how and why Mama had chosen to raise Lydia alone in the Valley for seventeen years.

Lydia ignored the tug that told her she didn't have time to reflect on the past.

With frigid fingertips, she nudged open the lid of the music box and slid off the top compartment holding her parents' wedding rings and a lock of her infant hair. Then, she grasped one of the envelopes, edges worn from the many times Dylan had held it and read the letter from within aloud.

Though Lydia had learned to read at a rapid pace during the lessons with her mother-in-law, Jaina, she had not yet attempted to read these letters on her own—despite having memorized every word.

Hands shaking, Lydia stepped beneath the lantern light.

June 17, 1904

Dearest Uncle Moses,

Though I am uncertain as to the exact date I will be sending this letter, today marks one month before my dear Lydia turns seventeen. These years have passed in a blur and I fear all my best intentions have been for naught. I should have heeded your offer to take us both in under your care those many years ago. The wounds from Mr. Sinclair were still too fresh for me to reside in the same city with him. In all honesty, I believed my plan to care for Lydia and retain our place here in the Valley would be dashed in no time. Yet, for reasons I will never understand, the Lord has kept us secure and safe and provided for our needs despite my dishonest efforts to hide Lydia from a life beyond the Valley.

I have allowed this ruse of our isolated life to go on far too long. And now, I fear Lydia has been dis-covered. By whom, I do not know, but I am asking you to do what you can to find out if Mr. Sinclair has sent anyone here to investigate. I would like to be prepared for the possibility before I find the best way to reveal to Lydia the truth about her father and her heritage. I sense she may know something as she took to a fever after my last journey into town and has not been the same since. To make things even more trying, the pain and tenderness in my limbs and joints is getting se-vere—yet one more thing I can no longer hide from Lydia—

Footsteps echoed along the wooden boards of the kitchen porch. Lydia slipped the letter into her pocket, her heart pounding as Dylan entered the kitchen, a rancid odor clinging to his presence.

Disheveled hair and dark circles beneath his eyes told Lydia he had never made it to their bedroom the evening before. How could she not know he hadn't laid beside her all night long?

"It's the sheep . . ." he rasped.

The lamb in Dylan's arms squirmed as he gripped the hoof and clipped away rotting flesh. His nose felt numb from the putrid stench, but it had to be done.

Dylan had already been sleeping deeply, Lydia snuggled at his side, when a gentle, yet steady rap at their bedroom door had awakened him in the middle of the night. Slipping away from his wife's embrace, he'd discovered it was Pete at the door.

After a profuse apology for disturbing Dylan's rest, Pete explained he hadn't quite fallen asleep in the barn when he'd heard distressed sounds coming from the sheep pen outside the barn. Unsure if the sound was normal, Pete went to investigate and discovered an ewe sprawled out oddly against the fence. Upon checking the ewe carefully, Pete knew the problem couldn't wait until morning.

At least a part of the flock had acquired foot rot.

The men had spent the rest of the night transferring the infected part of the flock to an unused corral. Without a wink of sleep, Pete had taken on the job as if his own life had depended on it.

Still, frustration compounded Dylan's weariness as the reality of the situation set in.

Both he and Lydia had been so certain this ranch was a part of God's plan. Why else would God have provided it the exact moment they needed it and for the exact financial requirement they had available with his inheritance? He believed there was a purpose and held fast to his faith despite the weariness that settled deep within his gut.

He knew that starting a sheep ranch wouldn't be easy. But how could he have predicted foot rot would disable half their starting herd, including the ram?

Now, he and Lydia would be facing a difficult spring. They had eight pregnant ewes and nearly twenty lambs. Lydia explained they were only a few weeks away from birthing—and as soon as the weather turned warm for spring, they would need to begin shearing.

Lydia crossed the stable floor and flopped down beside Dylan sitting on a bale of hay. "The uninfected sheep are secured in the back stall. I can tell already they don't like the close quarters."

Mud streaked her cheeks and apron bib. Hair clumped in frizzy knots down her fraying braid. She passed a towel soaked in disinfectant to Dylan and dried her hands on the underside of her soiled apron.

Yet, she smiled and her blue eyes twinkled in the dusty cloud of sunlight peeking below the roof of the stable. "No wonder Mama only kept a dozen sheep at a time. I only recall foot rot once before." She lay her head down on Dylan's shoulder.

"I should have hired more ranch hands at the start of winter," Dylan mumbled, avoiding eye contact with his wife. "And we should have limited the areas they grazed for at least two weeks after the move. The shepherd I spoke to warned me and I disregarded it due to the fact no animals had been here for weeks prior to us taking over the property." He swallowed against the putrid burning in his throat. The stench of rotting flesh still stung his nostrils.

Lydia should be able to leave the work to him and Pete, but it was more than a two-person job. He clenched his teeth, biting back frustration at also failing as her husband.

"No need to dwell on it." Lydia bumped her shoulder into his. "At least it's winter and you fenced off the far side of the pasture months ago. There's plenty of uninfected land for them to graze until we move the ewes into the barn."

"Yes . . . at least." He shifted his blank stare from the roof to his wife.

On the surface, she didn't appear as frustrated as he was. But then again, she didn't know, nor could she understand the financial implications of an infected flock. They would not be able to sell weaned lambs or acquire another ram until spring. By then, they would have lost too much income to recover.

After doing his best to wipe the grime from his hands, face, and neck, he reached for Lydia's waist. He needed to feel her close to him. Between losing his friend and the financial stability of their ranch, his wife's comfort was all he had to hold onto.

Nevertheless, she pushed away, the soft look in her eyes turning cold.

"Not now . . . what if Pete comes back from fencing off the infected pasture? Besides, we all need a hearty breakfast, not to mention another bath." She stood and scowled. She inhaled and shook her head. "At least we have Pete here now."

"Yes, I know. At least." Dylan parted ways with his wife without another word.

Fatigued arms and legs welcomed the hot water as Lydia wiped away grime that had made its way past her farm apron, shirtwaist, and undergarments. After treating the sheep all morning, both her and Dylan likely needed full baths, but they couldn't spare well water for a second bath in the same week.

She thought of how she'd spoke harshly after hearing of Dan and then, despite having made amends by the end of the evening, still pushed Dylan away in the stables that morning. Dylan was more than patient with her compared to how she'd witnessed Dan treat Hattie. If Hattie's love for her husband could still be so strong, why did Lydia find it so hard to receive Dylan's affections? There was a time when she'd only desired to be near him, when the work could always wait.

Perhaps it was the kindled feeling that Pete awoke that reminded her of how things had been in the first months she'd spent with Dylan as his wife. As tired as she was from the days' events, she had to make one last effort for reconciliation before sleep could take over.

FOUR

Dylan thrust the pitchfork into the pile of hay, forcing a layer of matted and soaked blades up from the mud.

Ammonia, dust, and dirt clouded the narrow corner of the stable, stinging Dylan's nostrils and coaxing forth a violent sneeze. He wiped his muddy brow and blew his nose before lifting the heap of soiled hay into the rusty wheelbarrow.

His chest grew heavy when he recalled the day he and Dan were entrusted with the errand of purchasing this exact wheelbarrow at the general store. They'd raced fast down the hill from Dylan's house, each falling and skinning a knee, erupting in the obnoxious laughter of nine-year-old boys—neither allowing tears to fall despite the pain. In those days, the idea of working to support wives or children never entered their conversations.

Now, Dylan felt like he had taken his friendship with Dan for granted—never imagining a day when he wouldn't see him on his visits to French Corral or listen to him describe the toils of working the mines. Their visits had grown sparse since he and Lydia had moved closer to Penn Valley. Though

Dan had chosen a much different way of life than Dylan, the bond they'd shared as young boys remained strong. Dan often confessed his wrongs to Dylan, during an occasional visit at the Saloon in French Corral or Penn Valley. Once Dan admitted that he had slapped Hattie across the cheek. Tears filled his eyes when he couldn't even remember why.

Eyes burning from the dust and stench, Dylan plunged the rake back into the pile, but the teeth stuck hard into the ground and forced a loose shard of the wooden handle deep into his calloused finger.

Gritting his teeth against a foul insult toward the rake, he kicked the tire of the wheelbarrow and stomped outside of the barn. He leaned against the cool outer wall of the barn and examined the splinter lodged into the crease between his middle finger and palm. He shook his head, blinking back frustration at how such a small thing could irk him so easily. It seemed to confirm he could hardly complete basic tasks without a setback. Running a farm on over fifty acres had showed to be much more work than he and Lydia could handle on their own.

So much for providing an easier life.

The squeak of the porch screen interrupted his thoughts. Beyond a newly planted oak tree and the entrance to the property, their two-story farmhouse sat on the top of a small hill. Golden morning sunlight edged above the horizon, washing over the lower half of the house and wrap-around porch. Lydia emerged through the doorway and allowed the screen door to slam.

Dylan's gaze fixed on her as she lifted her chin, closed her eyes, and raised her arms high. The sun's rays reflected off her flaxen hair and made her face and arms glow. She looked like an angel reaching to heaven in hopes that God would whisk her up for a flight through the clouds. Dylan knew she would accept the ride in an instant—not for escape but for the experience.

Dylan's frustration dissolved and a smile relaxed the wrinkles on his forehead. Realizing he hid well in the shadows of the barn, weariness coaxed him into adoring his wife from afar. He took a moment to watch her complete the morning tasks that had been delayed due to attending the sheep.

Lydia hummed while she descended the front yard toward the hen house.

The moment brought him back to the first time he saw her through the forest trees, one early spring evening nearly two years earlier.

He'd only gone to check on Emelyn of the Mountain, unaware of the girl who'd also lived in the isolated valley adjacent to but hidden from French Corral. Besides her presence surprising him, something more had captivated him. She had been skipping along a faded path that surrounded a pond at the edge of their property. The faint echoes of Emelyn called from behind her, and the girl replied with a loud and undeniable, "Yes, I know, Mama." Then she slowed her steps and crept along the path between the pond and the forest.

Dylan had tried to keep his horse still and steady, despite discovering that Emelyn of the Mountain was not alone.

Had she really been raising a daughter here all these years?

The girl stopped directly in front of the edge of the forest where, up until that moment, Dylan and his horse had remained hidden between evergreen trunks. Thinking she had spotted them, he tightened the reigns, willing his horse would somehow realize it should not move. He could not believe how close she was and seemingly oblivious to their presence. She crouched down and looked closely at a bush of some sort along the ground.

At first glance, she had looked like an ordinary farm girl, probably just a year or two younger than his eighteen years. Then Dylan noticed she was anything but ordinary. Bits of fading sunlight reflected off large eyes mostly shaded by long, light-brown eyelashes. Her cheeks, though hallowed and pale, stood firm on either side of her straight nose and supple lips. Thin lines of grime streaked her slender neck, revealing an obviously malnourished winter. Her worn, undersized dress fit snugly at the top and hardly covered her legs.

She wrapped bony arms around the skirt that reached just above pink knees. Bare feet with purple toes curled naturally over the uneven ground. She had to be freezing, but she didn't seem to care. It was more than beauty that emanated from her. Something about her pulled at Dylan and plucked at his heart.

Mesmerized by her intense focus on the plant she examined, Dylan tried to find a word to describe the feelings stirring within him. Then the girl shot up and began walking back toward Emelyn, a fistful of dandelions in her hand.

Dylan jerked and his horse shuffled its hooves before he could tighten his grip on the reigns again.

Then the young woman twisted her head back and looked directly toward him, eyes wide with what he could only define as complete terror. But her blind stare told him she didn't see him—she had only heard his horse. Risking their discovery, but unsure what else he could do, he had carefully turned his horse to face the forest and urged him through the trees as quietly and quickly as possible.

Despite her secluded life on the mountain, Emelyn was a vital part of the French Corral community. Her contributions to the general store and town folk had sustained French Corral well beyond most former mining towns. How she managed to craft and cook in such volume and quality was also a mystery. Yet, when asked, she gave credit to God as her provider and spoke of little else.

Now, Dylan had accidentally discovered there was more to Emelyn's life on the mountain. What he had not realized however, was that his discovery of this hidden girl, whom upon a subsequent meeting in the forest he learned was named Lydia—would change both of their lives forever. Looking back, he felt shame about his ignorant attempts to protect Lydia and Emelyn. He took full responsibility for Emelyn's death during the forest fire that had forced Lydia to leave the only life she had ever known and forced her to learn how to live in French Corral.

Still baffled at the random events over the following year that led to Lydia's ability and willingness to love him enough to become his wife, Dylan shook off his reminiscing and came back to the present.

He plucked the splinter out of his finger and wrapped his throbbing hand with a handkerchief. He gazed once more at his wife. Lydia was now singing a hymn while she retrieved eggs from the hen house that sat beyond the goat-grazed grasses at the bottom of the yard.

After a year of hearty farm food and Dylan insisting on taking on most of the manual labor of

the farm, Lydia no longer resembled a malnourished farm girl. Though still on the smaller side
compared to the heartier breed of Welsh women in
the area, her body was strong and firm and no
longer lacked the curves that symbolized the ability
to one-day mother children.

Children.

Dylan winced at allowing his thoughts to stray
to this subject. It had only been nine months since
their wedding, and though Dylan knew of couples
who did not get pregnant for a year or longer—he
had hoped Lydia would have been with child by
now. Shaking off yet another discouraging aspect
of how he'd failed as a husband, he returned to the
barn.

Lydia thought she caught a glimpse of Dylan
leaning against the barn wall while she walked down
the hill to gather eggs for breakfast. He was supposed to be cleaning out the horse stables, but she
resisted the urge to walk over and ask him why he
rested when there was still so much work to do before they could leave for French Corral.

She sighed and hummed until she recalled the
hymn's melody. Whenever she began to feel frustrated about the work that seemed to double by the
day, she would sing. The words would always calm
her spirit, despite their circumstances. She didn't
want her faith to falter after all God had already
brought them through. He would sustain her so
that she could sustain Hattie. He had to.

She walked back up the small hill to the porch,
gathering the edge of her apron to hold the eggs in

place while her other hand pulled open the screen door. After she set the eggs on the counter, she straightened her apron, retying tattered straps to tighten it further. She brushed her fingers over the strawberry-stained bib and wondered if Mama had worn this apron while pregnant with her. Her hands hovered over the lower part of her belly for a moment, flat as ever despite her arms, hips, and legs having thickened from hard work and heartier eating over recent months.

During one of Lydia's visits to French Corral in late autumn, Hattie told her that younger brides were known to become pregnant with a month of marriage. Hattie had given birth to Olive and been pregnant with Brian within a year of marrying Dan. But in the nine moon cycles since the wedding, Lydia's monthly had become staggered and no longer arrived with the full moon. Some months it arrived with the half moon, while other months it delayed until the new moon—offering temporary hope and then disappointment.

What if I can't get pregnant?

As if shooing a fly, Lydia batted the air. She would not feel discouraged even though she knew a pregnancy would prove her ability to fulfill all her wifely duties, as well as to please Jaina. Of course, Lydia also wanted a child—Dylan's child—to experience the outward evidence of their love for each other, to know how the elated joy she'd seen on Hattie's face after giving birth to Brian, felt on the inside—

Lydia caught her breath when Dylan's arms enveloped her waist from behind.

He pulled her arms into a hug around herself and he kissed the nape of her neck. She smiled and then grimaced as she breathed in the potent sour scent of soiled horse hay.

"I didn't hear you come in." She pushed his arms off her and turned to face him. She was not sure how comfortable she was with Dylan displaying such affection when Pete could walk in at any moment.

"If you are finished in the barn, the chicken wire on the hen house is coming loose. And we need another pile of wood for the stove."

Dylan shrugged and nodded, the small glimmer in his eyes fading with his grin while he turned back toward the door. "Yes, Ma'am. Pete and I will get it all handled before we head to French Corral to check on Hattie."

Lydia sighed and squeezed her eyes shut. Why could she no longer melt into his embrace without first thinking of what else he or she should be doing? Would intimacy come that much harder now with Pete and soon the other ranch hand and a housemaid around?

As difficult as it would be to give over her daily tasks to strangers, she knew it would be impossible for her to continue her reading and writing lessons with Jaina and keep up with the farm when winter ended. She hoped that spending a few days away to care for Hattie would make it easier for her to let go of the work and finally learn to rest.

FIVE

An overcast sky infused with Dylan's feelings and hovered over the smudge of a silver sun above the barn's roof by the time Dylan had loaded the wagon. The other ranch hand and the housemaid would arrive at the end of the day, so he needed to be back in time to greet them. There wasn't time to grieve the loss of Dan now. He had a ranch to run and a profit to make with scant resources to complete the task. After he dropped off Lydia with Hattie, he would go and speak with his father about his plan.

Dylan secured the rope at the back of the wagon and looked up at the house for Lydia. He was about to holler for her when the kitchen door swung open. Surprised, he watched Pete step outside. Was he carrying a laundry basket? Lydia followed behind him, resting her petite palm below his massive shoulder and then pointing out to the laundry line.

Lydia must have asked for his help to bring the wash out to dry, unaware that it wasn't a ranch hand's duty to help with laundry. Dylan snickered to himself and shrugged.

Dylan couldn't see the laundry line from where he stood. Maybe he should follow them around the side of the house to make sure his wife didn't make any further unsuitable requests of Pete when he had more crucial tasks to carry out.

Before Dylan reached the front of the house, Pete came jogging around the corner, a little out of breath. "I beg your pardon, Mr. Prescot. I soiled my shirt and was trying to wash it out myself when Mrs. Prescot offered to assist me."

Many words for a man who was so quiet the evening before. "Soiled your shirt, eh? Yep, flinging horse hay can backfire sometimes. It didn't take me long to keep a clean shirt hanging with the tackle. No time to be running back and forth doing laundry all morning." He forced a laugh, unsure if he was trying to set himself or Pete at ease.

Lydia emerged from the back yard, rubbing red hands together. "Sorry about that delay. My hands feel like ice after hanging the wet wash in that wind." She grinned and glancing back and forth between the two men. "I'm ready to leave whenever you are."

Dylan hesitated on the porch, wanting to be sure Pete was on his way back to the barn, before entering the house. "Go ahead and climb into the wagon. I'm going to grab an extra quilt in case you need it."

"I can grab it if you'd like, Mr. Prescot." Pete stepped alongside Dylan.

"Thank you, but you really need to finish up the barn and tend to the other tasks we spoke of this morning." Dylan nodded toward the barn.

"Yes, sir." Pete tipped his hat at Dylan, and then turned to Lydia. "Ma'am . . . Mrs. Prescot, have a safe journey and Godspeed as you comfort your friend in her time of mourning."

"Thank you, Pete. I will." Lydia curtsied and then parted paths with both men, making her way to the wagon.

Dylan shook off his thoughts again. What was this unease growing in his gut? He would have to take it to the Lord. Pete and Lydia were only practicing common courtesies, nothing more. It was just the first time he had seen her interact with another man this way. That was all there was to it.

Lydia floated between feelings of gratitude and grieving during the journey to Hattie and Dan's cabin. Normally, her mind filled with reviewing words and phrases from her previous lessons with Jaina and the time went by quickly. Dylan offering to take her to French Corral was indeed an answer to her prayer.

They had forgiven each other and enjoyed an intimate evening despite the gamut of emotions they'd experienced the previous day. Memories of Dylan's tender touch and enamored gaze reflected in the candlelight of their bedroom, gave her hope that they could overcome their present challenges.

Pete was already proving himself a great help from what she could tell. The work of two men would surely be better than one. Were her days of hard labor finally ending? For these things, she was grateful.

Perhaps she would not be so exhausted if she and Dylan had stayed in the Valley. They would be closer to Dylan's parents, reducing the time to journey to French Corral for her reading and writing lessons, and making impromptu visits to Hattie easier to come by.

The Valley that had encompassed her life from dawn until dusk, working her and her mama unto exhaustion day after day—now seemed like a pleasant escape. However, that life was now a distant memory. She no longer strove to simply satisfy Mama and please God by caring for the land and animals and sewing and cooking offerings for the angels. After coming to terms with and separating the fact from the fiction of her upbringing, Lydia's life now served a further purpose.

Though she still saw each act as an effort to serve God, she also embraced the full responsibility of being Dylan's wife. She had come to realize that despite Mama's intent to prevent Lydia from finding love—and ultimately heartache—that Mama had taught Lydia most every skill she would need to fulfill her duties as a wife.

Regardless of all the years Lydia had dreamed about what life would be like with a man at her side, the reality of married life hadn't taken long to set in. Yet, it would take her a lifetime to understand this man she now called her husband. What he ever saw in her—an isolated mountain girl who knew nothing of the outside world besides ancient Bible stories—was still a mystery.

Yet, he insisted on being her savior, a hero on a pale-colored horse who had emerged from the darkness of the forest's edge to reveal the light of the world beyond the Valley. He accepted her just as she was, yet his presence somehow inspired her to strive for more—to seek the truth and use it to find her true purpose. He made her want to be more than she ever thought she could be on her own.

Now, his willingness to take her to French Corral for Hattie proved his love was deeper than she could fathom. For this, she was prepared to offer a servant's heart and hand to him upon her return.

If she was honest with herself, though, she knew there was more. Yes, she wanted to please God and meet every need and desire of her husband's heart. There was also someone else she felt the need to please—someone else whose love and acceptance seemed to hover over Lydia and Dylan like a looming storm cloud. Lydia tried to justify her reasoning by convincing herself that if her mother-in-law, Jaina, was completely satisfied with the life her and Dylan led—that somehow that would mean she had also earned God's acceptance.

Part of Lydia knew this was wrong, but she could not stand seeing the look in Dylan's eyes whenever he became aware of his mother's disappointment. If it was important to him to have his mother's approval, then wasn't part of Lydia's role as his wife to ensure it as well? Jaina didn't like how much Lydia still worked. She had told her on more than one occasion she was convinced pregnancy would never occur unless she learned to rest.

Lydia had never lived a restful life and did not see how that had anything to do with becoming pregnant. However, she hoped that this time she spent apart from her husband—regardless of what Jaina may think about it—with her focus on Hattie and Dylan on training his new hires, would be worth it.

The wagon jostled and her thoughts merged to Hattie's loss. Feelings surged, reminding her of the days following Mama's death. She'd felt hollow, hopeless. Would Hattie feel this way? She had babies to care for too. Lydia could not imagine trying to care for a child while grieving the loss of her mother. She had completely forgotten about the farm animals for days after Mama's death.

Was that normal, or was it a sign that Lydia did not have the instinct of a mother—to put those who depended on her above her own needs?

She wanted to express all her concerns and questions to Dylan, but he seemed to be drowning in his own thoughts, blankly staring straight ahead. Would he be okay without her for a week? Though she wanted to be there for him, Hattie would need her more than he did.

What if Hattie hadn't heard yet? Would Lydia be the one to tell her?

By the time they crossed Bridgeport, Lydia's cheeks were numb from the crisp air. She pulled the quilt up over her face and blew into it to warm her cheeks with her own breath. This maneuver must have pulled Dylan from his daze, because he chuckled.

"Cold?" She felt his arm come around her and his hand grasp the side of her shoulder.

She lowered the quilt, cold air blasting her face. "If it wasn't for the wind, I would be okay. Do you think it will snow?" Though they were deep in the crevice of the mountain, a slate gray sky peeked through the tree branches.

"If it does it will be only flurries, nothing of significance."

He couldn't know. Nevertheless, she appreciated his effort to put her mind at ease about having to face extreme weather conditions amid everything else.

She tucked the quilt in tighter around her legs and ankles, covered it with a wool horse blanket, and scooted in closer to him. Sighing, she decided to ask him what he thought would be the best plan for Hattie.

"Do you think Hattie knows by now?"

"Yes, I do. They probably sent a telegram or contacted them with the telephone line from one of the other mines."

She had forgotten about that telephone line. Of course, they would have sent the message by now if the newspaper already had the information.

"Would she be able to contact her parents then? Maybe they are already on their way up here. Do you think she'll want me there?"

"She'll want you there, I'm confident in that. Her parents will want to control the details, but she will need you there as a friend. And Olive and Brian will need you too—especially since they see you more often than their grandparents."

Dylan sure knew how to build her confidence in moments of doubt. It was one of the ways she knew their love was true, and that he was meant to be her husband.

Yet, with the confirmation, in whirled another doubt. As soon as she thought the word husband, Pete's face fluttered across her mind. What did that mean?

Quick, think of something else . . .

"The babies . . . oh . . . Olive will be asking for Daddy no doubt. However, Brian probably won't realize Dan is missing at all. He's been gone so much of Brian's life." She felt sad that the children would not know their father. Somewhat like her, but at least they had photographs and a mother who would tell them about him. Tears surged behind her eyes and she bit her lip to ward them off.

She needed to be strong for her friend now. She had shed her tears the night before.

Dylan nodded. "You're probably right about that. Do you think we should pick up any goods from the store before we head to their cabin in case you feel you can't break away from Hattie? You know better than I what the children will need."

Despite Dan's temper, the only thing Lydia could think Olive and Brian needed was their father, and the security his presence and hard word brought to their mother. Hattie was a relaxed young woman, usually only putting forth effort when absolutely needed. It was why their friendship worked so well. Lydia learned firsthand by filling in the gaps where Hattie was unwilling. The women in town called her lazy.

Still, Lydia felt envious. Hattie had the choice, or so it seemed, to avoid some responsibilities. Now, she would not have such a luxury. Lydia would never admit it aloud, but she doubted that Hattie was capable of the full level of demands that raising two half-orphans alone would entail.

SIX

Dylan pulled the wagon to a halt several feet further from the Logan home than his normal stopping place, to avoid startling Hattie. There was no light coming from inside, no sounds of little ones stirring.

Lydia gripped Dylan's arm. She shivered and pulled herself close. Tears pooled in her eyes, but they didn't fall.

When they stepped onto the porch, Dylan took a moment and embraced his wife. "Hattie will be fine," he whispered. "With a friend like you, she'll be fine."

Lydia wiped her tears into Dylan's coat and stepped toward the door.

She tapped the door and turned to Dylan. "Maybe she's not here . . . or the children are napping."

Dylan nodded to urge her to try again.

Silence.

Then slow footsteps scraped from inside.

The door opened a crack, and Hattie's face edged into the light coming from the porch. Tear streaked cheeks and red and puffy eyes appeared confused at first.

"Lydia," Hattie whispered and dropped short of falling into Lydia's arms, as if her feet were unable to bridge the gap between friends.

Dylan caught her arm before she hit the porch floor, pulled her upright and then guided Hattie into Lydia's embrace. He stood back, feeling out of place as the women consoled one another.

Lydia sank to the floor of the doorway while gripping Hattie who clung to her as if her life depended on it.

"I want my husband . . . my husband . . ." Hattie wailed and dropped limp arms around Lydia's waist.

He couldn't leave them here like this.

"Come ladies, let me help you inside." Wrapping one arm under Lydia and the other under Hattie, Dylan lifted them to stand and led them inside. The cabin was dark and cold, and it took a moment for his sight to adjust and focus on the path to the bed—the best place he could think to take them.

He wrapped a quilt around each woman and located a few clean handkerchiefs. Then he set about to stoke a fire. His heart raced and his hands shook while he knelt at the mouth of the fireplace.

Dylan knew that drinking had spun Dan out of control. Although Dylan chose tonic water or wine whenever they drank socially, he had often felt a gnawing in his gut that he was still encouraging his friend to drink. When Dan confessed a desire to repent, Dylan only patted his shoulder and offered a weak, whispered prayer for God's mercy.

It wasn't until this moment that Dylan realized he'd usually joined Dan alone. He'd not made much effort to interact with any other men in town. The one's he did engage with acted more like fathers than friends.

He shook off a sudden wave of chills, unsure if it was the cold air creeping up behind him or the realization that he had lost the one person he'd called friend for most of his life.

Whines and whispers floated over from the bed. He felt like an intruder and needed to get a move on his additional reason for coming to town.

Kindling crackled. Small flames reached toward dry bark and protruding slivers of each log. In moments, orange light and oak-scented hot air coated Dylan's face. He stood, hesitated a moment, and then approached the bed gingerly.

Dylan rested his hand on Lydia's shoulder, unsure she would even hear him. "I'm going to go to my parents' house. I will check back soon."

Seconds later, Dylan eased his grip on the reins, allowing the horses to pull the wagon more slowly as they ascended the hill to his parents' house. This news of Dan would affect his plans in many ways. Lydia would want to be at Hattie's side if she could. Who would handle the laundry and the cooking while she was gone? The housemaid, Emily, he'd hired was supposed to be an assistant to Lydia. Would she stay on if it meant doing all the work alone?

He felt selfish thinking such thoughts, but the ranch could not run itself, and he couldn't run it without nourishment. Worse, not having his wife around would cause his mother to be that much more concerned about their marriage—and the prospect of grandchildren.

Dylan hoped Jaina would have compassion on Lydia in this situation.

His father would understand—he hoped. His parents were in the process of finalizing the sale of their house. If everything worked out as planned, they would be settled in their new home in Grass Valley just before Easter.

It was near lunch when he arrived. His mother invited him to join her in the dining room.

She had prepared one of her traditional French cuisines and expressed excitement in sharing it with someone. Though she had a cook at her beck and call, preparing meals from her homeland had always been more of a hobby than a chore—or so she told Dylan. His hunch, however, was that the cook could never quite capture the authentic taste his mother insisted upon.

"Your father is out in the vineyard, showing the new owner his methods, and other things I do not care to learn." A perfectly coiled curl rested on her ivory cheek. Sunlight glowed across her neck, reflecting off the jeweled gold necklace that complimented her navy-blue crushed velvet dress. Saucerwide eyes held a blend of annoyance and boredom. Even in her snobbery, Dylan's mother could dazzle him. She was the second most beautiful woman in his life.

"Mother, I don't mean to be rude, but there are more important matters at hand. I need to speak with Father. But since I have you all to myself for a moment, there is something I need to discuss with you regarding Lydia."

His mother's hand fluttered to her throat, and she pressed back a smile with her lips. "Please tell me it's so. She's finally pregnant—"

Dylan shook his head, dreading the look of disappointment he was sure to see cross his mother's face. "No, Mother, no sign of a baby . . . yet. For now, another matter has come up. Dan Logan was killed in a mining accident and since Hattie is sure to need Lydia's help through—"

"You have got to be kidding me. Dylan Brandon Prescot! Your marriage comes before any friend of . . . of hers. This is obviously why she has not been able to conceive yet. I knew it…I knew buying that ranch would continue to add stress on that girl. You know how hard she worked before you rescued her from the life of slavery her mother had devised for them in that valley."

Yes, he knew. All he had wanted was to give her an easier life, to take away the burden of a man's work so that his wife could find joy and rest for once. His shoulders fell and he turned his face away—staring at a painting on the wall.

"I know, Mother. I have failed her yet again—" His voice faded, and tears clogged his throat. He clenched his teeth.

As if his mother needed to remind him of all the reasons his wife needed to become pregnant.

Not only would pregnancy help him insist that Lydia reduce her workload, but it would prove to those who whispered and gawked at his marrying a mountain girl—that his wife was even more incredible than the average pioneer woman. Yet, even as he attempted to convince himself of this reasoning, he knew the truth. It was not the gossip reaching Grass Valley and beyond that concerned him if Lydia did not become pregnant soon.

If only his mother could accept their life as set apart—instead of striving toward the status quo.

Now, with the news of Dan's death, what his mother thought about him allowing Lydia to stay and console her friend created more anger than fear. He was frustrated enough with the daily difficulties related to the ranch—he did not need his mother's prying opinion. She didn't understand that giving Lydia space from the ranch could be beneficial in the end.

Jaina would insist that a wife's place was with her husband and nowhere else.

"Where is she now? You didn't leave her alone with some wild-eyed ranch hand, did you?"

"No, mother. I did not leave her at home . . . I left her with Hattie. She needs to be there for her friend. And in case it slipped your mind, Hattie's husband, Dan, was also my friend."

"What is all the yelling about in here?" Mr. Prescot's voice cut through the air hovering between mother and son.

Jaina sighed and pulled herself up straight. "Hello, darling. Dylan has just brought horrible news. Dan Logan was killed in a mining accident at Empire Mine."

"That is awful news, son. I'm sorry to hear that. Hattie must be devastated. Is Lydia with her, then?"

"Yes, Father, she is consoling her as we speak." Dylan felt his shoulders relax some. At least his father understood why Lydia wasn't with him. "I came to share the news, but I also need to discuss matters about the ranch with you—in private."

Dylan's father liberated a croissant from the center of the table and seemed to ignore his wife's raised eyebrow. "Darling, will you pardon us for the time being?"

Jaina pursed her lips in silent disdain.

Dylan glared at his mother briefly and then stood. "Thank you for the delicious lunch, Mother. We will visit again soon." He rounded the table and kissed his mother on the top of the head before departing to the den with his father.

Seconds later, his father sat adjacent to Dylan in one of two matching armchairs in the den.

"I understand the ranch is losing money by the day." Not surprising to Dylan, his father did not delay in discovering the real purpose of Dylan's visit. Mr. Prescot leaned in, an elbow on each knee and fingers clasped. "As much of a blessing as the land was to start, trying to do everything on your own to save the cost of labor has done you no good."

"I know, Father. I realize that now. I appreciate your willingness to let me take charge and not manage every element of things. You had faith in me after all the years I brought success for you here. Running a ranch is much different. And Lydia . . . well . . . my wife's needs are not what I expected either."

Dylan's father chuckled. "I imagine they are not. Nevertheless, what are your intentions?"

"I didn't want to have to ask, but I am afraid I will require one small loan to get us by until spring. We have had a . . . setback . . . and profits may not be what I projected. I am working on another investment idea to procure additional income in the meantime, as well as provide for my growing staff." Dylan hoped his father would not ask for specifics, for he had none.

Andrew Prescot crossed his arms and his legs. His jaw grew firm. "Son, maybe you should consider moving to Grass Valley as well. An experienced rancher is sure to purchase Rolling Oaks eventually. Let it go. Your marriage is not worth the stress and toil. God knows the strain it put on your mother and I the first couple of years we were up here. Lydia needs to be around people, learn to engage with society. Have you considered that she could put her dressmaking skills to use once again?"

Where was this coming from? It was as if his parents had already decided Dylan and Lydia's future. Dylan wasn't ready to expose Lydia to the world daily. He had tried to tell himself she wasn't ready, but truth be told, he wasn't sure he was ready. Especially after witnessing how quickly she had taken to Pete.

"What happened to letting me do this on my own?" Fear gripped Dylan. His father didn't realize how naïve Lydia still was about the world. He needed the conversation to stay focused on the business aspect of things.

"That ended the moment you came to me for more money. Dylan . . . you have business sense, but you are no rancher. Unless you can afford to hire out enough labor to keep you on the paper end of things and out of the fields, I don't see another option."

Dylan sighed. All his hours working the ranch had left little time for crunching numbers and soliciting contracts from buyers. Having Pete and Albert would prove beneficial in time. However, he needed a crew of workers. Who else would be willing to work for only room and board for months until they turned a profit? Who would be safe to leave alone with his wife during times he needed to travel for business?

"I've hired a housemaid and two ranch hands—the first arrived last night along with the news about Dan. With Lydia otherwise detained with Hattie, I'll also need a second housemaid. Is Violet Marks still looking to stay in the area?"

"That would be a matter for you to discuss with Mrs. O'Shea. However, you will be hard pressed to find local laborers if the mines continue to turn profits. But let us not discount the possibility that God will provide in another way."

"If you and Mother would have decided to stay here, I suppose we would have had the option to move into the upper level—if only temporarily. But without that option, and no reserves to cover the cost of living elsewhere . . ." Dylan couldn't bring himself to utter the fact a move to Grass Valley and living with his parents may be their only choice if they couldn't successfully run the ranch with limited resources.

Andrew sighed. "Son, I commend your efforts thus far. Do not lose hope yet." He leaned in and patted Dylan's knee, then winked. "I suppose I can draw out an additional reserve—but it will need to be paid back promptly. And it comes with the condition that you will use a portion of it to run help wanted advertisements in the Morning Union and other newspapers from here to San Francisco. If you agree, I'll loan whatever you think you need."

Relief emerged even though Dylan did not like the idea of having strangers on his property. This was why he had hoped word of mouth through people he knew would be enough. What choice did he have now? He had trusted referrals from Dan for Pete and Jason for his cousin, Albert, as a second ranch hand. Obviously, even that approach did not bring guarantees. All he knew about Pete was that he was a widower and a hard worker by Dan's account alone.

"Thank you, Father." Dylan rose from his chair and reached his hand out to his father. A twinge of guilt settled in his stomach as he made firm eye contact.

Though his father couldn't know it, a portion of this loan would also be used to serve some unmet needs of his marriage as well.

SEVEN

Lydia clung to Hattie for a long while after Dylan left. There were no words. Only long sighs followed by shudders and deep sobbing with a shower of tears.

Hattie's dead weight only made the agony within Lydia that much harder to bear. It was her friend who had lost her husband. Nevertheless, the grief—the torment emanating from Hattie—seeped into Lydia's heart and soul. What could she say?

Hattie couldn't have her husband back.

Not ever.

"Come . . . let's sit up." Lydia forced out the words. "I'll make you some tea."

She placed a pillow under Hattie's back and tucked the quilt in under her chin. The moment brought her back to the day Brian was born. So much joy and life came forth from this bed. Now it would only serve as a reminder of a space Dan would never occupy again.

Lydia rubbed the tears from her cheeks with her sleeve. She had to be strong for Hattie. Stronger.

She searched the room for the children. Locating them had skipped her mind the moment Hattie had fallen into her arms. Neither Olive nor Brian were present in their single-room cabin. The cot Olive slept on appeared undisturbed. A flour sack and a basket of linens sat inside Brian's crib. Hattie's mother must have taken them already.

It seemed strange that Hattie had not joined them. Why stay here alone in her sorrow?

The important thing was that she could focus on Hattie and comforting her here and now.

Lydia started the water for tea and added another log to the fire. She hadn't noticed how freezing the house was until she pulled away from Hattie and the brisk air shot through the gap in her opened coat. Had Hattie gone the entire night without heat?

When Mama died, Lydia had been partially prepared for the news. She understood Mama might not survive the forest fire. However, Dan worked for one of the safest mines in the country. "Accident free," he used to say. Hattie probably never thought of the possibility that the mine could take his life.

Hattie's sobs echoed in the room and shook the bed. Lydia went to her and held her. "Jesus . . . Jesus comfort Hattie in this moment. Assure her you will be her guide and her strength as she requires it."

This was Lydia's first attempt at praying for someone else. She did her best to duplicate the prayers she had heard many people say on her behalf after Mama died.

Hattie would make it. Her children needed her. Hattie had little lives depending on her to stand strong and look to the future—to distract her from the pain and void left after losing a husband. It was more reason than Lydia had when she lost Mama.

Once the fire roared and dissolved the chill through the room, Lydia located some biscuits and served tea on a tray at the end of the bed. The silence between friends was peaceful. Hattie cooperated with Lydia's efforts and even managed a small smile of thanks. A plan for supper would need to happen soon, but for now, Lydia felt Hattie only needed her presence as sustenance.

It was late afternoon before Hattie spoke. "My mother has the children," Hattie whispered and sipped the last bit of tea.

Lydia nodded and pulled a comb through Hattie's unkempt hair. Knots of frizzy curls matted beneath the back of her neck made it difficult to avoid tugging on her scalp. Hattie did not complain. Her tears and shuddering had subsided for the moment.

"They insisted I go with them, but I couldn't—not yet anyway." She sighed and leaned into Lydia's tugs.

Lydia's heart sank. Of course, Hattie wouldn't stay on here. The only reason they had not already moved was in large part due to Dylan and Lydia still being relatively close. Dan's drinking habit was also a big reason. He couldn't have Hattie's parents close enough to see his nightly routine and witness how often he left Hattie alone when he wasn't working.

It didn't seem fair after all Hattie had sacrificed for a husband who mostly left her alone—but maybe God was making a way for something new. It hurt to think that plan might mean a more distant friendship.

"Are you sure moving in with your parents is the only option?" Lydia made herself speak without emotion, despite the despair she felt about her friend living nearly a day's journey away.

Hattie nodded slightly. "As much as I look forward to your visits, most days I am alone. Besides, my parents need help at the mercantile. And I need an income if I am going to keep caring for my little ones. Funds for half-orphans hardly provide for necessities. There's no reason for them to live in squalor, not when I have my parents to provide shelter and additional income."

"You can stay with us at the ranch and help me bake and finally let me teach you dressmaking techniques . . ." Hattie and two little ones running around might not set well with Dylan. She should probably discuss the option with him first.

"No . . . I could not add that burden to you. My parents have two extra rooms at their house. They are happy to take us."

"Then I'll go with you. If the mercantile is as busy as you say, who will care for Olive and Brian? I can stay at the house, sew dresses, and prepare the meals."

"And be apart from your husband?" Hattie shook her head, but something in her voice made her sound hopeful for the first time all day.

"It would only be for a few weeks. The ranch has consumed Dylan lately and with training the new hires, he might be okay with me being away until spring. He hardly has time for me anymore and when he does . . . well . . ."

Hattie turned and looked up at Lydia, a sideways smile emerging past her pained expression. "Well?"

"He's not interested in talking . . ." The topic used to be one to bring giggles, but now it became a reminder that despite the frequency of the intimate times she and Dylan shared, her monthly continued to arrive on schedule.

"At least he is still interested. Dan and I . . . were having troubles in that department."

Lydia shook her head. "Never mind about my troubles anyway. Let's get you settled for the night. Dylan will be back any time. He'll understand and I'm sure some time apart will do us some good. He can focus on the ranch without feeling obligated to me. He has hired two ranch hands . . . Pete Evan is there now and—"

Hattie raised her eyebrows. "Pete? The widower? Maybe it is best you stay with me for a while."

"Why is that?" Lydia would not admit how just saying his name caused a flutter in her chest.

Hattie laughed and surprised Lydia at how quickly her mood could change. "You didn't notice? Wow, Dylan definitely did a good job captivating you if you didn't."

"Notice what?"

"How incredibly handsome and charming he is. He first time I met him, even I couldn't help my heart from racing even though I had given birth to Olive only weeks earlier."

Flustered at recalling her own heart rate while she had served Pete the night previous, Lydia changed the subject.

"When did you tell your mother that you'd be ready to leave?"

Hattie shook her head and pressed puffy lips together. She glanced around the room, ran her hand across the empty side of the bed. "I said I would send a telegram within a few days. I can't imagine leaving yet . . . not until I have retrieved the good memories Dan and I shared to hide in my heart and mind forever." A tear dripped onto her cheek, but she smiled. "There are some not-so-good memories I am happy to leave."

Hattie was probably referencing the frequent arguments and the emotional wall Dan had built that rarely let Hattie in. Yet, she'd loved him anyway and would have stayed in French Corral forever to honor him and keep distance from her parents.

Hattie turned to a lighter topic and began sharing memories with Lydia—many of which led the women to laughter. By the time Lydia had heated up a portion of the meal Clara had brought earlier in the day, Hattie seemed to have built up an appetite. The thick sorrow that had filled the air upon Lydia's arrival had thinned to acceptance.

Nevertheless, Lydia knew how quickly the loss of a loved one could swing one's mood. She had felt guilty for allowing joy into her heart after Mama had died. Hattie was a strong woman, but grief was not an easy burden to bear.

"How soon do you think you will be able to come to Grass Valley?" Hattie's voice sounded nearly normal, as if in everyday conversation.

"I imagine—if I can convince Dylan it is for the best—I can be down within a couple of days." Her confidence swayed as she considered that Jaina may not be so keen on the idea.

"What about now? Will he let you stay here and help me pack things?"

"You probably didn't notice my belongings on the porch, but Dylan brought me here to stay for now. He'll be checking in before he heads back to the ranch. So I'm here if you need me to be."

Hattie pulled her hands into a single clap and looked surprised. "Oh good. You can't know how much having you here for the past few hours has helped my spirits. Perhaps he can send word to my mother that you're here, so she doesn't worry?"

"Of course."

"Did he say he was going to his parent's house? Last I heard, their move to Grass Valley is nearly final."

Lydia nodded, and a twinge in her chest brought reality to the situation. One by one, the people of French Corral, whom she had come to know and love as family, were leaving. Even Jason and Clara Roberts were packing up their store to partner with Hattie's parents at the mercantile. And with Hattie and her children moving on as well, before long Dylan would be all she had.

Questioning why God would allow so many events to unfold and lead to another kind of isolated life, discouragement sunk Lydia's spirits. She did her best to hide them in the presence of her friend, but a desire to distract herself emerged.

EIGHT

Twilight veiled French Corral in evening shades of navy, lapis, and indigo as Dylan pulled up to Hattie's cabin. The women's chatter echoed to the porch, and though indecipherable through the wall, seemed upbeat from Dylan's interpretation.

He paused, thinking of how much Lydia had grown accustomed to life in French Corral, their brief time as newlyweds at her home in the Valley, and then as a rancher's wife in Penn Valley. Now, more changes and choices lay ahead. Thank God in heaven she seemed to adjust well. But how many of these changes were due to his own misjudgment?

Perhaps he should have considered his father's offer for them to live in the upper level of his parent's house that past summer. After Lydia's grandfather, Mr. Sinclair, had taken back the land of the Valley and made it clear he would not accept her as family, their choices were few.

Instead, Dylan had felt the need to make some distance and avoid the hovering eye of his mother. When the ranch became available days after he and

Lydia had returned from San Francisco the previous summer, Dylan was sure this was where God was directing their path.

Dotted with clusters of oak trees between rolling grassy hills, he and Lydia chose the name Rolling Oaks Ranch. Fully stocked with a two-story house, a barn and plenty of land for raising cattle and sheep, he saw no reason they couldn't turn a profit and recoup his early inheritance within the year.

Now, the whole concept seemed foolish.

He knocked on the sun beaten door of the Logan home.

Lydia welcomed him with a brief kiss at the door and showed him inside.

He drew a deep breath and weighed his choice of words before speaking. Most of what stirred in his mind could not be spoken aloud. He began with his attention toward Hattie. "How are you faring, Hattie?"

Hattie sat up on one side of the bed, a tray of half-eaten biscuits and an empty teacup at her feet. Though invisible, it seemed as if she had placed a solid line between her and Dan's side of the bed—quilt neatly laid out, the top folded down and pillow fluffed beside her own as if she expected him to come lay beside her at any moment. She folded her hands around her elbows and nodded. "Much better with Lydia here, thank you."

Lydia wove her fingers through Dylan's as she stood beside him at the foot of the bed. "She's happy to know I can stay for a few days and help her with moving."

"Moving?" His wife didn't seem disappointed enough at her announcement. Dylan suspected there was a plan in the works to keep the friends from parting so soon.

Lydia nodded. "After the funeral at French Corral, there will be a memorial service at Empire Mine." She watched Hattie as she spoke, a questioning tone in her voice. "Hattie plans to stay in town with her parents after that. The children are already there. However, she will need help until she can secure a nanny."

Here it comes. "That's what her parents are for, right?" Dylan attempted to sidestep what he thought would come next.

"Well . . . not exactly." Lydia turned to face Dylan. Her smile didn't soothe him but instead, it made his heart race in a disturbing way. "I have offered to go with her . . . I realize I should have asked first, and you can say no . . . but the kids already know me and—"

"Please excuse us for a moment, Hattie." Dylan clenched his jaw and tried not to increase his grip on Lydia's hand as he led her outside.

What was the Lord doing here? He had just decided that Lydia was better off at the ranch, adjusting to one stranger at a time. He desired his adoring wife back—the young woman whose gaze had said he was all she needed. He wasn't prepared for her to insist on independence this way. He honestly thought her apology the night before would have deterred her from taking initiative for a long while.

"Dylan, let me explain," Lydia said once he shut the door and they were alone on the porch.

He felt like the only husband in the Sierras whose wife not only did not know her place—but worse—didn't even realize she had left it.

"Let you explain? No, I need to explain." He shook his head and stared into the darkening sky for a moment before turning back to face his wife.

Lydia nodded and her bottom lip began to quiver. "I don't understand what's happening between us. I've done it again, haven't I?"

"Sweet Lydia." He cupped her cheek with one hand and searched her eyes. Nothing in them told him she was trying to be defiant. "I'm struggling as well. Our first months at the ranch were idyllic. We worked together, rested together, and enjoyed every moment to the fullest."

He sighed when she smiled at his words, her lips pressed together in agreement, accompanied by a tear-filled gaze.

"I will not hide my apprehension." Dylan raised an eyebrow to establish his authority despite the fact her eyes were melting him at the core. "And I need you . . . plead with you . . . to discuss things with me before you decide in your heart what you will do."

She pressed her hand over his on her face. "I will! And I knew it the moment I said it—that I should have asked you first."

He brought her closer and kissed her, more for his own comfort than for her benefit, while he determined what to say next. He held her face close to his, sorry that he may have coaxed out the solitary tear sliding down the side of her nose.

"I'm hoping this will work out for the best. I will know more in a few days. Then I'll have delegated to Pete and Albert and see if Emily will accept the added responsibility of cooking. I will return for the funeral and take you home. Then, we will discuss it and I will decide what's best. Only then will I permit you to stay in Grass Valley as a temporary nanny for Hattie's children."

Lydia nodded and sighed. "Whatever you decide, I promise to be the respectful . . . and obedient wife that you deserve."

Her voice faded with each word. More than obedience, Dylan wanted her heart to be in it. Why didn't he believe it was?

The week Lydia spent with Hattie became an overwhelming chore of physical toil and emotional exhaustion. Between thoughts over her words to Dylan and concerns over Hattie, her mind rarely rested. No matter where her mind wandered, the work required to care for and prepare Hattie for moving never ceased. Hattie's house soon became a constant stream of townsfolk coming to bid condolences, assisting with loading Hattie's belongings, and keeping plenty of prepared food at hand to nourish all.

Though Lydia was glad to be a part of the efforts and have an opportunity to visit with the same folks who'd comforted her and made Mama's death bearable—by the end of the week, she was ready to go back home.

Her opinion of how to handle affairs for Hattie were mostly disregarded. Hattie's neighbors and the other townsfolk didn't have to guess what needed to be done. Whenever she thought she knew the best course of action, someone would chime in about why it wouldn't work or how another way was better. They were experienced in the routine of helping the grieving and efficiently packing up a home ready for abandonment.

Lydia felt even more useless when her *monthly* arrived, requiring additional laundry as well as discretion while Hattie's house remained full of both friends and strangers. Before long, Lydia stopped offering a voice and became available by hand and heart alone.

This time, all eyes and efforts were on Hattie's comfort. Orders came from Mrs. O'Shea, Clara, and even Jason about what to do and how to do it.

"Take the laundry off the line, fold it, and place it in that crate there . . ."

"Stack those pots and utensils in that trunk . . ."

"Kindly reheat the stew . . ."

All the while, Hattie kept quiet on the bed, bouts of tears followed by long naps and silent staring. Whenever Lydia found a free minute to sit with her friend, she tried to coax out a smile and find a glimmer of that easy-going woman who had emerged ever so briefly the day Lydia had arrived. But to no avail. By the time the day of the funeral arrived, Lydia numbly succumbed to demands and requests, her mind focused on silent prayers for Hattie.

Lydia considered the promise she had given Dylan and doubted her heart's intent. Her thoughts came from a place of internal battles on unfamiliar ground. It was what she wanted and knew Dylan desired—so why did she doubt her ability to follow through? Without being able to talk about it with Hattie, Lydia felt overwhelmed. She pressed the uncertainties of her own will aside and focused on the tasks before her. Even then, she felt ill-equipped.

Upon Dylan's return, Lydia relished in his embrace, holding fast to the feel of his arms around her as she pushed away thoughts of ever losing him.

On the way home, she didn't speak of the possibility of going to Grass Valley. She would leave it to Dylan to initiate discussing the topic.

Unsure she had what it took to care for her friend, her resolve dissolved. However, she missed Olive and Brian and wanted to provide for their needs—especially if Hattie continued in her state of despair. God willing, if Dylan allowed her to go, she would use her time away from home to discover a way to find satisfaction in her evident future of continued isolation.

NINE

Dylan guided Bailey around the back of the house to graze after inspecting the fencing Albert was repairing. Spotting Lydia's gingham print shawl on the porch post, waving in the cool breeze, he thought it odd that Lydia would not be wearing the shawl to keep warm. He scanned the yard and saw her at the laundry line. His wife had been quick to catch up on incomplete chores upon her return. Among the intertwined shadows of near-bare branches, it took a moment for Dylan to see that someone else stood under the oak tree, partially hidden by the swaying sheets along the line.

His heart rate surged upon the realization that it was Pete. His stomach twisted. Pain paralyzed him like a noose cutting off his heart from his head. How did Pete seem to find a reason to hover near the house repeatedly, despite the many duties he was to accomplish far from there? With Lydia's back to the pasture and Pete's view blocked by the laundry line and Lydia, Dylan willed brick-heavy boots forward to get a better idea of what was happening between his wife and his hired help.

Lydia's pace of removing the laundry was at a near standstill. She kept folding the same sheet in her hands, leaving the remaining linens flapping in the breeze. Pete and Lydia appeared engrossed in deep conversation and completely oblivious to Dylan's approach.

Dylan cleared his throat and Lydia jumped.

"H—hello." Lydia quickly dropped the folded sheet into the basket. When she reached for a pin and began to remove another sheet, the breeze kicked up and blew it to the ground.

Pete lunged forward and scooped it up. As he handed the sheet to Lydia, he looked directly at Dylan. "Mr. Prescot, sir, I'll be happy to take Bailey back to the barn for water."

Dylan handed the reins over without hesitation and gave forceful nod. "You do that, Pete. And when you finish, you can join Albert at the east fence. Those repairs need to be completed to-night."

If he had not so desperately needed Pete's help, he would have dismissed him from the ranch that instant.

Lydia bit her lip and focused on folding the re-maining items left on the laundry line, frightened that she had once again done something to disap-point Dylan.

Several minutes earlier, Lydia had descended the porch, about to grab her shawl when Pete raced past her toward the oak tree near the laundry line. She froze, clinging to the sides of the empty basket between her hands.

Pete leaned a thick hand against the trunk, hunched forward, and began coughing violently around the back of the tree. When the coughing fit didn't stop, Lydia had hurried over to see if he was all right. The muscles across his back bulged through his shirt. His legs stood staunch and thick like an ox straining against the weight of a plow. She rested a hand on his shoulder blade, but he waved her off.

Still, she stayed close, the scent of oak dust and pine needles emanating with each spasm until his fit ceased. When she stepped back to begin taking down the laundry, she kept eyeing him to ensure he was fine.

Once Pete recovered, he turned around but remained in the shadows of the tree limbs. Cloud-filtered sunlight seeped between bare branches and illuminated his chicory-blue eyes amid the shadows.

"My apologies for startling you, Mrs. Prescot. This cough has been improving but occasionally, a fit will take me unawares. If I'd known you were here, I'd have faltered out by the road."

"I'll make my mama's recipe of tea blended with herbs for you this evening. Does everyone who works the mines get such coughs?" Lydia asked, compelled to hear him out as compassion filled her soul.

"The physician said the cough could linger for years but working outdoors should keep it from getting worse."

It didn't seem right that he would have to suffer this coughing illness after devoting his life to the mines. Lydia was so caught up in his story, she hadn't noticed Dylan approaching them.

Why had she felt instant shame once she'd known her husband was near? How could she be so easily consumed by this stranger, overwhelming concern filling her heart? Would every man she met captivate her this way?

In the silence hovering between them while she waited for Dylan to respond, Lydia began to desire distance from the ranch. She needed an opportunity to separate herself from these moments where her heart and her mind insisted on playing against each other.

The knot in his stomach growing, Dylan waited for several moments to allow Lydia time to explain. Would she offer a reason for their conversation or explain why Pete had strayed so far from his task of chopping firewood on the other side of the house? The answer appeared to be no as she proceeded to retrieve and fold the remaining laundry in silence, her back to Dylan.

Was she unaware at how improper it was for her to be speaking to Pete in such a secluded setting? He hadn't anticipated the need to educate his wife on proper conduct with other men. Had his mother not injected these norms into Lydia's lessons?

He shook off a vision that crossed his mind of what may have transpired had he not spotted them. Pete had to know better—his shameful expression prior to heading to the barn revealed it. Why would he risk his new job, and his hide, to steal moments and speak with another man's wife?

Dylan swallowed hard and tucked his thumbs into his front pockets. "I suppose now is as good a time as any to let you know I've decided to allow you to help Hattie in Grass Valley."

Continued isolation wasn't helping his wife learn proper etiquette and societal norms. She'd need to observe and learn firsthand if there was any hope at all.

Lydia turned to him, lit eyes contrasting the odd frown at the corners of her mouth. She pulled a hand to her lips and sucked in a breath. "Thank you." She heaved the loaded basket of linens from the grass and gave Dylan a quick kiss on the cheek before heading toward the house.

For several moments, Dylan stood there, not sure what to do next. He was confused about everything that had just transpired. At least Lydia seemed happy about the decision. Before her time in Grass Valley was up, he would speak to Pete. Then he would finalize his plans to rekindle the passion he'd shared with his wife only a few months earlier. He forced down fleeting thoughts of hesitation and uncertainty and hastened his mind to the tasks that needed finishing before he could take her away.

That evening, Dylan decided Lydia needed a distraction from any unintended thoughts she may be having about the hired help. How could he explain to her the line between polite and making the wrong impression? Distraction seemed a better tool than stirring up a discussion that could end badly. This way, he would avoid revealing his own insecurities a not risk looking like a fool in case he was imagining things.

Music box in his hands, he ascended the stairs to their bedroom, where Lydia was completing her packing.

"I thought you could take along pen, ink, and stationary and write Uncle Moses a letter while you are in Grass Valley. Mother says your penmanship is coming along nicely."

Lydia squealed, and then bit her lip. "Do you think he is still in San Francisco? The last letter is dated over ten years ago."

Dylan could see hope waning in Lydia's eyes.

"There is only one way to find out." He smiled and winked.

"Thank you." Lydia retrieved the music box from Dylan and placed it on the window bench with her other belongings ready for the trunk.

Then, she joined Dylan at the end of the bed, and rested her head on his shoulder.

Grabbing his hand in hers, she squeezed. "Are you sure about this?"

"About what?"

"Taking me to Grass Valley? I feel like I'm abandoning you."

"I'm sure." He returned the squeeze and pulled her hand to his chest, pressing into the beat of his heart. He grazed her forehead with his other hand and searched her eyes—still so innocent and trusting. "I'm going to work hard to ensure you come back to a home that offers some rest and work only for the things you love doing."

A shy smile replaced her pensive gaze. "I am looking forward to living with running water and electricity for a time. Though I am sure caring for Hattie, Olive, and Brian will be a close match to the demands of caring for pregnant ewes and their newborn lambs." Her eyes sparkled and she laughed.

"It will be good practice." Dylan tapered his grin before he drew her in for a serious kiss.

That night, while he held her close, he prayed for a breakthrough in the coming weeks. His confidence as provider was weakening. What if he could not sustain the ranch? Would Lydia's faith in him also falter?

Visions of worst-case scenarios haunted his dreams—a rundown shack on the edge of town for their home, him forced to become an accountant for some shady gambling establishment while Lydia became a waitress preyed on by drunken miners. Their babies—if they had any—dirty and crying in their cribs while Lydia sat exhausted and unresponsive in a creaky rocking chair.

Lord, please show me the way. I will not believe this is the plan you have for us. Show me how to provide a good life and one that will allow us both to honor you in every way.

TEN

Before dawn, the steady tap of raindrops against the window woke Dylan. Rubbing sleep from his face, he ushered his weary limbs into motion. Rain would not make the day's journey an easy one. The earlier they could get going, the better.

Less than an hour later, near-freezing rain whipped around the carriage as Dylan clung to drenched, slippery reins. Lydia nestled in close to his side, the familiar grip on his arm a reminder of her dependence on him. He scanned the road ahead for ruts and puddles and guided the horses around anything that could jar them enough to throw a wheel.

With each aversion, a small voice within told him that God held their future in his grasp. When the carriage hit a hole, Dylan hadn't seen beyond misting sheets of rain, he realized seeing or avoiding every potential set back in their future was not possible. He steadied the carriage, fighting doubts that seeped into his spirit like the streams of icy rain flowing into his collar.

Freezing through wet layers of garments, Lydia clung to Dylan for more than just warmth. Hattie revealing her own attraction toward Pete echoed in her mind and stirred feelings Lydia could not explain. She felt something for Pete as well—but she didn't know what to call it. Hattie made it sound so obvious and seemed to be making a joke. Yet, Lydia hadn't shared how Pete sparked her insides either. Was this something she should share with Hattie when the time was right?

Dylan was hers now and forever. He would be the only man she would ever be this close to.

Ever.

The words of Elder Scott echoed in her mind—
And what God has joined, let no man take apart . . .

At the time she spoke them, Lydia hadn't understood her vows completely. Though she intended to fulfill them. Of course, she would remain faithful to her husband. Other men hadn't been a problem until then. Jason, Dan, customers at the Inn—none of them had made her insides tingle. But she didn't understand that another man may enter her life and draw her in as Pete had. None since Dylan awoke the fluttering, the sensations that seemed to wake up after months of feeling dormant. How had the fervor between them ceased so soon after she and Dylan had said their vows?

If she dug deeper into her emotions, she knew what she desired most was to feel that way for her own husband again.

Rain splattered across her cheek and she nuzzled her face into Dylan's arm. His strength penetrated through his damp jacket as he guided the reins. She thought she felt him shiver. Would her affection for him resume during their time apart? Would there ever be a time when her marriage would not seem like an endless stream of unanswered questions?

In frigid silence during the remainder of their journey, she prayed and willed that God rid her of any inappropriate feelings for Pete or any other man. She desired to love her husband—and her husband only—deeply and devoutly for the rest of her life.

Hattie's parents' house was on the south edge of Grass Valley. The town, full of narrow, yet steep hills, reminded Lydia of a miniature version of San Francisco. Although trees instead of ocean bordered its inhabitants, the town held an intoxicating charm, and a welcoming presence. Even in the murky weather, brick buildings, colorful store signs and Victorian-style homes created a dream-like state of calm.

"You sure you understand how to send a telegram should you need anything?" Dylan's hands gripped firmly on her waist didn't want to let go. Cold rain dripped from his hat and splashed onto Lydia's cheek.

Dylan removed one hand from her side and, using his thumb, caressed the cool water into her cheek instead of off it.

Lydia nodded, the security of his firm, strong hand on her face creating a swirling sensation in her belly.

He pulled her closer, warm breath tingling more than just her frozen face. "Let's get up to the porch. Soon we will go from sopping to soggy."

The Williams' home was a modern bungalow, according to Dylan, who had pointed out the different style houses along the ride. Thick white beams bordered a deep porch that spanned the front of the pale-green home. A mist from the wind-whipped sprays of rain covered the wide slats of the porch floor. Lydia took her steps with care, unsure how her arrival would affect the children, or the strict routine most likely established by Mrs. Williams.

The door handle jingle echoed through humid air. At first, it appeared nobody stood at the opened door. Then chubby fingers curled around the edge of the bottom half of the door, followed by round, wide eyes.

"Lylia!" Olive squealed and leapt into Lydia's wet coat. She turned her head back toward the house, undeterred by the damp wool and yelled again. "Brian . . . Momma . . . Lylia is here!"

Mrs. Williams and the children gathered at the doorway, but Hattie did not appear or make a sound from within the house.

"Hattie is resting," Mrs. Williams said with a glint of worry in her eyes. Then she pulled out a smile and scooped Brian onto her hip. "The children and I were having a snack while we waited for you. I've got to get back to the store as soon as you're settled."

Mrs. Williams took Brian back toward the kitchen. Olive stayed attached to Lydia's coat and skirt, and pulled until Lydia followed her to the fireplace, where they warmed their hands and waited for Dylan.

Dylan brought up Lydia's trunk and other belongings and set them inside the doorway. When he joined them by the fire, he slipped around to the side of Lydia not blocked by a small child and slid his arm beneath her coat and around her side. His grip was firm as he pulled her into the crook of his shoulder and chest. His eyes spoke volumes, his smile downcast.

Lydia had no words—unsure of how this separation would affect them. How could she reveal her apprehension now that they were already here? She had seen him, felt him, spoke with him every day for over a year. What would it be like to be so far from his presence?

Olive clung to Lydia's leg, whining for more biscuits and jam. Lydia caressed the child's pine-nut curls and attempted to relinquish Dylan's hand from her ribs. "I will be fine . . . and very busy. Violet will also be arriving to assist Emily. And with me out of the way, you'll be able to fully focus on the ranch and have ample time to work out a solution about the sheep. Just remember Albert and Pete must rotate night shifts with the pregnant ewes." Focusing on work seemed to be the best escape from relentless emotions lately.

"I love you," he said firmly, pulling her yet closer, demanding she meet his gaze.

Deep pools of willow-green plucked at a place deep in her heart. "I love you. Now smile so I can remember you in a happy state." She leaned up and kissed his cheek, holding it for a moment before tracing the indent of his dimples with her lips until they met his own.

He took her breath away, kissing deeply. Her smile broke their bond and she wished they could have just one more evening alone before he parted.

He could still wake the butterflies after all.

When Lydia asked Mrs. Williams where Hattie was, she only pressed her mouth shut, shook her head and sighed. Then she pointed down the hall toward the bedrooms. "She won't leave the room."

Within a few minutes, Mrs. Williams gave instructions for Lydia to take charge of the children and dinner and hurried back to the store. With Brian immersed and gobbling up his biscuits and jam in his highchair, Lydia stood on the porch and watched Dylan race down the walk. She waved goodbye while he turned the carriage around and headed toward town. She ignored the wind pushing rain onto her face until Olive's whining about the cold turned into wails from the doorway. When Brian toddled over asking for more biscuits, Lydia turned her attention to the children.

After cleaning up biscuit crumbs and jam remnants on the table, chairs, and floor, Lydia brought the children into their nursery to play. Once they were occupied with dolls, books, and blocks, Lydia proceeded to the other end of the hallway to seek out Hattie, who had yet to appear.

With the quiet sounds of the children playing behind her, Lydia approached the still, silent, and shadowed hallway. Each step creaked the floorboards, announcing her arrival to the partially cracked door Lydia assumed led into Hattie's room. She nudged the door, the hinges squeaking in protest. With heavy curtains drawn, it took a moment for Lydia's eyes to adjust to the darkness. Though the room was cooler than the rest of the house, the air felt heavy and thick, as if the weight of Hattie's sorrow had overflowed from her and into every corner.

Lydia located a gas lamp sitting on the round table near the door. She turned the cool, metal switch until it clicked. Soft, pale-yellow light emanated only a few feet in every direction, but enough for Lydia to locate her friend lying on the bed.

Hattie faced the window, lying in her nightgown barefoot and still atop the wrinkled quilt. Lydia sat down, placing herself in the crook remaining between Hattie's waist and the edge of the bed.

Lydia remembered days when the loss of Mama seemed greater than others did. How long had Hattie been like this? Mrs. Williams had not revealed details, only a look of concern. Lydia rubbed Hattie's shoulder, but her friend did not respond with even a blink. Her eyes red-rimmed, fingers clutching a handkerchief. If not for the slow rise and fall of her chest, Lydia would have wondered if her friend were still alive.

"Hattie," she whispered. "Hattie, I'm here."

Lydia looked around the room for a quilt. One lay draped over the back of the chair beneath the window. She opened the window a crack, thinking the cold and damp, yet fresh air should wake Hattie's senses. She found a pair of stockings in the bureau and pulled them over Hattie's purple toes. Then she cloaked the quilt over her, tucking it in behind her back and shoulders and under her feet.

Had Mrs. Williams given up on her basic needs for care? Or, had Hattie refused her mother's gestures?

Hattie still didn't move, though she sighed once, her breath lapsing as if the act of sobbing now took too great an effort.

Lydia lit the lantern on the nightstand and turned on the two remaining lamps in the room.

"Have you had lunch yet?"

Hattie closed her eyes and pinched her lips together, then turned her face into the shadow of the pillow.

Lydia's stomach tightened. She hadn't an appetite after Momma died. But Hattie needed nourishment to keep up her strength for the children.

"Lilia?" Olive's loud whisper was followed by a flurry of socked feet padding the hardwood floor in the hallway. When she came to the doorway, she stopped and peered at the floor.

"I am saying hello to your mama, Olive. You need to stay with Brian and play nicely."

Olive looked up at Lydia, tilted her head, and nodded. Her eyes darted to Hattie, then back to the floor.

"You can come see her for a moment."

Olive's eyebrows raised and her mouth parted with a small smile. She scurried to the side of the bed and reached up. Lydia lifted her to Hattie. Olive instantly wrapped her arms around her mama's neck and then kissed her cheek.

With what seemed like great effort, Hattie found her own small smile, and patted Olive's bottom. "Go now . . ." she whispered, tears pooling in her eyes. "Mama will see you for dinner."

However, when dinnertime arrived, Hattie was sleeping soundly. Since Olive didn't ask for her, Lydia did her best to distract the children by seating them by the fire and telling them Bible stories about rainbows, angels, and miracles. Thankfully, Olive seemed undeterred once bedtime arrived, her eyes growing heavy with sleep only moments after Lydia tucked her in and said prayers. Brian required a bit more cajoling, but eventually lost the fight after a long session of Lydia humming hymns and swaying to the sound of the storm outside.

Fatigued and somewhat frustrated at the lack of help by Hattie's parents, sleep did not come easy for Lydia that first night. She already missed Dylan terribly and uttered a prayer for his safe return home and success in his business-related endeavors. She relived the moments of their farewell until sleep finally took her into the morning light.

ELEVEN

The carriage wheels sloshed and careened along the uneven street as Dylan passed the rock quarry and ascended the steep incline on Neil Street. Turning right on Mill Street, Bailey nearly collided with a bike messenger crossing the intersection from the left. Dylan yanked on the reins, and a sheet of pooled rainwater spilled onto his lap from the carriage canopy.

Dylan's heart thudded. He hadn't even looked in that direction. The last thing he needed was to have to replace a bike or cover the medical costs of some stranger. The boy looked more embarrassed than angry at the near miss, and quickly sped around the carriage before Dylan could prompt his startled horse to continue. A half block down, he brought the carriage to a stop.

Veering his thoughts from his heart to his head, Dylan focused on business matters.

He shook as much water as he could from his hat and coat, and careful not to slip on the stone steps, entered the Morning Union building. A half-dozen conversations and tapping on typewriter keys filled the warm, dry air.

Dylan placed an ad for a ranch hand and an additional housemaid. Even with Violet coming, he knew her help was temporary.

Back outside, the wind had picked up. At first, Dylan thought the rain had slowed. It wasn't until he slipped on the last step that he realized the rain had turned into sleet. As soon as he started to fall backward, he wrapped his arm around the metal railing between the steps.

"Are you all right, sir?" A man on the other side of the steps leaned down and lent a hand.

Grasping the bar had slowed his fall only enough to keep him from banging his head on the upper step. His bottom side had hit hard enough to cause a shooting pain up the side of Dylan's back.

He took the man's hand with gratitude. "Yes, thank you. I'm fine . . . didn't realize the steps were icy."

As soon as Dylan stood upright, the man tipped his hat and fled up the steps and into the building.

Dylan checked his watch. If he didn't start heading home within the hour, he might need to stay at the Anthony House in Penn Valley—yet one more expense unrelated to investing in the ranch. He chastised himself for believing that he could make the trip and back in a single day during harsh weather.

A glance up at charcoal-gray clouds indicated there was a good chance this icy rain would soon be turning into snow. Between the slippery sidewalk and the twinge in his back, his pace slowed. He prayed the movement would work out the kink by the time his errands were complete.

While on Mill Street, he purchased a new dress and parasol for Lydia at the department store with the funds he'd allocated for that exact purpose.

This was the first part of a surprise he was planning for them the coming spring, and the reason he needed to maximize the remainder of the loan from his father.

Whether they ended up living in a shack or not, he felt an urgency to remove them from the toils of ranch life, if for only a short time. He hoped a new solution would surface once they took some time away. A naïve and maybe even irresponsible gesture at best, but he couldn't risk his wife and ranch slipping away all at once.

He had grand plans, and once the details were in place, he would reveal just enough to compel her curiosity and gain excitement. The dress and parasol would be one of many surprises once they arrived in the city. Originally, he was going to take the loan from his father and bring Lydia to San Francisco for a surprise getaway before the lambing season began.

However, between the trials of a reduced flock and Dan's passing leading Lydia to comfort and assist Hattie, he decided to delay the trip until after Easter. For now, he would invest his remaining resources to seek alternative means of income while maximizing the use of his new hires. Come spring, Dylan hoped that things would look promising and enable him and Lydia a reprieve.

At the post office, the ache in Dylan's side had grown into a throbbing. Trying his best to ignore gloomy thoughts about his trip home and handling labor-related tasks about the ranch on his return, he focused instead on the letters he was sending. The one to his grandfather's house, attention to Miss Gracie, contained a request to arrange for theater tickets and dinner reservations upon the planned arrival date of April 15.

Then, he mailed Lydia's first letter to Uncle Moses and a second one that he had written in more detail, where he wrote about their life in Penn Valley and how Emelyn's unfortunate death and Mr. Sinclair's resolution to exile them had forced their move. His hope was that Uncle Moses would understand Lydia's need to be accepted by family and treat her as such.

He knew Lydia would be overjoyed at the prospect of meeting her mother's uncle, and he was not about to let her hopes be dashed—again. He needed confirmation from Moses before attempting to make a personal call. Moses was her only connection to her parents' past and a part of her mother she may never know otherwise.

Dylan prayed for a good return on their efforts—for once—and began his journey home.

Cold air and light snow clung to him and increased the pain that surged up his back with every bump. A folded quilt behind him, he urged the carriage forward through the rapidly darkening sky. The Anthony House was still hours away.

By the time he entered Pleasant Valley Road, every rock and bump sent a stabbing pain between his hip and lower back. His hands were icy wet inside of his gloves, and his face was numb from the constant barrage of snowflakes that had increased in size and stung as the wind blew them his way. More than once, he'd had to recover parcel purchases that toppled into the frozen mud after the carriage blundered over an unseen hole in the road.

Finally, a dim house light blurred in the distance. After turning on what he hoped was the driveway, the carriage lantern bobbed back and forth and revealed the landmarks that confirmed he was nearing the Anthony House.

It was a grueling night of sleep. Between the unending throbbing in his backside and concerns that Pete and Albert had managed all overnight tasks, Dylan found it difficult to rest. Nevertheless, his bed was warm. With Bailey watered, fed and likely finding warmth alongside other horses in the livery stable, Dylan knew he could do nothing about his worries until daylight anyway.

While a silver line of morning sunlight peered over the edge of the foothills, Dylan braced himself against the cool, still air. He urged Bailey back onto Pleasant Valley Road. The crisp, hard ground caused the carriage to bump and jiggle the remaining journey home. Dylan stiffened with each movement, overcompensating to one side to minimize the stabs of pain to the other.

The dawning sun eventually melted the white world that surrounded him, finally warming the tops of his legs shortly before the rooftop of house at Rolling Oaks Ranch came into view. Bracing himself, he snapped the reins. The sooner he could be home, the sooner he could begin his plans—even if it meant delegating everything to Pete and Albert while he nursed his injured backside.

Pete and Violet met Dylan at the carriage before he could even pull it to a complete stop. With few words, they set to work immediately and seemed undeterred by Dylan's back injury.

Pete walked alongside, clutching Dylan's satchel in one hand and the store parcels in the other. "We're glad you made it home safe, Mr. Prescot. You had us worried when you didn't return last night. Nobody was expecting snow."

If Dylan needed to steady himself, he would have no choice but to grab a hold of Pete. Given he felt he may buckle under the pain at any moment, he was never more grateful to be near a man of Pete's stature.

A ceiling-high stack of firewood along the side of the porch assured Dylan of his hired hand's efforts while he'd been gone. Relieved, he entered the toasty-warm house. Pete had no doubt worked through the day and night since Dylan and Lydia's departure.

Once inside, Pete gave a report for the past day and a half. "We had some cows wander back into the coverage of trees at the edge of the field after dark. I sent Albert to round them up while I fed and watered the cattle back at the corral. I filled in a gap around a few fence posts sagging in the mud as well. Shortly after dark, we'd accounted for all the livestock, pregnant cows and ewes included."

"None wandered onto the infected land? How are the horses?"

Pete remained close to Dylan but didn't offer a hand to assist him in sitting. "The fencing around the infected land is still secure. Horses were fed and watered and returned to the stables before the rain turned to snow."

Violet stood silent in the doorway between kitchen and living room.

Dylan nodded at her, trying to cover his grimace with a smile as he adjusted his position. "I'll take my supper in here, Violet. And if you can locate an aspirin in the medical supplies in the shed, I would appreciate it."

"Of course, Mr. Prescot." Her curious gaze turned to disappointment and she shuffled away.

Did she expect a summary of Hattie's condition or some sort of town gossip? Dylan had more important matters to address.

Pete leaned toward Dylan and with a low voice said, "I know you're not partial to hard liquor sir, but I do have a stash in my room . . . if you need it to dull the pain."

Had he done that bad of a job hiding his discomfort? Feeling weak and justifying that a drink might welcome a decent night's sleep, he obliged.

Moments later, the two men clanked their glasses together and raised them. Albert entered, expecting to be late for the afternoon meal. Pete poured another drink, but Dylan put his hand up to signal they would all be finished after one glass each.

Dylan felt odd sitting in his living room with these two men who, though strangers, held the fate of his ranch in their hopefully capable hands. He resisted the urge to enjoy a few more drinks and attempt to get to know these men better while his wife was not around.

However, he could only allow a few moments for pleasantries before focusing again on preparing the ranch for lambing and other tasks. Attempting to keep his motives of understanding Pete's intentions hidden, he addressed the men equally.

"I trust Violet and Emily have fed you both well since Lydia and I departed?" He made sure his gaze settled on Pete when he spoke his wife's name.

Pete held eye contact and nodded. "Every four hours with the diligence of your wife, Mr. Prescot."

Albert agreed. "And may I add that Miss Violet wouldn't retire last evening without keeping a lantern lit in case of your late return."

Never thinking of Violet as more than an arrogant schoolgirl, the gesture caught Dylan off guard. There was a good chance that her princess complex had dissolved now that her parents and sister were in Oregon and she was left on her own.

Dylan took a swallow of the harsh liquor. "To my dismay, I'll need to spend the afternoon here resting my back. If this weather doesn't let up, our workload will double, and I can't afford to be down for one more day. Albert, with your history at the sheep ranch in Montana, you'll stay close to the barn and look for signs of ewes ready for birthing. Pete, the cattle and horses will be your charge in addition to keeping the fencing mended and ensuring no animal or human sets foot on the pasture containing foot rot."

Albert and Pete placed their empty glasses aside and stood, nodding in compliance to Dylan's delegations.

Violet appeared at the door with a linen towel woven between her fingers. "Dinner is at the table."

TWELVE

For the first week, Lydia felt as if she were caring for three children. Hattie required help for everything, not willing to handle even her most basic personal hygiene. Lydia even ended up spoon-feeding her a couple of times. How could she be worse than the day she got the news? That evening she had been talking to Lydia. That evening, she seemed to accept the news and be willing to move on.

Hattie had quit nursing Brian, who now took bottles several times a day. A grueling task, especially when the milkman came late, and Brian's fussing became hysteria. Lydia's heart broke every time the sobbing child pulled at the rubber nipple and gazed down the dark hallway. Sometimes he refused to eat even though she knew he was hungry. What he wanted was his mama, and no amount of milk from a hard, glass bottle would satisfy his need.

What had seemed to be a random, late winter storm turned into weeks of freezing drizzle, snow flurries, and dark skies. It was as if the heavens themselves were mourning along with Hattie.

Mr. and Mrs. Williams would make a brief appearance each evening, and then retired to their bedroom only to be up before Lydia and back at the store. She had a hunch that this had not been their routine prior to her arrival.

When she finally coaxed the children to sleep and spent a few minutes telling Hattie about their day, she then slipped down the hallway to her own room. Each night, the cold sheets would remind her of the absence of Dylan's warmth. At least she could still look forward to sharing a bed with him soon. Hattie would never feel Dan at her side again.

Stuffing down feelings of frustration for having to figure out everything on her own, she focused on what tasks she could complete. Thankfully, Olive was an observant little girl and knew where everything was from extra bedding to baking supplies.

The Williams had a Chinese immigrant couple as servants, Ernie and Edie, but their English was poor, and Lydia found communicating with them difficult. However, Ernie kept the fireplace stoked and handled the grocery deliveries while Edie prepared the main meals. This left Lydia to the sole care of the children and Hattie from dawn until dusk.

It wasn't until late evening that she could sit and ponder the day and the feelings she'd suppressed in the name of serving and providing for Hattie and her children.

Lydia mourned for her friend—not her friend's loss—but for the person her friend used to be. She missed the giddy Hattie with a smile of mischief who never tired of life, even on the duller days.

One afternoon, while Hattie and both children napped, Lydia decided to explore. A room in the back hall had piqued her curiosity. Hattie's mom had referred to it as her sewing room. Out of the many tasks her and Mama completed in the Valley, sewing was always something they had done together.

The door stood ajar, not making the slightest squeak as Lydia pushed it open enough to enter. Various fabrics lay folded in piles on a long table against the sidewall. Wools, calico cottons, satin and silk. Boxes with folding lids were stacked on another table near a desk-like contraption that took Lydia a few moments to recognize. She had only seen drawings in the Sears catalog. Never one up close. She didn't understand why Mama had never brought one to the Valley.

It was a sewing machine.

Lydia ran her hands over the smooth metal top, rounded and shiny black. Metal popped out here and there in the form of springs, knobs, and wheels. How quickly could she make a dress with this machine? How would she ever learn to use it? Mrs. Williams didn't seem to have time to teach her. Even if Lydia could coax Hattie back to her normal self, she'd told Lydia she'd never been interested in sewing, despite her mother's insistence that it was a necessary skill.

Inside one of the narrow drawers, thread spools sat side by side in shades like sunset hues from every season. The other three drawers held needles, shears, a small tin bottle and various tools Lydia could not identify. Then she eyed a booklet—a *magazine*—if that was the correct word for it.

Opening it, she found page after page of drawings of various dresses and patterns like the ones Mama used to bring from the angels, which Lydia now knew were probably from the Robert's General Store in French Corral. They had only sewn about six patterns, duplicating the design until they had mastered the cuts and stitches.

The myriad of colored fabric complete with customized, embroidered accents mesmerized her. There was more fabric variety than she'd ever seen at the general store in French Corral. One of the dress patterns looked nearly identical to the dress she'd worn the night her and Dylan had spent in San Francisco shortly after their wedding day.

Locating a piece of chalk and a blank sheet of tracing paper, Lydia began drawing a revised pattern. She loved the dress, but she had also considered ways to change it—if only slightly. First, she wasn't too fond of her shoulders showing. Instead of a separate drape, she drew in a sleeve that covered the front neckline in a half-circle, leaving only the very tops of the shoulders showing. Next, she took colored pencils and drew in a different embroidered pattern—one with larger flower blossoms, with equally prominent vines and leaves.

The drawing was crude at best but was enough for Lydia to make the alterations as she went along. Whether she used the sewing machine or not, she decided to ask Mrs. Williams if she could at least use the materials in the sewing room to hand stitch the dress. Holding the fabric and imagining sewing again stirred bittersweet memories of Mama. Maybe taking up sewing dresses could also bring in extra income and take a portion of the burden from Dylan to provide through ranch profits alone.

That evening, Mrs. Williams smiled for the first time since Lydia's arrival. To Lydia's surprise, Hattie's mother was more than willing to stay up into the night to show Lydia the workings of the machine.

With the rest of the household asleep, Mrs. Williams turned on the electric lamp and gestured for Lydia to stand and watch where her shadow would not cover the machine.

"I suppose we can start with a tour of each part of the machine. This one I purchased through Montgomery Ward, not as esteemed as the Sears' models, but high in quality all the same." She went on to describe the names and function of each part. Odd terms such as head, feed, tension, and shuttle reminded Lydia more of the task of herding sheep or cattle rather than of sewing.

Nevertheless, she memorized every detail, having faith that in time, each part and mechanism would prove its purpose.

Then, Mrs. Williams demonstrated how to insert the spool and wrap the thread around and through knobs and rings and springs until she finally poked the end through the eye of the needle facing toward the table. More thread wrapped around a wheel-like disk no larger than a small coin that sat below a metal hatch set underneath the tabletop. In a swift rotation of the black wheel attached to the end of the machine, Mrs. Williams dropped the needle down through the metal door and brought it back up to instantly reveal both threads pulled out together.

"The machine works to stitch front and back at once, using the spool above for the main stitch and the bobbin below to connect the stitches on the backside. Hand me those strips of blue wool there and I will demonstrate."

Lydia retrieved the fabric pieces and handed them over.

Mrs. Williams lined them one over the other and smoothed them flat before laying the edge beneath the needle.

"This metal grate is the foot press and allows me to control how fast the thread comes through the machine." She held the fabric taut and began pumping her foot at a slow pace.

A perfectly even line of zigzag stitching appeared in less than a heartbeat.

Lydia gasped. "May I try?"

"Of course," Mrs. Williams beamed and stood.

Lydia's entire world of possibilities amplified. Over the next several hours, they used up every bit of scrap fabric in the room. Lydia patiently watched, and then quickly duplicated an array of stitches.

The sound of the machine's whirring echoed through her mind while she tried to sleep that night. Rest seemed impossible while visions of satin and lace flowing through her fingertips like liquid gold made her heart thrum with the potential.

The next morning, Mrs. Williams gave Lydia permission to use anything in the room as well as her charge account at the mercantile to order whatever else she needed. Lydia would be able to sew garments with existing patterns or her own creations without limits.

Something awakened in Lydia over the following few days. She rushed through tasks involving the children and Hattie, though she still completed them thoroughly. Every free minute she had was spent either thinking of the next step or sewing her new dress design. After her first attempt fell short, she immediately tore through the seams and started again. Before the end of the week, she'd sewn three dresses and could hardly recall the few brief hours she'd spent sleeping in her bed.

Yet, she felt exhilarated and energized. Since the Williams' home was connected to electricity, it allowed her to sew all the way through the night until Mrs. Williams had to ask her to put it off until morning due to the machine's wheels echoing down the hallway. Lydia apologized, sorry that she'd kept them awake by the noisy machine, but not sorry about her progress. Her eyes had been so focused the sound hardly resonated upon her own ears.

One evening, about a week later, Lydia's eyes grew dry at her intense focus on a hem that kept kinking. She'd already pulled the stitches and re-sewn it twice.

Someone knocked on the door.

"Sorry," Lydia whispered toward the door, assuming it was Mrs. Williams asking her to quit or work on hand stitching. "I am about to be finished for the night."

The doorknob turned and Hattie's slippered feet scooted into the room. Her ebony hair hung in silken ringlets in front of her shoulders, contrasting an ivory nightgown and alabaster complexion.

"I couldn't sleep." Hattie's voice rose beyond what had become her normal, strained whisper.

Lydia waved her the rest of the way into the room. "I hope I wasn't keeping you awake. I think I've got the tension set wrong for this hem, but I didn't want to bother your mother."

Hattie shook her head. "I can't hear a thing from down the hall with my door closed. I was relieved to see the light coming from below the door." She glanced at a wingback chair in the corner, strewn with fabric scraps. "May I take a seat and join you for a while?"

Was that a small smile on her lips?

Relief flooded Lydia's heart. "Of course, just toss those scraps onto the ottoman."

Hattie complied, tied her robe strings, and sat down. "I think I am ready to venture out of this place."

Lydia pulled her chair closer to Hattie and reached for her friend's hand. "That is wonderful news. We'll plan an outing with the children as soon as this rain and snow decide to move on."

Hattie nodded. "That would be nice, but I was thinking that you and I could do something alone first. The Bon Ton Orchestra usually holds a social dance every Saturday night. I am sure Mother will be happy to watch the children once she learns of our plans."

"That would be nice." Lydia did her best to hide her enthusiasm. Not only was she glad her friend was emerging from her bedroom cave, but she was excited for a chance to see the town.

"That fabric is beautiful," Hattie said, nodding at the dress in Lydia's lap.

Lydia went on to describe how she'd converted the pattern from the booklet and used a combination of fabrics. This was the third dress she'd sewn, and she couldn't get over how fast the machine made the process compared to hand stitching.

"Of course, it is faster when I don't need to undo and redo my work. I may end up sewing this hem by hand if I can't figure out the problem."

Confessing she knew a bit more about sewing than she had previously let on, Hattie offered to help.

It wasn't until the early hours of morning, that each of them revealed sleep was finally calling. Grayish-blue light pressed past streaks of rain on the window at the end of the hallway as the women parted toward their rooms. Although the wooden floorboards chilled her feet, warmth filled Lydia's chest. She had not fully realized how much she missed Hattie's friendship until that moment.

THIRTEEN

The next morning, while the children finished breakfast, Hattie transferred from her bedroom to the living room sofa. She remained in her nightgown wrapped with a quilt and opted to stay home while Lydia took the children outdoors for the afternoon.

"Are you sure you won't come with us?" Lydia asked one last time.

Hattie tucked the quilt edges beneath her legs and folded the extra length beneath her chin. "I'm not ready for the outdoors or facing the townsfolk quite yet."

Lydia sighed, and proceeded to the outside storage shed where she wrestled the baby carriage from the entwined grip of various yard tools. Unlike her friend, she longed to be outdoors and for a chance to explore the town of Grass Valley with the children in tow. Dylan had insisted Lydia be chaperoned whenever she left the house, but she believed having the children with her would suffice.

"Where we go, Lilia? Brian going too?" Olive chirped from the porch while Lydia latched the shed door.

Lydia pushed the carriage to the bottom step, and then grabbed hold of Olive's hand to take her back inside.

"We are going to the clothing store and the next stop after that is a surprise."

Hattie smiled when Lydia and Olive joined her on the couch. Brian lay sleepy-eyed on Hattie, one chubby cheek pressed against her heart. He had not left her side since she had emerged from her room.

Lydia thought she would need to fight the poor babe to come with them. But, when he observed Olive getting her coat on, he squirmed to the floor, and toddled over to pull his coat off a low-hung peg on the wall.

Hattie laughed and gave Lydia a look of relief.

Lydia secured the ribbon below her chin, aware of the significant breeze despite the sunny day. "Are you sure you'll be fine alone?"

Hattie waved from the front doorway. "Yes, I will be fine. I might even dare to wander to the backyard and begin pruning rose bushes before you get back."

Reassured, Lydia encouraged the children to wave goodbye to their mother, and then maneuvered the carriage down the drive and onto the sidewalk. Brian sat up straight, fat fingers clasped on the edges of the basket as his wide eyes glanced to-and-fro at the houses, blossoming foliage, and other spring-clad scenery along their path. Olive assisted pushing the carriage and told a story half-filled with gibberish, half-filled with intelligible words, about everything within their sight.

"Gama's store is ova there . . . that bird sings at my window in da morning . . . that moto car looks like Papa's . . ."

Brian attempted to add his own perspective with gurgles and squeals or by simply bouncing in his seat and pointing.

Their joy reflected what Lydia felt in her heart. She was amazed that a simple thing like a child's smile could bring her weary spirit back to life.

With her three dress designs neatly wrapped in paper at the back of the baby carriage, Lydia entered the clothing store on Mill Street. Olive and Brian quiet at her feet, she bribed them with a treat if they promised to behave while she spoke with the store clerk.

But first, Lydia took a moment to observe the array of clothing displayed in the windowsill and through the store to the back wall. It was her first time inside and her heart fluttered at the sight. Walls and racks held garments in every color and style she had only seen in black-lined drawings inside the Sears catalog. She glanced briefly at the mostly men's clothing at the front, a blend of wools and hint of cigar smoke dominating her senses. The combination brought her back to the scent of her grandfather's house, and with it, bitter memories. She dismissed them with a wave of her hand, intent on eventually seeking out new memories of love and acceptance.

"Lilia, where are the dresses?" Olive tugged on Lydia's coat, her soft voice like a young bird chirping for food from its mama.

"I'm not sure, Olive. Let us ask that woman at the counter."

The woman smiled with tight lips, staring at the children as if they were unwanted merchandise. Narrow eyes accompanied a deep, scratchy voice that surprised Lydia. "May I help you, Miss?" She raised her chin and kept her glare on Lydia.

"Do you sell dresses here . . . rather . . . would you be interested in purchasing one of my custom designs?"

The woman started to laugh, then huffed and shook her head. "Your custom designs? Who are you?" She jutted her head forward like a hen ready to pounce on a worm.

"My apologies." Lydia smiled widely, confident that her name would be of no consequence once the woman saw her dresses. "I am Lydia Sinclair Prescot." She raised her own chin and extended her gloved hand toward the woman.

The woman brought her bare hand forward, fingers hanging limp like strands of moss. A second after the brief handshake, she whipped it back behind the counter. "Mrs. Purington. My husband and I have owned this store since its inception back in eighty-five and we've yet to purchase anything made by a local . . ." She shot a glance at the children. "Homemaker, I assume."

"Oh, these aren't my children, Mrs. Purington. They are only in my care while their mother mourns the loss of her husband. My husband and I are from French Corral . . . Penn Valley presently. My mother and I used to make dresses for the general store—"

The woman's expression changed instantly. "French Corral? We used to place regular dress orders with the Roberts General Store every month. Then last summer, they said they were no longer available. Such a shame really, with the alternatives to order from Sacramento or San Francisco at higher rates and longer waits. Are you claiming you made those dresses?"

"Yes, my mother taught me while she was alive. Her mother was a dressmaker in San Francisco before that."

The woman reached beneath the counter, an authentic smile forming on her lips. "Would you children like a lollipop?"

The children nodded quietly and looked at Lydia for approval.

Lydia smiled and nodded. "But Olive, you must stay right here and watch that Brian stays seated in the carriage."

Olive bobbed her head and giggled. After handing Brian his lollipop, she held the side of the carriage and sang a single repeating line of a lullaby to her brother between licks.

Lydia pulled out the paper packages and placed them on the counter. "These are my first designs using a sewing machine, however I hand-stitched the embroidered patterns."

The woman carefully examined every seam, pulled on each button, and ran her fingers across every fold and pleat. Her smile revealed satisfaction until she looked back at Lydia. "These are . . . of acceptable quality. I will take them on consignment and once sold, will provide a store credit equal to twenty percent."

Twenty percent? Lydia didn't want to appear ignorant. She hoped that the difference would be enough to purchase additional fabric and still make some profit. She didn't want to have to explain to Dylan why they would owe Mrs. Williams for mercantile purchases upon his return.

She agreed to the terms and signed the required paperwork. Then she perused the woman's section of the store until the children finished their treats.

Afterward, she took the children to their grandparents mercantile, where she enjoyed a brief reunion with Clara and Jason. The mercantile merger had gone very well, and they were enjoying life in the growing town. Clara was thrilled that Lydia would be making dresses again and promised to put in a good word for Lydia to Mrs. Purington.

With the small allowance that Dylan had provided, Lydia decided to purchase a bolt of lace for a new dress, a pattern, and several yards of cotton-checked fabric needed to make men's work shirts. If Dylan saw she could also provide for their own basic clothing needs, she hoped he would agree to the investment of their own sewing machine.

When Lydia and the children returned to the Williams' home, Hattie sat on the front porch with a half-sewn quilt square in her lap. Olive raced up the steps and wrapped her arms around Hattie's neck with a squeal.

"Your hands are sticking to my hair, child!" Hattie giggled, squeezed her daughter in a loving embrace, and then showered her cheeks with kisses.

Upon seeing such affections bestowed upon his sister, Brian wailed and reached toward the sky from his place in the carriage.

"Yes, Brian, you can get kisses, too." Lydia stabilized the carriage and scooped up Brian.

She was about to burst with the news of consigning her dresses in town, but she held back and watched Hattie love on her children. The warming breeze danced between locks of hair and swept across the edges of Brian's coattails and Olive's dress skirts. Lydia felt like she was intruding on a private moment between a mother and her children, but the blessing of observing it kept her there.

When Saturday evening came around, Hattie seemed to have returned to her normal self. The house filled with her and the children's giggles.

Lydia felt her face glowing as well, relief washing over her that there was hope once again for her friend to feel joy and happiness. Once Mrs. Williams took the children to their room for the evening, Lydia and Hattie could hardly contain their laughter as they tried on dresses and hats and primped for the dance.

"If only I could cinch my waist as narrow as yours." Hattie turned from side to side, hands on her hips as she observed her reflection in the mirror.

"If only I couldn't cinch mine at all," Lydia said with a smile, attempting to joke while keeping down why she wished it were true.

Hattie turned to Lydia, grabbed each of her hands, and pulled them to her chest. "You will become pregnant soon enough. You know I didn't mean anything by it. They say the fuller figure is coming back in fashion, you know!" Hattie winked.

Lydia shook her head with no way to avoid returning Hattie's contagious smile. Tonight, they weren't going to dwell on what they didn't have. They would be two friends enjoying a social event for all it was worth in the moment.

Dusk settled on the horizon behind the Williams' coachman while he waited at the base of the walk. Clasping their gloved hands together, Lydia and Hattie strode in unison down the path from the house to the street. Once they sat in the carriage, Hattie took on a serious expression for the first time all day.

"Now, Mrs. Prescot, I will be giving you a brief lesson in the correct mannerisms for a married woman during a social event in which she is not accompanied by her husband." Hattie's eyes sparkled despite her pursed lips.

"What do you mean?" Lydia's heartbeat quickened in her chest.

"Exactly why I need to provide the lesson, my dear." Hattie raised a single eyebrow. "Officially, neither of us should be out without escorts. But my mother is so eager for me to meet a suitor she is allowing the exception since she's sure anyone who may know of us won't be at the social dance to gossip about it anyway."

Lydia cleared her throat, sensing Hattie's giggles were only a pause before she made her point.

"Nevertheless, we should exercise some caution. There's no way to avoid your captivating appearance. Without evidence that you have borne children, and with those innocent blue eyes, you will be sought after tonight."

"Sought after?" Heat pricked her neck.

Hattie bit her lip.

Lydia thought her friend was trying to hold back a smile.

"Oh, I need to come out and say it, don't I?" Hattie waved her hands and let her smile emerge. "You are a beautiful woman, Lydia. The extra weight you've managed to acquire since you've become a wife seems to have only added to the desirable places—if you know what I mean." Hattie winked and glanced at Lydia's bosom, which did seem to appear more prominent in her new dress design. "And Grass Valley has far more single men than it does available women. Until we make it clear you are married, the men are sure to flock around you like bees to the first blossom of spring."

"What am I supposed to do?" The thought of numerous strange men surrounding her, brought both fright and excitement. Somehow, she knew that these mixed emotions could lead to trouble without a plan.

"Smile and be slightly rude if that is at all possible. And try not to make eye contact any longer than you need to properly introduce yourself."

"What about you?" Lydia didn't know if there were proper mannerisms for a widow, but she imagined Hattie would eventually want to find another husband.

"I will be . . . taking inventory." Hattie laughed. "But I won't leave your side, I promise."

Though Lydia was glad to have the warning, part of her didn't want to have an expectation about their evening. Especially now that Hattie was indicating they were on the cusp of an evening she thought Dylan would not approve of. Teetering between telling Hattie to have the driver turn around and a burning curiosity if her friend was right about Lydia attracting other men, Lydia gulped a breath of cool evening air laced with the aroma of rose buds from a nearby garden.

People were always trying to warn her and protect her. How would she ever learn to traverse life's challenges on her own if she never crossed into unknown territory? She was tired of never being able to experience an event in life without feeling limited by her lack of knowledge or someone guarding her every move. It wasn't like she was going to the social dance alone. Certainly, Hattie wouldn't let

the evening go beyond an innocent evening among
friends.

FOURTEEN

When Dylan heard the horses approach outside of the barn, he removed his gloves and wiped his face with a clean handkerchief. Nevertheless, his mother was already climbing down from the carriage before he could reach her.

"Mother, I am right here. I could help you down."

Jaina looked up, her chin raised high and her lips a straight line. "I can manage, Dylan. But thank you."

She finished lowering herself to the ground with grace, and then slid her gloved hand into the crook of Dylan's waiting elbow.

"Since it's such a beautiful spring day, I thought we'd have our visit out here," said Dylan as they approached the enclosed porch behind the kitchen. "Emily and Violet have prepared a light lunch and dessert for us to enjoy with tea. How's Father?"

"That sounds wonderful." Jaina patted Dylan's arm. "It has been too long since I have enjoyed an afternoon with my son." The corners of her mouth turned up slightly. Then she bent her wide-brimmed, white-straw hat, blocking the bright sunlight with dancing shadows across her face.

The porch was shaded nicely, joined by a cool breeze that came in waves through the screened windows.

Dylan and his mother ate their meal for several minutes without speaking. Jaina nodded and smiled in approval at the finger sandwiches and garden salad topped with cantaloupe chunks.

Violet stood silent like a fixture in the doorway. "Anything else I can get for you?" She shuffled her feet, her gaze lingering a little longer on Dylan than he felt comfortable with.

"No, thank you, Violet." Dylan poured a second serving of tea into his mother's cup.

Jaina unfolded and refolded the napkin on her lap several times, and then cleared her throat. "I suppose I should explain why I am here."

Dylan's heartbeat quickened. "Go right ahead, Mother. I'm all ears."

"I have tried to stay out of things. I know I say things here and there, but I can no longer hold back. Unless you have news to share with me today, I am concerned about Lydia's continued . . . barrenness."

He knew this was coming. He had hoped she would not say anything, but he had unintentionally provided this opportune time for his mother to speak her mind.

"Lydia has been in Grass Valley for two weeks now . . . I don't see how—" He took a deep breath and pressed his lips shut.

Jaina's expression did not appear deterred. "We have no idea what type of nourishment—or malnutrition—Lydia suffered all those years alone. She could have had an illness that will not allow her to bear children. I've consulted two physicians—one in Grass Valley and another in San Francisco—and they both said the same thing. If, for any reason, her body suffered during the time she transitioned from a girl into a woman—well, it could mean that there is no hope."

What? "You have no way of knowing if that's true. What are you saying, Mother? Lydia seems perfectly healthy to me. Sure, she was a little on the thin side when she first left the Valley, but we all were after that winter. And look at her now—stronger than ever and has a good amount of weight on her in all the right places—"

"I did not come here to listen to your excuses. I think there is hope. And a simple solution. Lydia needs rest. She needs rest from this hard life of unending work from dawn until dusk."

He thought there must be more. "Mother, I realize I'm your only son and that without offspring, the family line ends with me. But it hasn't even been a year yet. And it's been hard work—as much as I try to get Lydia to rest, she won't. She is used to working hard and staying busy. It's a part of who she is. Besides, without as many demands for physical work these past weeks, she must be getting more rest, despite assisting Hattie, than she would be if she were here."

Dylan folded his arms and would have stood up if it weren't for proper manners.

Jaina cleared her throat. "I will not have my son be shamed even more. It is bad enough you married a girl from the mountain. Your father and I have tried to protect you from the gossip—but you must know . . ."

"I know mother . . . I know! You think I haven't heard the snickering when I am in town. People don't have a clue who Lydia is, yet they assume she is stupid and dirty and unable to . . ."

Jaina reached for his hand, her scowl turning to an empathetic frown. "I am so sorry . . . it was the very thing your father and I tried to avoid—and did, thanks to his discretion—when we first moved to French Corral. Unfortunately, news of the girl on the mountain spread long before your engagement to her."

Dylan's body tensed and he clenched his jaw. Blood pounded through his ears as he tried to hide any signs of discomfort. His mother had no right to hide him from the gossip or attempt to mend it with her suggestions. He could handle this on his own—he had to. How else would he prove to her and everyone else that he and Lydia had a unique purpose in God's grand design?

"You should know I don't care about what others think. Lydia and I need each other and believe God put us together for a reason. All you ever taught me was to work unto the Lord. Why this sudden concern?"

"Where is your wife, Dylan?" She crossed her arms now and raised a stiff chin.

"She . . . she is in Grass Valley with Hattie. You know that."

"And did you agree with her going?"

"Well . . . not exactly . . . but I knew she needed to. And we needed some space—I mean . . . there is so much for me to do here, I thought if she spent some time there, I could get things in order with our newly hired help, complete projects in preparation for spring and be more . . . available when she returned."

Beyond the outside patio, Pete approached the side of the house, guiding the horses into graze on the grasses. Dylan watched for a moment, knowing that above anything else, Pete was the real reason he was so willing to let Lydia stay away.

"Pete seems like a hardworking fellow. He should be lifting your burden somewhat."

"Yeah, he is helping in some ways, Albert too. He has a lot to learn still, but he has a knack for it—this life seems to come naturally to him."

"So, you've been helping Lydia with her reading then?"

Dylan shifted in his chair, trying to steal his eyes from Pete and center them back on his mother.

"Dylan? Lydia's reading lessons . . . how have they been going?"

"I haven't managed to assist her. She's been on her own—to my failure. I lose track of time so easily in the field. When I remember, and return to the house, she's already finished. She is a dedicated student." Dylan sighed and looked out at Pete again. "All right, Mother. I get your point. I need to spend more time with my wife and do what I can to ensure she is not working herself ragged."

The conversation moved to other things, such as how life was faring in Grass Valley and how Mr. Prescot was getting accustomed to his role as board member at Empire Mine. Though they ended their visit with smiles, Dylan felt unsettled. He knew he shouldn't be so concerned with what his parents thought, but their approval did matter. Without it, the tension between him and Lydia would only grow.

"We'll see you tomorrow evening after I pick up Lydia from the Williams' home, then?" Dylan pressed a firm son's kiss into his mother's cheek before helping her up into the carriage.

"Yes, and that should give you plenty of time to consider my suggestions. You know I only want what's best for the both of you." Jaina leaned back and held her hat secure as the carriage surged forward.

Dylan delegated ranch tasks to Albert and Pete and dedicated the remainder of the evening to paperwork and correspondence. He eventually created a plan to offset most expenses by selling the weaned lambs by summer. Unfortunately, it would nearly wipe out his flock for the next year. He needed to find another way to generate income to pay back his father and prove he could manage the ranch without further help.

Firelight flickered across the bookshelf. Dylan slid his overflowing leather file in between dog-eared book bindings on the topics of sheep ranching and vineyard farming. He scoffed at his own naivety and false sense of pride, and glanced out toward the barn, nestled in the shadows of dusk.

Lantern light flowed from the doorway, the dark outlines of Pete's giant arms and tall stance making Albert look like he was David about to fight Goliath if it weren't for their relaxed postures.

For we wrestle not against flesh and blood, but against principalities, against powers, against the rulers of darkness of this world . . .

Somewhere deep within, Dylan knew that Pete was not the real threat. There were unseen forces attempting to rip apart God's plans for him and Lydia. He took the recollection of scripture as a prompting to keep Pete on for now. And if the Lord willed it, He would provide a replacement in due time. There were too many other things Dylan needed to address, things that were obvious hurdles, and not possible hindrances.

He'd also need to explain the time and expense of a trip to San Francisco that would satisfy his father considering his recent loan. It would cause a significant financial pinch, but if he leaned on gaining his mother's support, there was a chance his father would keep any protest to himself. Jaina would not be concerned about the financial strain—she would support the idea of a getaway, and likely take credit for the idea that the couple needed rest and dismiss any long-term consequences. Her contradictory reasoning more humorous than harmful most of the time, Dylan hoped his mother's concern would override his father's doubt.

Regardless, Dylan still planned to ask his grandfather for yet another loan—not to spend but to have on hand, in case any purchase contracts did not follow through. He needed a back-up plan to account for the unexpected. In addition, having a reserve that could reduce Lydia's stress levels to a minimum would require nothing of her that she did not desire to do on her own.

She enjoyed sewing dresses, baking and gardening. If he could afford to cover the cost of paying help for everything else, then she may finally have the life she deserved—a life of more leisure than toil.

The bed seemed colder that night than it had since Lydia left. Perhaps it was because Dylan knew that come morning, he would gather his bride into his arms and bring her back home. Though the thought should have brought him comfort, he couldn't shake a sense of uneasiness. The scent of lavender had all but faded from Lydia's pillow, but

Dylan still breathed in any trace as he pulled it to his chest. The one thing that kept him from a restful night's sleep was his eagerness to feel Lydia near him once again. Had she also missed him and longed for his embrace? Had she experienced at least some rest, despite assisting Hattie and caring for small children?

Her last letter to him had been short and vague. Somehow, he knew her carefully chosen words were not only due to her limited writing skills. A small amount of dread filled his heart. He sent a silent prayer of protection over Lydia, and knowing that rest was more productive than worry, he eventually drifted to sleep.

FIFTEEN

When Lydia stepped out of the carriage, her head swayed and her heart thumped. Finely dressed women and men stood along the perimeter of the outdoor gathering. In one corner of the courtyard, men stood atop a raised platform, each with a different instrument blaring in response to each man's hands or mouth. The sound was invigorating, yet overwhelming. Immediately, Lydia noticed a small group of men tip their hats and smile at her and Hattie.

Hattie giggled and grabbed Lydia's arm. "Remember, no mention of my status as a widow. There shouldn't be anyone here that knows me or my parents."

Lydia could hardly hear Hattie's words over the blares and twangs of instruments.

They sat on raised chairs at a small table located a few feet away from where the group of men stood, their eyes fixed on the young ladies' every movement.

Hattie glanced toward the men and curtsied, then turned her back to them and faced Lydia.

"Mother hates that I should have to wait six months to even consider a suitor."

Lydia shook her head and tried to raise her voice above the noise. "That is one rule I can understand. It would take my heart months if not years to get beyond anything happening to Dylan."

Hattie scooted her stool close enough to Lydia to whisper in her ear. "What you and Dylan have is different than what Dan and I had."

"I know he was harsh with you at times . . . but from the story you told at my bridal shower I was sure that the love between you was still strong."

Hattie's eyes moistened. She pressed her lips together and her chin began to quiver. "Oh, it was. But I was miserable all the same. I would only confess this to you but . . . I grieved more over my relief than over sadness from his death. It's hard to explain the weight that has lifted from me since I no longer need to fear one of his fits of rage."

The topic of conversation was unexpected. Why bring up Dan now? They were here to enjoy themselves, not bring up painful memories.

With Hattie's last words, the song ended and a buzz of voices and laughter from the crowd replaced the sound of instruments.

A gentleman from the group standing behind Hattie walked toward them. With a twinge in her chest, Lydia bit her lip and lifted her chin to Hattie, as the gentlemen approach. His companions followed closely behind.

Hattie moistened her lips and replaced her frown with a smile before she pivoted casually in a half circle to face the men.

Lydia took a deep breath and rotated her knees behind Hattie. Her hands fluttered about her lap, unsure where their proper place should be.

"Good evening, ladies," the first man said, pulling his bowler hat to his chest with a bow. "I am Maxwell Jenkins. My comrades and I are only passing through town." His light brown hair was combed into neat lines from the top of his head to each ear like freshly sown soil in early spring. The style accented pencil-thin eyebrows atop large brown eyes. His mustache, again no thicker than a line of ink, lay sketched above straight, full lips.

He smiled directly at Lydia.

Her heart couldn't help but flip. She drew herself back and nearly fell off the back of the stool.

Maxwell reached to steady her and one of his comrades stepped behind her. "Are you all right, Miss?"

Hattie belted out a laugh and looped her arm inside of Lydia's. "She's fine." Hattie plunged her hand, fingers pointed down, toward Maxwell. "This is Lydia and I am Hattie. We are pleased to meet you."

Maxwell gripped Hattie's fingertips and she hopped down from the stool.

Hattie's smile dazzled alongside her ringlets of nearly black hair cupped around her porcelain complexion. Lydia steadied herself on the stool and planned to sit and observe. But as soon as Hattie had captured Maxwell's attention, the man who had stood behind Lydia came around the front of her and offered his hand.

"Name is Jackson . . . Jackson Miller."

Lydia inhaled, sat upright and extended her hand. "Nice to meet you, Mr. Miller."

He formed a crooked smile, looking more like a young boy with his ashen hair and blue eyes. "Please, call me Jackson."

Lydia nodded and allowed Jackson to help her from her seat.

The third man in their group stood back, his eyes shifting around the room. He moved the drink he held from hand to hand while he tapped one toe.

When Lydia managed to make eye contact with him, she reached her hand past Jackson toward the third man. When she did so, Hattie's eyes grew wide and her jaw twitched.

Lydia hesitated, realizing she probably was not supposed to initiate a greeting. The man shifted his glass again and met her hand halfway.

A look of relief crossed his face and his shoulders dropped. "Pardon me, Miss. I . . ." He shifted his feet once more, and then bowed. "Allow me to introduce myself. I'm Alex Miller, brother to Jackson here."

Jackson slapped Alex's back and pushed him closer to the group. "Yes, my shy brother Alex is not one for social gatherings."

"Can we get you ladies a drink before the band starts up again?" Maxwell raised his eyebrows and directed his hand toward a man standing behind a long, high table stacked with an array of bottles and glasses.

Hattie spoke up before Lydia could think of how to answer. "Ginger ale would be fine, thank you."

Jackson nodded at his brother. "Alex, would you mind getting these ladies each a glass of ginger ale?"

Alex shifted his jaw to one side and then smiled. "Of course. It would be my pleasure." The brightness in his eyes faded before he turned and walked away.

With drinks in hand and music blaring, the men dominated the conversation, appearing eager to entertain and impress the women. Lydia followed

Hattie's lead, repeating her friend's laughter and gestures. When everyone finished the drinks, Maxwell asked Hattie to dance. Hattie shot a look of apology, indicating she was about to break her promise. Glad that Hattie was enjoying herself, Lydia nodded her approval.

Alex excused himself seconds later, leaving Lydia and Jackson on their own.

"So, Miss Lydia, you've hardly shared a thing about yourself." His shoulder brushed against hers, the music forcing them to stand near to hear each other speak.

She half-expected him to ask her to dance as well. Hattie had not told her she shouldn't dance— but Lydia was not comfortable with the idea. Talking with these strange men was enough unknown territory for her this evening.

"I hope you don't find it rude of me not to ask you to dance. I find it hard to keep a conversation going on the dance floor."

Lydia nodded, smiling in relief.

"Tell me about yourself. Surely, you've had an adventure or two if those blue eyes don't deceive me."

What could her eyes have revealed to this stranger?

She had been quiet content in only listening and responding in kind. What could she say about herself without revealing her marital status and having to explain why her husband had not accompanied her? Although Hattie had not directly told her not to mention it, Lydia was confident it probably was not a good idea to reveal it. They were already violating proper standards and didn't want gossip reaching the William's circle of acquaintances.

She clasped her hands behind her back, fingering her wedding ring beneath her gloved finger.

"There's not much to tell." Lydia shot her eyes toward Hattie and Maxwell on the dance floor.

"Well, have you lived in Grass Valley long?"

"No, I don't live here. I'm staying with Hattie for a few weeks while my . . ." She glanced down at the embroidery she'd added to her dress. "While I reestablish my mother's sewing business."

If I talk about Mama, I may not need to mention Dylan at all.

He nodded. "Sewing business? Is this one of your creations?"

"The dress isn't, but I added this embroidery here. We used to sew everything by hand, but with access to Hattie's sewing machine, I have a few more designs in progress."

Relief flooded Lydia's chest. Jackson seemed very interested in all the details of her sewing methods and of her plans to sell her dresses in town. He even offered to spread the word to his mother and sisters.

Engulfed in the conversation, Lydia hardly noticed Alex joining them until he handed her a second drink.

This one didn't taste like ginger ale. It took all she could to avoid grimacing at the pungent, burning sensation filling her mouth. But she sipped anyway. Soon, the tension caused by unfamiliar surroundings and people dissipated. She began to feel relaxed enough to enjoy herself and the attention both men held on her. After a while, she decided she wouldn't even mind if one of them asked her to dance.

Her glass was half-empty by the time Hattie and Maxwell joined them again. The moment Hattie spotted the drink in Lydia's hand she replaced her grin with a glare.

Lydia could have stayed there the whole night through. Any worries had long fled her mind. She was enjoying herself and the company of these gentlemen at her side. She felt like Jaina—at the center of attention and fully in control of her audience.

Hattie took the glass from Lydia's hand and set it on a table. "If you would pardon us, Gentlemen." Hattie curtsied and placed her hand inside Lydia's arm.

Lydia curtsied as well and offered a smile toward Jackson before Hattie whisked her off.

Lydia hadn't noticed the doorway into a building along the back of the courtyard where clusters of women filed in and out. Inside, there were several groups of chairs and narrow couches along two walls. The back wall was a huge mirror bordered along the bottom with a shallow counter where several women stood chattering while preening in their reflections.

Hattie led Lydia to an empty corner and pulled her face to Lydia's ear. "I think this was a mistake. We need to make up an excuse and leave right away."

"What? Why? I am just starting to enjoy myself."

"Exactly. Have you mentioned that you're married yet?"

"No, I didn't know if I could. We were discussing my sewing and plans for selling dresses. Have you mentioned you're a recent widow?"

"It doesn't matter what you are talking about. It only matters that you both appear very interested in each other. And what were you drinking?"

"I . . . I don't know. Alex handed it to me, and I didn't want to appear rude by not accepting it."

Lydia's eyes blurred for a moment and her head felt foggy. She leaned back against the wall. "It's stuffy in here. Can we go back outside?"

"Not until you agree we need to leave. Thankfully, those men are just passing through and nobody will need to know about us meeting them."

Lydia didn't understand why Hattie's voice held such urgency. "What do you mean? You seem to be enjoying yourself as well."

"I am . . . I was that is. I am afraid we have given these men the wrong impression. If my mother had realized this was possible, she would never have let us come."

"What was possible? Hattie—"

Hattie leaned in and whispered in Lydia's ear. "I'll explain once we get back in the carriage. Please, trust me. We must go . . . now. They think we're prostitutes!"

SIXTEEN

His heart filled with hope about their future, Dylan returned to Grass Valley to bring his wife back home. Lydia greeted him with a deep kiss that warmed parts of him he'd forgotten existed in past weeks. The embrace that followed felt sure to have contained the promise of a later encounter.

"Dylan, I've missed you! I have wonderful news!" Lydia beamed and his heart jumped when he thought he knew what she would say next.

"The department store has placed a special order for my customized dresses. I created a new design and brought it in last week on consignment. The gowns sold immediately to a wealthy patron from Sacramento. She wants six more dresses for her own store immediately!"

Hopes dashed and feeling foolish that she would announce a pregnancy—but not wanting to destroy his wife's enthusiasm—Dylan brought her in for another embrace. He rubbed his disappointment into her shoulder and then nuzzled her neck. He inhaled, savoring the sweet scent of lavender he'd missed. "That is . . . that is great, sweetheart . . .

wonderful news." When he gazed into her eyes, he saw something different, as if a part of her innocence had vanished. There was a confidence, yet a hesitation about how she seemed to draw back the longer he stared.

She smiled and straightened her shoulders. "Now that I've learned to use a sewing machine, I can make dresses much faster. I also taught herself to alter patterns and customize them to meet modern trends. And the best part . . . they're willing to pay double if I can have the order completed before Easter."

"Are you able to bring the sewing machine back home with you?" He hoped she didn't intend to stay on longer.

"Not exactly." Her shoulders fell. "I was going to ask if I could stay one more week and perfect the pattern." She tried to kiss him again, but he pushed back.

Between Lydia's elation and the passion overflowing from her gaze—of having a purpose, and the chance to bring in extra income—it was difficult for Dylan to deny his wife's request. This could be the answer to his prayers for another source of income as well to distract Lydia from interactions with Pete or any other hired help for that matter.

"I have a better idea. My parents have invited us to stay at their house this evening. I have some business matters to discuss with my father and if all goes well, I'll purchase you your very own sewing machine on the way back home?"

She jumped into his arms, showering his face with kisses. "Thank you! Now I'll be able to contribute to our needs as well."

She could not know how those words hurt. He should be able to provide fully for their needs. Didn't she know that being his wife was all the contribution he needed?

Grateful to be home again, Lydia first ventured to tend her garden the morning after their return.

The air stood still as bees buzzed and humming-birds floated nearby—their slender beaks poking in and out of bright pink trumpet vine blossoms. The vines had overtaken the garden fence since she'd been gone.

She shook her head and cupped the petals of one of the flowers. "As pretty as you are, you still need a guiding hand to keep you under control."

Visions of the strange men at the social dance fluttered through her mind and she felt ill at the thought of what could have happened. Hattie promised not to say a word to Dylan about it, but that wasn't what concerned her.

She knew she had enjoyed the attention of those men too much—so much that she was afraid to even tell Hattie. Like the vines of the plant she held, there was a part of her that had wanted to keep on going. She knew it wasn't a part of God's plan, but the desire to gain the knowledge of all things in this life was stronger than ever before. Her time in Grass Valley had awakened a part of her that she hadn't known existed.

Regardless, being home again made her feel safe. There was little temptation—and much to keep her busy. Even if her thoughts strayed, she was limited in what she could do about them.

The sewing machine fit nicely in the enclosed porch between the winter washroom area and a worn wooden table that had been left behind by the previous owners. She had the view of rolling hills, clusters of oak trees, and her corner garden.

She could also watch the men complete work on the ranch when she wasn't focusing on her sewing. Having Violet and Emily at the house to handle the inside chores also gave Lydia more time to sew dresses and still feel productive without as many physical demands.

The rhythm of needle and thread notching into the fabric, the pull and turn of the seams, soon became a task that did not require much thought. The task would set her mind to wandering in the same way milking Megan had while she was living in the Valley. Megan remained her primary confidant. Lydia milked her every few days for that very purpose. That was something she never wanted to give up. Milking Megan connected her to her mother's memory, just as sewing did.

As spring showed signs across the meadow, the season brought forth a surge of other memories—walks with Mama, meeting Dylan, and the disappointing encounter with her grandfather the previous spring. He had forced her to leave her childhood home and begin a new life with Dylan at Rolling Oaks Ranch. But as much as she and Dylan had tried, it seemed impossible that this place would ever feel like home to her. It was a constant reminder of all that was lost—her parents' lives, the life Mama had created, and then her grandfather refusing to accept her and ordering her and Dylan to leave without recourse.

Lydia pushed soil colored silk between the prawn foot and thread plate and pressed the treadle with her foot in a steady rhythm. Her grandfather's fiery eyes still burned in her memory. The brown silk reminded her of the walls in her grandfather's dark den. He was such an angry man. He hadn't even given her a chance to explain or plead for more time. There must be a way to win his heart or at the very least, his willingness to accept her—his only grandchild—as family.

Months ago, Dylan helped her write to her Uncle Frank, her father's brother and her only apparent ally in the Sinclair home. But Frank hadn't replied. Maybe he'd also decided to reject her and any memory of his brother.

When Lydia wasn't sewing, gardening, or cooking, she'd search out Dylan on the property. It seemed he spent more time focused on the concerns of the ranch than he had prior to her trip to Grass Valley. More than once, he'd used the excuse that he was heavily laden with supervising or delegating tasks, and often needed to work himself. More than once, he'd broken his promise to help Lydia with her reading lessons before the midday meal break.

One afternoon, after finishing and admiring at length the fourth of six dresses for the Sacramento order, Lydia sat on the back of the porch facing the horse pasture and the road. She couldn't understand how Dylan continued to work so hard despite having two hired hands. He should be sitting here on the porch, helping her with her reading.

So, she chose to view the open pasture sprinkled with wildflowers instead of the enclosed barn that imprisoned her husband, while she practiced reading.

"... that your pereg ... peregrine ... perigrin-a-tions in this metro ... metrop-o ... lis have not yet been ex—"

Footsteps creaked around the corner. The thud and rumble of logs tumbling on the porch broke her concentration enough that she gasped. Assuming she would see Dylan, she was about to chastise him for startling her when instead, Pete poked his head around the corner.

"Pardon me, Mrs. Prescot," he rasped. Then he cleared his throat before tipping his hat.

SEVENTEEN

Lydia gulped. She had managed to avoid Pete aside from mealtimes ever since her return and she had hoped to keep it that way. "It's nothing. I was only trying to understand this passage here and hadn't heard you come up to the house." She tried Hattie's suggestion of a cold and rude response but didn't feel successful.

Pete stepped forward and looked toward the book. "May I?"

Lydia's heart leapt at his approach. He nearly took up the entire width of the porch with his arms expanding like large branches on either side of a wide tree trunk. The smell of freshly cut wood and earth intoxicated her senses. She handed the book up to him, hoping he wouldn't notice her fingers twitching.

"Charles Dickens, eh? My pa used to read this to us as little ones. Shall I read it to you?"

Would Dylan be upset if he caught Pete away from work and once again in the presence of his wife? If he did, Lydia would remind him that if he took a break now and then to help his own wife, then maybe the hired help wouldn't have to step in. At least she would think about saying it anyway.

She knew Dylan understood how important it was that she learned to read.

"Yes, please."

Pete sat next to her on the wicker bench. Lydia scooted as close to her side of the bench as she could. Thankfully, Pete seemed aware of his size and kept to his side, avoiding physical contact with Lydia's waist and leg.

For several minutes, Pete read, and Lydia re-read the passages until she could read them without faltering. He was very patient and explained about the period of the story and other details Jaina had not described.

Upon the sound of galloping coming up to the house, Pete and Lydia stood in nervous unison and rapidly parted to opposite ends of the porch. Relief and then embarrassment flooded Lydia's face in a wave of heat when she saw one horse chasing another across the pasture.

Pete cleared his throat and wiped the edges of his lips with a handkerchief. "I better be getting back to the wood pile."

Lydia curtsied and stepped backward toward the screen door at the other end of the house. "You've been very helpful. Thank you." Nearly running into the screen, she yanked the door open. She needed to release herself from his presence to take a full breath.

Her heart fluttered until she crossed the living room and entered the kitchen. The pounding in her chest seemed to echo between the hushed kitchen walls.

Hattie's warning resonated in her mind. This man was captivating her by his presence. But would he try to draw her in on purpose? Of course, he would know better. His job—even his life—could be in the balance should Dylan feel this man had inappropriate intentions toward Lydia.

Yet, her mind kept drawing her back to the few moments they spent on the porch—alone. Pete's eyes, his voice, his smell, his patient method of reading to her and explaining. He made her feel safe and insecure all at once. But she dared not to speak of her thoughts aloud to anyone. She would simply need to find other things to occupy her time, other ways to avoid these interactions where she and Pete would have any chance to be alone.

Violet entered the kitchen, arms clad with baskets overflowed with garden vegetables.

The men would all be arriving for their afternoon meal shortly.

The stench in the barn forced Dylan and Albert to wrap double handkerchiefs around their mouths and noses.

"Does it normally smell so terrible?" Dylan heaved soiled hay into the wheelbarrow. He held his breath until the debris finished floating and fell to the ground.

"This is the last of the contaminated stables," Albert said, scooping up a muddy mess of decomposing hay mixed with sheep dung.

Dylan gagged—glad the cloth around his face hid his repulsion.

"But, yes sir, Mr. Prescot. You'll never forget it either. Just a hint of this come next season and you'll be taking precautions in an instant."

"I can't express enough gratitude for the help from you and Pete. Between your knowledge of sheep ranching and Pete's productivity—when he's working anyway . . ." With his words, Dylan realized that he hadn't heard the echoes of Pete chopping wood for quite a while.

"Shall I go fetch him, Mr. Prescot?" Albert stuck his hay fork into a patch of clean, soft soil.

"Thanks, but no. Tracking him down only wastes more time. Have we all the pregnant ewes inside clean stalls?"

There had been no answer to the "help wanted" advertisement Dylan had placed weeks earlier. Regardless of Pete's disappearing acts, they needed more than three men to tackle all the needs of the ranch through summer.

Dylan took a step outside the barn, inhaling fresh spring air and looking up at the house. Could Lydia have detained Pete to help with something at the house? Dylan didn't have time to check on Lydia either. With her extra tasks of sewing dresses and reviewing her reading—

Her reading!

He had forgotten about his promise to help assist Lydia with her reading lesson during his midday break. He shook his head with disdain for himself and how easily he could get caught up in work, forgetting his wife's needs. More doubts that he had the knack for running a ranch flooded his guilty heart.

But what could he do now? He couldn't afford any more losses. Any day now, every one of them—including Lydia, would be on watch around-the-clock to assist with birthing lambs to ensure every sheep survived.

"Excuse me, Albert," he hollered back inside the barn. "I've got to head up to the house. Finish up here and then come join us for lunch. We'll finish laying down the clean hay I the empty stalls this afternoon."

Albert nodded and got back to work.

Dylan thought of his original intentions upon bringing Lydia home. He had wanted to tell her of his plans for their trip to San Francisco, but she'd been delighted to be home again. She had pranced around the garden, uninhibited as she hummed a hymn and greeted the rows of vegetables and clusters of herbs. He felt a fool as he stood and watched, unaware of how she'd captured his attention. He hadn't seen her again until later that evening, due to the back up of chores while he'd been gone the previous day.

His failures mounted in frustration. He exchanged his contaminated books for his usual pair and ascended the path to the house.

Adding to Dylan's financial pressures, buying the sewing machine and fabric had strained his existing resources considerably, even if he considered them an investment. He may have no choice but to travel as far as Sacramento and then North to locate new buyers. It would be a challenge to find multiple farmers willing to take newborn animals that may have been exposed to late winter foot rot. Pete and Albert would need to master their tasks and work longer hours while he was gone. It seemed impossible to achieve without a miracle.

Only then could he take Lydia on their holiday to San Francisco without concerns looming upon their return. Logic told him he should postpone if not cancel before Lydia knew of it. But he'd received a letter from her Uncle Moses while she'd been in Grass Valley. Moses was thrilled to hear from them and couldn't wait to meet Lydia. Despite all that Rolling Oaks Ranch demanded—Dylan's marriage and uniting his wife with family would take priority.

A pile of fresh logs lay unattended at the chopping block.

Where was Pete again? He should have had all the firewood completed by now. Dylan hesitated, and then finished chopping the stack himself—knowing every minute was one less he'd spend with his wife—and then headed up to the house. At least this would give him an excuse to apologize to Lydia for forgetting about her reading lesson.

His stomach growled. He'd only have time to eat now.

As he came up to the side of the house, he thought he heard voices on the other side of the porch. Then a screen door slammed, and Pete strode around the corner.

"Pete, there you are." Dylan lifted the stack of logs in his arms and raised his eyebrows.

"My apologies, Mr. Sinclair . . . I . . . uh . . . was headed back down to grab another load. Is there more?" Pete seemed flustered, out of breath even.

"Yes, one more stack. I'll take a meal break while I'm up here. Once you bring that last load up, join us for a quick meal, then it's back to work." Dylan dumped the logs and entered the kitchen through the covered patio door.

Lydia and Violet stood with their backs to him, working at the sink.

When neither woman acknowledged that he'd entered the kitchen, he risked the element of surprise. He slid up behind Lydia and nuzzled her neck before grabbing a hold of her waist and turning her to face him.

Instead of giggling and returning his embrace like he hoped she would, she looked stunned to see him. Seeing her swallow hard, and press her lips together, he figured she was upset about him missing the reading time.

"Lydia . . . please. I didn't exactly forget . . . time slipped—"

She pushed away and turned back to the sink without a word.

Great, now what?

"So, what do you ladies have for us working men to eat?" His shoulders refused to relax as he took at seat and saw Lydia's copy of David Copperfield splayed crooked in the center of the table. "Pete and Albert are on their way up."

Violet grimaced and raised her eyebrows, glancing at them and shaking her head. It wasn't the first time she'd appeared displeased to be in the center of a marital rift. "We have leftover broccoli and chicken casserole, and fig pudding. Shall I put on a pot for coffee as well, Mr. Prescot." She turned her frown into a smile before she finished speaking, and then curtsied.

"Violet, no need to address me formally. You're a friend. Thank you. And, yes, coffee would be great. We have a long afternoon ahead of us and it looks like rain clouds on the horizon."

As soon as Pete entered and took a seat, Lydia made an excuse to leave the kitchen. Dylan hastened his meal, ensured his farmhands understood the details of their evening work, and then went to locate his wife.

EIGHTEEN

Lydia sat on the bed and looked at the grazing meadow beyond the front yard. This ranch was indeed beautiful. The spring brought varieties of wildflowers that had never bloomed near her home in the Valley. Dozens of rolling hills, with clusters of large rocks and oak trees, provided secluded spots to sit and ponder, or to pray. Maybe she would take a walk before getting back to her sewing.

The warm spring breeze wafted in through the window, caressing her face in invitation with sweet scents, confirming her thoughts. She needed to get away from the demands of this house and seek the Lord for direction about managing the sudden barrage of men in her life.

How did she get to this place of an unsettled heart? She was back home now, yet she found another sort of work to do which kept her from the one thing that seemed to bring her peace. It had been so long since she'd felt connected with the land again—to have time to wander and to daydream.

She had worked long and hard with Mama as a child and young woman. But with only the two of them, the demands on her heart and mind had seemed less exhausting. Now she had a large home with their new housemaid, Emily, and her friend, Violet, to share in the chores and work involved in feeding and cleaning up after three men. When there was time to spare, she found joy in reading lessons and fulfilling sewing orders.

Yet, resting in the Lord's presence and trusting for His provision were, just as—if not more important. It seemed like weeks since the last time she and Dylan had sat by the fire while he read scripture, then prayed before they conjured up dreams of all the plans God had for them.

Footsteps tapped the stairs in an even rhythm until they stopped at the doorway to the bedroom. She was almost afraid to turn and see who it was.

Pete would not dare come up to her room, would he?

"Sweet Lydia . . . please understand . . ."

Lydia dropped her shoulders and exhaled. It was Dylan.

She went to him, hesitating for a moment as shame filled her with the reminder of her thoughts on the porch while Pete sat at her side. But she went to her husband anyway and returned the embrace he had tried to give her in the kitchen.

"I understand, Dylan. I do. We are both tired and worn. As much as we try to find rest, it seems we only make more work for ourselves. Come, come walk with me. It is a beautiful day and the clouds are still far off."

Dylan raised his eyebrows and pulled her even closer. His eyes still knew how to swoon her innermost parts. He leaned down, kissing her ever so gently on the mouth—like a butterfly's wings brushing a rose petal.

She nearly pulled him into the bedroom but thought better of it when she noticed Emily at the base of the stairs on her way up with an armful of folded linens.

Instead, she reached for her husband's hand and led him down the stairs after Emily entered the landing. Heading out the back door, they avoided the men in the kitchen and cut through the horse meadow to the open field behind the fence.

Dylan kept a tight hold on Lydia's hand. How blessed to have such a forgiving and understanding wife. She could see life in a way he never could—and would remind him of the important things he easily forgot while distracted by the tasks and toils of his responsibilities.

The breeze stirred the grass and muffled out the house, the ranch, and all the duties behind them. The clouds were a lot closer than Lydia had said they were. But he didn't care. It seemed forever since it was the two of them, alone, with only the land beckoning them forth.

They walked in silence for several minutes. The calming sounds and senses of this great land they now owned eased the burden of their uncertain future.

"Sorry I forgot about the reading time. Were you able to get through some on your own before preparing lunch?"

Lydia sighed, an odd smile crossing her lips. "Yes, I got some reading done . . . on my own . . . but a passage was troubling me when—"

"When?" Dylan slowed their stride.

Lydia cleared her throat. "Um . . . when Pete uh . . . well . . . Pete startled me, and I explained I was having trouble and then he . . ."

"He what? What did Pete do?" Dylan stopped and pressed his heel firmly into the ground. His pulse rose and his jaw tightened.

Lydia shook her head. "Nothing . . . he offered to help me read the passage. I didn't know what to say and I wanted to finish the page . . ."

Dylan took a deep breath. Lydia seemed as disturbed as he did. One more breath and he tried to think reason. Was Pete only trying to help? It still wasn't right. But getting angry with his wife was not the way to go about resolving things.

Lord, help me.

Did his wife know how to refuse a man's advances? How could he talk to Pete without risking losing his tempter and firing him, or worse—appearing like a jealous husband only to end up a fool for what could be a simple misunderstanding?

"Dylan? Are you all right?" Lydia stepped closer.

"Fine, darling. I'm fine. That was . . . uh . . . very kind of Pete to offer his help. But I should have been there. I should be making more of an effort to spend time with you."

Lydia's eyes sparkled as the sun escaped from behind a cloud and illuminated her face. The breeze blew wisps of hair along her neck, urging him to tuck them behind her ear. He drew his hand beneath her chin and pulled her to him. She was dazzling.

Pete had to notice her beauty, her innocence— the curves that seemed to have formed overnight.

Dylan would have to attend to his wife without faltering. And their week in San Francisco would surely reignite the passion they had shared as newlyweds. He leaned in to kiss her the same moment the clouds covered the sun as if to provide a bit of privacy to their interlude. They stood feet away from a group of oak trees bordered by a several large boulders.

With the smell of rain filling the air, Dylan prayed the rain would hold off for a few minutes longer. Then he pulled away for a moment, breathing in the lingering scent of vanilla and jasmine that emanated from Lydia's hair and skin.

"I have something to tell you. Let's go over there to those trees in case it starts raining."

She followed his lead, holding his one hand with both of hers. Once beneath the trees and out of sight from any wandering eyes coming from the stables or barn, Dylan pulled his wife closely and kissed her deeply. Then, he led her behind the rocks to embrace between a moss-covered boulder and a couple of large oaks.

Lydia giggled when he tried to untie her apron strings. "Dylan . . ." Her voice was weak and though she tried to protest verbally, she allowed him to continue.

The rain started as a patter on the tree branches, but within minutes, it began to pelt. Dylan and Lydia ignored the spring storm, their hearts and minds on other things. By the time the storm passed, the two of them caught their breaths, holding damp clothes to their skin and laughing between kisses.

"Sweet Lydia . . . it has been too long since we've shared such a moment. I love you . . ." He kissed her again, and then kissed the raindrops from her cheeks, neck, arms, hands.

"I love you," Lydia whispered. "If I wasn't catching a chill, I would say we should stay here for the rest of the afternoon. I miss these moments with just the two of us . . . where nothing else in the world seems to matter . . ."

"Me too, darling . . . me too. Which leads me to what I wanted to tell you."

Lydia sat up, pulling her sleeves back over her shoulders and buttoning the back of her dress. "What is it?"

Was that a look of worry or excitement in her eyes?

"I've a surprise. Please don't ask how I managed. That's a secret." He winked and paused until her eyebrows rose with anticipation. "I won't hold you in suspense any longer. I have planned a trip . . . a long-needed trip for only the two of us."

"A trip? To where?" Her smile grew, her cheeks glowing in a hazy ray of sunlight.

"We're going to spend a full week in San Francisco. I have made all the arrangements. We will stay at a grand hotel, take in a show at the theater, and see all the things we didn't have a chance to see before."

Lydia sat on her knees and clapped. "Oh, Dylan! Really?" She fell into him, hugging him like a little girl who had opened a long-awaited Christmas gift. "I don't even care how you planned this. One day I think I want to be here, but then work tasks keep me from all I adore . . . including you."

Dylan laughed, absorbing Lydia's excitement. "And one more thing."

"What? I'm already bursting at thinking of all the fun we will have . . . alone." She smiled slyly.

Dylan sat against the rock and adjusted his boots, purposely pausing to add suspense now that he had Lydia's full attention.

"Dylan!" She nudged his shoulder.

He felt his dimples emerge but kept his gaze low as if his boots retained more of his interest. "Uncle Moses returned our letters."

"What? You wrote him as well? You promised not to keep any more secrets from me." Lydia sat back on her heels, brushing her loosened hair with her fingers before twisting it back up beneath her bonnet. She raised eyebrows in contrast with her grin, her voice laced with disappointment.

"I only wanted to make sure he was still in the city. I didn't want to get your hopes high only to have them dashed."

Lydia closed her mouth, and her eyes widened.

"He continues to live with the Samuel family on Folsom Street above their tailor shop. The business is quite successful serving the elite families of the city. He was delighted to hear you were doing well, but very sad about Emelyn's death."

Lydia's cheeks fell flat at the name of her mother.

"He said he would love to see you while we are in the city, which may work out well since I should probably pay a visit to my grandfather while we're there."

Lydia stood, pulling herself in a hug when the breeze kicked up again. "Is this why you've been working so hard? Do whatever you feel is necessary to prepare the ranch for our absence. I still have two dresses to finish and plenty else to do to prepare the garden . . . oh . . . what about lambing season?"

Dylan stood while she spoke, and then pulled her close. "You're shivering. We will take the train from Grass Valley on Easter. All the sheep should lamb by then."

She looked toward the house, the clouds were floating off and sunlight twinkled in the moisture across the meadow between them and the horse pasture. "I'm sure between you and the sunshine I'll warm up in no time." She leaned up and kissed him firmly, then grabbed his hand and started back to the house.

NINETEEN

Friday April 13, 1906

Lydia secured the clasp on her suitcase and headed toward the staircase. Her bag was heavier than she expected, so she had to balance one step at a time to keep the case from pulling her down. When she reached the bottom, footsteps clamored on the porch near the door. Assuming it was Dylan, she called out.

"Help here! This is heavier than I thought," she grunted through her words, pausing on the step in hopes her husband would relieve her of the grip before her fingers gave up.

Pete emerged through the door. The sunlight behind him created a golden outline that emphasized the muscles on his thick neck, arms, and legs. He practically took up the entire doorway. Lydia sucked in her breath, trying not to look too surprised.

"Whe-where is Dylan?"

In one stride, Pete was at the bottom of the stairs. He retrieved the suitcase from Lydia's grasp without a word. Only his breath hit her face, a mixture of licorice root and alfalfa. The warmth of his frame hovered across her arm.

At first, she didn't let go. He tugged and she looked up, trying to see his eyes in the dark shadows of the foyer. When he took hold of the suitcase, she fell forward, not realizing she was leaning toward him.

With a single arm, he caught her by the waist, and pulled her toward him enough for her to gain her balance. "Whoa there! I didn't mean to make you lose your footing."

Yet, his hand lingered at her waist for a moment.

Without thinking, Lydia allowed the moment—absorbing the length and breadth of his hand and how it nearly covered her entire hip. He felt so much stronger than Dylan.

She shuddered.

What am I doing?

She blinked and stepped back, straightening her posture. "Dylan? Where is he?"

Pete cleared his throat and turned his face. Morning sunlight streamed in, illuminating his square jaw, round nose, and the deep pools of his sky-blue eyes.

The best she could describe his appearance was that like the beautiful and strong warrior angels Mama had described in the stories she'd told.

"Dylan is still with the sheep . . . one is struggling with birthing what he thinks are twins. He asked me to come find you. Albert is assisting with another birth, so more hands are needed now."

"Oh my . . . will you take the suitcase to the wagon, please?"

Lydia rushed past him, ignoring the sensation of brushing into his chest as she flew out the door.

A few minutes later, she joined Dylan in the barn.

He crouched over on his knees, back facing the entrance to the stable. A tiny, wet sack lay near his knee.

Lydia rushed toward it. A small lamb squirmed, fighting to get free of the membranes. It mewed like a kitten, weak but still alive. Lydia grabbed a cloth from a pile in the corner and quickly wrapped the lamb. Then she set it beside its mother, hoping the heat coming from her body would keep it warm for the moment. The ewe didn't move.

"How's the mama doing?" She whispered.

Dylan shook his head and rested his chin on his chest. "We just lost her," his voice cracked. "The other one is still inside. What do I do?"

He looked up, his eyes welled with tears, his face streaked in red and brown.

Lydia bit her lip. "This happened once in the Valley. The mama sheep died before giving birth to a single lamb. I need a blade . . . sharp enough to open her up."

Dylan stood, pressing his lips together. Tears dripped onto his cheek. Lydia wasn't sure if he was sad about the life lost or frustrated about the prospect of losing three sheep to the flock.

"What about that one? How will it survive without a mother?" He asked, and then he turned toward the door and headed to the wall of tools.

"This one will be fine as soon as I get it suckling on another ewe. But time is short if we are to save its sibling."

Within seconds, Dylan had traded the blade for the lamb, holding it close and wiping it dry while Lydia worked on the unborn one.

All the lambs should have birthed by now. Lydia had wanted to stay in the barn through the night. But she hadn't slept for a day and half and Dylan insisted she rest before they left for Grass Valley. Exhaustion had won the fight, and she'd conceded. But now she regretted not insisting she sleep on a hay pile in the corner. Not only would she have been here to assist, but she would have avoided yet another unbearable encounter with Pete.

Inhaling deeply and willing her pulsating palms to still, she prayed.

Lord, take my thoughts captive. I give them to you for I know they are not your will. Free me and give me strength to focus in this moment.

She exhaled her breath strong enough that it disturbed the dry blades of hay surrounding the motionless ewe.

Faint grunts and cries echoed between the walls in the barn.

Mama had done the cutting before. Though unsure of her own strength, Lydia still had to try. Taking in a deep breath, she wiped the tears from her face and chin with her sleeve, and then pulled the belly of the ewe taut. Hoping to avoid nicking the membrane surrounding the lamb, she sliced along the side, pressing hard. The abdomen opened easier than she'd expected.

She dropped the blade, wiped her soiled hand on her apron and then plunged both hands into the opening.

Feeling for the fullness of the sack and accounting for a head and four hooves, Lydia squeezed slightly and pulled the slippery bundle into her lap. This lamb was larger than the other one, a good sign it would survive.

The lamb lay limp in her arms at first. She set it between folded knees and pressed her hand in waves up and down its back and abdomen until it jerked, bleating like a newborn human baby.

"Quickly, to the next stable." Lydia ordered Dylan while nudging him on. "Take that cloth and rub it hard on those lambs there. We have to make these ones smell like her own for her to be willing to nurse them."

Dylan followed orders without question.

It took some coaxing, but eventually both newborns were sucking away on their surrogate mama.

Dylan wrapped an arm around Lydia's waist and leaned his head on her shoulder. "We make a good team . . . you have no idea how grateful I am that you knew what to do. I wasn't prepared for that."

"I wish we could thank Mama in the heavens. She taught me how." Lydia smiled through her own indebted tears.

"Everything work out in here?" Pete's deep voice echoed from the barn entry.

Lydia sighed and turned around. "Yes, Pete. We saved the lambs, but sadly the mama didn't make it."

Pete's figure, dark and outlined by sunlight, made it even more apparent when his shoulders fell and shook as if he too, were crying. "I . . . I am sorry to hear that." He stepped back abruptly and started to walk away.

"This is no time to shirk responsibilities, Pete," Dylan barked.

Lydia's stomach sank at his tone.

"I need you to work with Violet to prepare this ewe for our future meals. No waste allowed around here when it's perfectly good eating."

Pete tapped his palm on the doorframe. "I need a few minutes and I'll be back to follow your orders, sir."

With sweat, mud, and blood mingled into his furrowed brows, Dylan turned back to Lydia. "I'll handle cleaning up the other stable and Albert should be able to keep an eye on the lambs while Pete and Violet prepare the ewe. Have Emily draw a hot bath first and I'll be up soon." Dylan kissed her forehead, and then frowned when his gaze rested on Lydia's soiled blouse and skirt.

He shook his head as if to apologize and nodded toward outside.

However, when Lydia stepped outside expecting to see Pete on the way to the house, she heard his coarse cough coming from the side of the barn.

Why did the news of losing the ewe seem to upset Pete so deeply?

Recalling her earlier prayer, she knew rounding the corner to locate Pete and find out more was not a good idea.

Despite her mind's resistance, her feet followed Pete out to the corral.

Her heart pounded. She had to know why she felt drawn to him—once and for all. With Dylan otherwise distracted, this could be her final chance. She would not return to these unsettled feelings again. During their journey, she would tell her husband about the thoughts and feelings she'd been having and that she knew they were wrong.

"Pete . . . Pete wait," she called in a loud whisper.

Pete was already several strides ahead of her. She ran to catch up. He stopped beneath the shade of a poplar tree on the other side of the corral.

When he turned, undeniable tears glistened in his eyes. He started coughing and tried to look away.

"What's wrong? Are you okay?" She drew near him, attempting to act more like a mother comforting a child.

But in her heart, she was a curious woman finding an excuse to touch his arm for the pure sensation of it one last time.

"My . . . wife . . ." He shook his head. "It probably seems silly to you, but it reminded me of my wife and child. I lost them both in childbirth—" He coughed again, pulled a handkerchief from his pocket, and covered his face.

Wife and child?

"I didn't know you had a wife . . . I'm so sorry." Her heart swelled with compassion for him, and all reason blew away with the morning breeze. "The strangest things will trigger memories for me about my mama too." She rubbed his arm, trying to comfort him.

For a moment, her thoughts went back in time, recalling the day Mama died. The fire, the smoke, all the strange people and surroundings. Then her thoughts strayed to Hattie losing Dan.

Why does there have to be so much death, so much pain in this world?

"You should be getting back to the house before Dylan goes looking for you." Pete rubbed his face with his handkerchief and patted Lydia's hand, which still held his shoulder. "Besides, I'll need to get on Mr. Prescot's orders in a jiffy."

Lydia nodded, realizing she'd briefly forgotten about her present obligations. She cleared her throat as heat crept up her cheeks. "Yes, I better get going. But please, make yourself at home while we're gone. When we return, don't hesitate if you feel the need to talk about it. Sometimes it helps me to recall the good memories too."

She smiled at him, and realized she'd somehow known he'd suffered loss—sensing a connection due to her own loss of Mama. Relieved, she believed there was no harm in consoling him. The odd feelings had faded the instant she learned about his past.

Feeling she had done right to offer him a chance to speak about his pain, she returned to the house.

Dylan thought long and hard to figure if there was something he could have done to save the ewe, but nothing came to mind. It was part of the business. *You gain some and you lose some*. At least she had twins, which may turn out to be a blessing so long as they both survived. And since the ewe was perfectly healthy before the birth, they would be able to utilize her meat and coat to help ease the cost of food for feeding everyone while he and Lydia were in San Francisco.

Wondering why Pete was taking so long, Dylan fumed at yet another of Pete's disappearing acts. As he started searching the property, it took him a moment to recognize Pete and Lydia standing beneath the poplar tree on the other side of the corral.

He stopped short and refocused his eyes. Now he was certain.

His wife and his farmhand stood at an intimate distance. Her hand was indeed caressing his arm. Heart pounding like a sledgehammer inside his chest, it took everything within him to stay still and not bolt in their direction.

Just wait.

He sucked in his breath, and stood still, watching and waiting. After a moment, Pete stepped back and rubbed his face with a handkerchief. Dylan knew now he wasn't imagining things. There was something going on between the two of them.

Whether they knew it or not.

When Lydia began heading to the house, Dylan began to stride toward Pete.

"Mr. Prescot," Albert said from behind.

Dylan pulled back his boot and stomped it into the ground. His fists dug into his thighs and he clenched his jaw before he turned toward Albert. "What is it?"

Albert frowned, his hallowed eyes growing wide as his throat bobbed. "W-would you like me to help Pete with the ewe? The last lamb is birthed and nursing strong."

Dylan relaxed his fists at his sides and sighed. "Of course, Albert. Thank you. I was about to give Pete . . . final instructions before Lydia and I head out."

The interruption gave Dylan the moment he needed to recoil his rage and think logically. Could he risk scaring away Pete with a confrontation? Not now. But he would be on the lookout for Pete's replacement while in the city.

Besides, if things went as well as he'd hoped, he would capture any part of Lydia's heart he'd lost to Pete. Shifting his stride from the corral to the house, he went to join his wife and make final preparations for their journey.

TWENTY

Lydia prepared dinner alone while Violet helped Pete disassemble and divide the ewe carcass. Lydia purposefully faced away from the window separating herself from their hired helpers, muffled voices sounding at ease compared to the tension she felt each time she encountered Pete. She tried to reason with herself that the pressure in her chest was due to exhaustion.

Yet, whenever her thoughts strayed to her encounters with Pete that day, the pressure intensified.

She decided it was best to remain quiet during dinner and let the men dictate the conversation. Thankfully, when the five of them sat and began the meal, nobody attempted much more than small talk.

Later in the evening, Lydia filled a small basket with biscuits, almonds, and dried figs for their journey to the Prescot home in Grass Valley. The other packing was complete with their trunks already on the way to the train station.

Violet pulled a jar of pickles from the pantry shelf. "Why aren't you bursting with excitement?

You're about to experience a lavish Easter dinner—French style—and a romantic week in San Francisco."

Lydia gulped. What if Pete hadn't urged her to leave when he did? What if she had kissed his check instead of only caressing his arm? Her mind also involuntarily repeated the moment they'd had at the bottom of the stairs. Pete's firm hand on her waist; the turmoil in his eyes that she now understood.

She'd be facing her mother-in-law within hours and she didn't want Jaina to sense her distracted thoughts.

Forcing a smile, she looked Violet in the eyes. "I am . . . excited . . . but exhausted. Saving those lambs this morning took what strength I had recovered from sleeping last night."

Violet raised her eyebrows. "If I recall, you were in the Valley alone last Easter. I'm not exactly positive about how the Prescot's celebrate, but I can give you an idea of the meaning behind the typical traditions if you'd like."

Lydia had politely declined the invitation from the O'Shea's the previous spring. Dylan had proposed only days earlier. Uncertain of how the folks of French Corral would take the news of their engagement, she had decided it was best not to take attention away from their celebration.

"Whatever you think would be helpful. I regret that I missed it last year . . . and it would be nice to visit and not feel I am getting another lesson from Jaina."

Violet snickered. "Nonsense." She rolled her eyes. "Jaina will enjoy showing you the customs and traditions . . . mixing in her posh French culture with every opportunity."

There was little to support Violet's claim—considering Jaina's privacy all the years in French Corral—but Lydia understood her meaning. Though it was difficult for her to grasp most of the time, Lydia was slowly learning how people might say things for their effect, even if the specifics couldn't possibly be known.

Lydia looked forward to understanding more about Easter and its meaning. She hoped to learn more about her mother-in-law in the process. She still found it difficult to grasp that Jaina had been born on the other side of the world and traveled thousands of miles between shores and across land. She couldn't fathom the scope and difference between Jaina's life there and here. Perhaps Jaina would share more about her past while they prepared food together.

But that was not the reason behind her melancholy mood.

Violet added a stack of napkins to the picnic basket and closed the lid. "Is there something else wrong?"

Distant voices told Lydia the men were near the wagon below the house. Dusk at hand, the men could only accomplish so much before dark. She went to the window to confirm, spotting Pete mounting a horse and heading toward pasture while Albert walked in a hurry toward the barn. Dylan stood and watched the men for a moment, then appeared to be securing the wagon.

There wasn't time to delay what she felt she should do. On a whim, she decided that Violet was a neutral party to the other issue clouding her enthusiasm.

Lydia took in a deep breath and sat at the kitchen table. "Yes . . . it has to do with Pete."

Violet's eyes grew wide as she fumbled to take a seat across the table.

Dylan took full advantage of his position as owner and supervisor of the ranch while he barked orders to Pete and Albert for hours without ceasing. He could see the men were exhausted from the lambing and meat preparation, but weary frustration calloused his ability to care.

"Pete, check the perimeter fence for repairs."

"The perimeter was checked—"

Dylan shook his head and pointed toward the pasture. "Do it again . . . we've had rain that could have loosened posts."

"Albert, I want fresh hay in every stall in the barn—we can't risk contamination of any sort."

Albert nodded and obeyed, despite having had laid fresh hay less than twenty-four hours earlier.

Light gray clouds lay across the sky like a blanket—a silvery sun glowing along the horizon. Rain was possible. Dylan checked that all was secure in the wagon, and the canopy enclosed enough to prevent any water damage.

With his farmhands far away from the house, Dylan did his own perimeter check. He nailed a loose piece of garden fencing and filled several pails of water from the well for Violet to use for watering if needed. Lydia would want her garden to flourish while they were gone. Warm spring temperatures could shift to sweltering summer heat in a day—even in early spring. Though he didn't know about the needs of growing anything besides grape vines, he knew water was important and would save Violet the time knowing both her and Emily would be plenty busy.

He scoffed at his own foolishness. *What man do I know that thinks of such things?* But his mother had long admonished his unique sensitivity toward women. She'd even claimed in a private moment where neither his father nor Lydia could hear—that this was likely what had won Lydia's heart whether she knew it or not.

So why wasn't it enough to keep her attention from another man?

Boiling inside despite the chilly evening air, Dylan decided to cool off by chopping the remaining pile of wood before Pete returned from the pasture.

"Lord . . . what am I to do?" He spoke in unison with each chop, the crunch of ax hitting wood keeping anyone but God from hearing his words. "I . . . *pray* . . . for a clear . . . *answer* . . . that extends . . . *beyond* . . . my . . . *feelings* . . . this moment. I fear my . . . *rage* . . . and my inability to see . . . *clearly*."

CHOP!

CHOP!

CHOP!

Keep thy heart with all diligence; for out of it are the issues of life.

Was this God's answer? To guard his heart—or to show Lydia how to guard hers?

Or perhaps it was to hold fast to trusting a part of his heart he knew true above all else—that his love for Lydia was stronger than his doubt. And it was stronger than the short-lived attention of a seemingly desperate farmhand.

As twilight settled, the air smelled sweet like rain even though the sky was clear. Lydia lay in bed alone, waiting for Dylan to join her. The curtains danced to-and-fro along the edge of the windowsill. Bats flew about, their pitched squeals echoing between the barn and the house. Then, her eyes caught on the handkerchief nestled beneath the side table lantern near the bed. She sat up a bit, moving the lantern aside and grabbing hold of the handkerchief.

The blue embroidered angels had begun to fray. Holding the edges, she brushed her thumbs across them. *Mama, what did you know before you died? Did you and Father ever face such challenges?*

Lydia scoffed at the thought. Mama had kept Lydia from knowing anything about men. Mama was the reason Lydia didn't know what to do. She hated feeling anger toward her in these moments.

What would Mama say if she were here?

She wished she could read better. Did the Bible speak on how to manage difficult feelings as a wife? Elder Scott may have insight. But the thought of speaking to him about such things seemed improper. All she could recall were her wedding vows—

. . . to love and to cherish, till death do us part . . . those whom God hath joined together, let no one put asunder . . .

No matter what she had done to avoid Pete, they continued to share isolated encounters. Was this a *temptation?* Should she tell Dylan about what was happening, even though it was only happening in her mind?

If only Hattie or Mama were here. She and Hattie had shared enough intimate friendship moments that she could tell her anything. But was it so wrong to talk to another man? Nothing about Pete indicated that he was less than a good and honest man. He was hurting. Why couldn't she console him?

Thankfully, she didn't regret confiding in Violet—at least not now. There was still the matter of Violet's confidence, but Lydia believed Violet's sincerity. She also began to understand why Pete appeared undeterred by their encounters, after Violet had explains a few things earlier in the kitchen.

Apparently, Violet managed to coax information out of Pete while Lydia was in Grass Valley. Though she hadn't found the opportunity to share with Lydia, nor felt it was appropriate. But with Lydia's confession, Violet finally explained.

Pete was still in such deep mourning, that he was unaware of how his actions might appear—at least that was Violet's impression. She had warned him after witnessing their encounter at the laundry weeks earlier. Apparently, Violet had watched the entire scene from the upstairs window!

Though they were not able to finish their conversation, Lydia came away with one conclusion. She would need to convince Dylan to find a replacement for Pete upon their return. Mourning or not, his presence awoke things in Lydia she could not deny. With Violet confirming Lydia's feelings were a temptation, she had to find a way to remove it once and for all—regardless of whether Pete recognized the danger.

Footstep bounded up the stairs and the door flung open. Lydia spun her head toward the door, heart leaping until she saw a grin across Dylan's face. He strode in and closed the door, not slowing his pace until he reached the bed. Then he pulled Lydia from her covers and kissed her with more passion than he had in months.

Going limp, she expected him to continue with his regular motions.

Instead, he tucked her back into bed, and then kissed her forehead. "Good night, my bride." He lowered the lamp flame.

Lydia watched his shadow move around the other side of the bed where his silhouette removed his clothing and slid into bed beside her. Then he rolled over with his back toward her. Soon, his deep breathing indicated he was asleep.

Normally, a kiss like that meant more to come.

Confused, Lydia eventually fell asleep with a partial sense of relief. If Dylan knew or suspected something regarding Pete, his love for Lydia had not faltered in the process.

If anything, his kiss hinted at his plans for their week in the city—a week Lydia hoped would dash any doubts about their marriage and lead to the one thing that would ensure their future together—a child.

PART 2

"And the Lord said, Simon, Simon, behold, Satan hath desired to have you, that he may sift you as wheat: But I have prayed for thee, that thy faith fail not; and when thou art converted, strengthen thy brethren."
Luke 22:31-32, KJV

TWENTY-ONE

Saturday April 14, 1906 - Grass Valley,

California

"Where can I help?" Lydia scanned Jaina's kitchen for an apron.

Jaina chopped garden vegetables at the center block while her servant, Lyn prepared the lamb at the sink. Unseen and savory flavors burst from the lids of piping pots at the back of the stove. They blended with cinnamon and vanilla. Lydia's mouth watered though the thought of eating a full meal brought a lump to her throat.

Jaina shook her head. "You can help by taking a seat over there and telling me all about your plans for the city."

Bordered by potted rose bushes and green-leafed plants, an oval mahogany table sat with two matching chairs in the center of a nook nestled into the side of the main kitchen area.

Lydia sat, finding no comfort in the hard, cold chair which contrasted with the warming kitchen air.

"Dylan says you're going to stay at the Palace Hotel. It's quite magnificent." Jaina's words came faster than the rattling of her knife lopping off carrot tops and cubing large white onions. "If you get a room at the top floor, the view of the city is incredible at sunset."

Remorse flowed in waves across Lydia's insides, and she felt fatigue and nausea all at once. Dylan had gone to great lengths to plan an extravagant weeklong adventure between all the demands of the ranch. Meanwhile, Lydia had been too distracted by her sewing and their hired hand to realize it.

Jaina didn't seem to notice a shift in Lydia's demeanor. But that didn't lighten the weight inside her chest. While Dylan was in the other room convincing his father that their trip was necessary, his mother talked as if they were about to attend a town picnic.

Scooting her chair closer to the walkway, Lydia sat up straight, pushing the events of recent weeks behind her as she anticipated the sights, entertainment, and anticipated romance in the week ahead. "Yes, at first he thought about the Fairmont, but they are still constructing parts and he didn't want that to hinder our experience. More than the hotel, I can't wait to watch the opera. I have never seen a story performed before . . . let alone one told with songs."

Slipping the broad knife blade beneath the orange and white medley, Jaina cupped her hand beneath the edge of the counter and slid the pile of vegetables into her palm with precision.

Lydia sucked in a little breath, expecting a stray piece to fall to the floor anyway.

Yet, without dropping a single morsel, Jaina glided the few feet to the stove, and tossed the carrots and onions into a cast-iron pan. Steam spit and spattered for several moments while Jaina stirred briskly with a wooden spoon. Soon, the vegetables calmed to a sizzled and the steam subsided.

Her back to Lydia while she stirred and sprinkled in various dried herbs, Jaina finally responded. "You'll love the opera, I'm sure of it. Dylan was wise to acquire your tickets in advance as I hear they are now sold out. Witnessing a performance by Enrico Caruso is likely something you'll only experience once in your lifetime. I know you enjoy stories. Watching them play out is an experience everyone should have, regardless of social status."

Lydia felt goose bumps along her arms at the words. The words 'social status' reminded her of one of Mama's first diary entries and the disappointment when Charles' father—Mr. Sinclair—would not let her mother attend the theatre due to her status as a vendor's daughter. What would he think now of his granddaughter attending?

Lydia rubbed her arms, forcing a smile past whatever unseen force kept trying to dampen her spirits. "For years, I imagined what it would be like to watch the stories Mama told."

Jaina poured the sautéed herbs, onion, and carrots into the bottom of an oval roasting pan. Lyn set the lamb over the layer of vegetables and herbs, covered it with a heavy cast-iron lid, and then inserted it into the oven. Jaina stirred simmering flageolet beans and crème, lowered the flame, and then joined Lydia at the table.

Jaina smiled and then rested her palms over Lydia's hands in her lap. "Now, how have your reading lessons been going?"

Heat crept up Lydia's neck. The mention immediately brought her last reading lesson—and Pete—fresh to her mind. Surely, she could not hide her reaction from Jaina now.

"Fine." She chewed the inside of her lip and pretended to be fascinated with the shiny green leaves on the plant near the window. "Fine . . . for what I can do on my own. I have been writing too. Did Dylan mention we have written to both of my uncles in the city?"

"No, he did not." Wide eyes and a curt reply told Lydia her attempt to change the topic had gone awry.

Did she speak out of turn? Was there a reason Dylan had not told his mother about that part of their plan?

"Frank hasn't replied yet, but my Uncle Moses—Mama's uncle—says he would like to see me while—"

"Just remember, Dylan has planned this trip mostly for the two of you to spend alone." She winked in a way that made Lydia blush.

Lyn began cracking eggs into a large white porcelain bowl. But when Lydia began to speak, she saw Lyn hesitate, not cracking another one until Lydia paused.

"This may be my only chance to learn more about Mama. And if I can reach Frank as well . . . maybe he can bring my grandfather to his senses."

"Mr. Sinclair is not worth your time as far as I'm concerned. Although I am not thrilled that your mother's family is of Prussian blood, I'm elated you've the opportunity to reunite with another family member." Jaina shifted in her seat and brought her voice low. "But onto other things before it is time for us to eat."

Jaina reached in her apron pocket and pulled out a blue glass vial. She leaned forward, pressing the container into Lydia's palm in a way that would ensure the maid would not see it. "Don't let Dylan find this or see you take it. It's a little helper—an old remedy for promoting fertility. Simply add several drops to a cup of your tea when he won't notice."

Palms sweating and heartbeat accelerating, Lydia swallowed the lump in her throat. This woman did want a grandchild—badly. But why not tell Dylan?

"It helped Andrew and I conceive Dylan."

Lydia nodded. "Thank . . . you?" She didn't intend for her gratitude to come out as a question.

As if she had expected Lydia to reject her gesture, Jaina sat up straight, shifting her smile into a straight line between hardened cheeks. "Is it possible for you to accept help without having all of the information? Can you understand that getting pregnant is essential at this point? My son needs this. He needs to know you can mother his child. Why is that not enough?"

"Jaina . . . I . . . of course it is. I want that too." Lydia shook her head, confused at the sudden shift in Jaina's tone. "I am not questioning the importance of getting pregnant. I want to leave it in God's hands . . . let him decide when. Is that so wrong?"

"God's hands?" Jaina huffed. "We play a part in His handiwork as well. We make choices . . . or circumstances trump His original design. This is only a means to help . . . to possibly repair any damage you may have suffered all those years in the Valley."

Was she hearing this right? She had not suffered in the Valley.

The heat spread to her cheeks. If Lyn had not been in the room, Lydia would have surely raised her voice.

Instead, she spoke firm, yet soft. "Jaina, I appreciate what you have done to help me enmesh with *normal* society. Nevertheless, allow me to make one thing as clear as the glass in that window. My mother provided for my every need in the Valley—every need. I will not sit here and listen to you accuse her of somehow stripping me of the ability to bear children."

Lydia's heart raced. It took great effort for her to breathe deep enough to keep from feeling light-headed.

Jaina's eyes grew dark and she flung the towel from her shoulder onto the table. "You really would not know, would you? You need to trust me—and Dylan. And stop insisting on understanding when obedience should suffice."

She stood, tongue outlining her teeth while her jaw twitched, not loosening her glare on Lydia.

Jaina spun around and went back to attending the dinner preparations. When Jaina and Lyn began to arrange the platters, Lydia knew the conversation was over.

Mama used to quiet Lydia's curiosities too—though not with such accusations.

Would Jaina ever fully accept her as her daughter-in-law? She trusted Dylan more than she did Jaina. But didn't trust also involve understanding?

Lydia exited the kitchen without another word.

Dylan and Mr. Prescot stood in the parlor, overlooking the street from the bay window. Their discussion hushed as soon as the kitchen door clicked shut behind Lydia.

Dylan turned to face her, a teacup and saucer in his hand. "Lydia, sweetheart, how is dinner coming along?" He smiled, though his dimples remained hidden.

Lydia nodded, afraid her voice would shake if she spoke.

Dylan met her at the doorway and kissed her cheek. "Is everything alright? You look flustered?"

"I'm fine," Lydia managed to whisper. Then she curled the corners of her mouth until her cheeks ached. "Kitchen getting a little warm is all."

TWENTY-TWO

Sunday April 15, 1906 - Downtown Grass Valley Easter Sunday Services

If someone had asked Dylan what the minister at his parents' church looked like, he couldn't say. Dylan couldn't keep from watching his wife—tears glistening in her eyes as she took the communion cup and biscuit. Lydia hadn't taken her eyes off the minister the entire service. Watching her hear the full Easter story for the first time was like hearing it anew himself.

She'd cupped her hand over a sob when the minister spoke of the crucifixion, elaborating on the scripture and emphasizing the pain and suffering Christ had endured. Then he flipped back, reading the Last Supper and reminding the congregation of Jesus' command to embrace his death and resurrection as a fulfillment of the new covenant.

"And as they were eating," the monotone voice of the minister read, his voice echoing between stained glass walls and the hardwood floor. *"Jesus took the bread, and blessed it, and brake it, and gave it to the disciples, and said, 'Take, eat; this is my body'."*

A tear spilled down Lydia's cheek as her teeth pressed into the bread.

Dylan put the whole piece in his mouth, and then curled his fingers between Lydia's. She held fast to him, squeezing and shaking her head slightly while she chewed. Dylan gave her what he hoped was a reassuring smile and nod.

"And he took the cup, and gave thanks, and gave it to them, saying, *'Drink ye all of it; For this is my blood of the new testament, which is shed for many for the remission of sins.' "*

The minister must have gestured in silence because a moment later, those sitting behind and beside Lydia lifted their cups and drank.

Lydia lifted her cup and Dylan drank in unison with her. Then he pulled a handkerchief from his vest pocket and handed it to Lydia.

Andrew and Jaina Prescot exchanged pleasantries with other members of the congregation after the service, introducing Lydia with an odd air of pride and indulging grins. Sensing her requirement to play along, Lydia shook hands and nodded her head with vigor. The train for Sacramento would be leaving at noon, so there was little time for detailed introductions. Strange how what she assumed the standard post-service ritual contrasted with the tone of the minister's teaching. Lydia couldn't understand why no one else appeared impacted by the story they'd heard.

Before long, the four of them began to walk through town toward the Prescot home. The words of the minister repeated in Lydia's mind and formed a vague yet clear image. This place where Jesus had lived, died, and ascended to Heaven sounded nothing like the world in which she lived now, yet she could not deny the power this story held over her heart and spirit. Deep within her and beyond doubts of her ability to fulfill God's purpose, bits of truth began to string together from the life she'd lived with Mama. God wanted to prevent his people from experiencing the hardships resulting from sin. Mama had tried to keep Lydia from those hardships for as long as she could.

Pink dogwood blossoms sprinkled the sidewalk, the branches arched over them from the yard of the house they passed. Along the low fence of the next house, fat black bumblebees flitted in and out of purple blossoms snuggled deeply within thick vines of dark green leaves. Warming air filled the sunny patches, while a hint of the cool morning still clung to the shadows along their path.

Dylan and Andrew strolled ahead, leaving Lydia at Jaina's mercy. With the short time they had left before boarding the train, Lydia prayed Jaina would either remain silent or choose a neutral topic for their conversation.

"*Joyeuses Pâques!*" Jaina piped, tilting her chin and catching the shadow of branches and blossoms across her cheek.

Lydia brushed her fingers across the pointed tips of a white picket fence, unsure of how to respond to the strange words uttered from her mother-in law's lips.

"Happy Easter, Lydia. This is how you say, 'Happy Easter' in French—*Joyeuses Pâques!*"

Lydia nodded, but didn't dare try to mimic the phrase.

Jaina clapped and pulled clasped hands into the sunshine. "I think I will tell you about the day the bells flew back to France." She flung her arms into the air as if she were about to take flight herself. "Now, it is truly only a story—but one day you *will* need to know it for your children."

The hope and childish gaze upon Jaina's face made Lydia wonder if the minister's words had shifted something in her.

Grateful for a topic of little consequence, Lydia nodded, feeling her own childish grin emerge. "Of course, Jaina. I would be delighted to hear it."

Dylan's father strolled at a snail's pace beside him as they ascended Bank Street. Dylan spun the end of a rosemary branch in between his fingertips, still in awe at the sight of his wife grasping a portion of the Cross and Resurrection of Jesus. He couldn't know his wife's mind, but the conviction he felt was clear. He needed the reminder of who sat on the Throne of Thrones—and it wasn't Dylan Prescot. It was time to give control back to God— regarding the ranch and his marriage. No matter what outcome he hoped for in the coming week, he would accept it all as a part of God's plan for him and Lydia.

Dylan chortled. His mother was telling Lydia the children's story about when the bells flew back to France on Easter Day. Jaina spoke in a loud whisper, seamlessly blending English and French phrases, as she walked with Lydia several paces be-hind.

He wished his mother had waited until they'd re-turned home from Easter Services, so he could watch Lydia's reaction to this story as well. But there wouldn't be time since they'd decided to walk instead of taking a carriage to and from church. Would Lydia know it was only a silly story parents told their kids as an excuse to lavish them with sweets while helping them remember the Easter story? He would offer to explain more once they boarded the train that afternoon.

Lydia giggled—the sound sweeter than any chocolate egg an angel might drop into the garden. To hear laughter from his wife was a treat indeed. And it gave him hope that joy was around the bend.

Andrew Prescot cleared his throat. "Your mother is quite the influence, son." He chuckled and shook his head.

Dylan didn't respond. What kind of conversa-tion was his father about to embark upon? He hoped it wasn't going to be too serious.

"I tried to reason with her, with you, and even God about the timing of this trip, but my attempts are of no avail." His father glanced back and then quickened his steps when they turned on Bennett Street. "Except for the obvious need for the two of you to have some time alone without the demands of the ranch and managing your new employees, she reminded me that Lydia needs to connect with her family no matter the cost. All in all, I would have done whatever possible if there was ever a chance to reunite your mother with her family."

At his father's words, Dylan's footsteps felt lighter. Though he had convinced himself that what his parents thought did not matter—their approval still brought comfort to his soul.

"Thank you, Father. When you didn't protest yesterday, I assumed you were choosing to keep the peace in the name of Easter."

His father waved as if shooing away an invisible insect. "I was. . . in part. But I also had not decided yet. However, God has a way of putting us in our places. I've been so concerned about the financial security of your ranching venture—I've lost sight of all you and Lydia have overcome. Though you have been more fortunate than your mother and I were in our early years, you face a set of obstacles that I cannot fathom."

A knot settled in Dylan's chest. They were only a few houses away from arriving at his parents' house.

"What do you mean?" Could his father somehow know about the challenges that Pete presented?

"That, son, is more than I have time to expound upon. However, heed fast to holding your position as protector over your wife this coming week. I sense the enemy is on the prowl with you two." Andrew shook his head.

Dylan thought he saw his father's eyes grow moist. His heart rattled against his chest and he would have stopped if the women weren't so close behind them.

"Father? Do you know something that I don't?" He withheld the urge to pull at his father's coat tails, knowing Lydia and his mother would surely see it as a sign of duress between men.

Andrew shook his head, sighing deeply before speaking in a quick and loud whisper. "I only know that my dreams of late are smothered in warnings of impending doom. Perhaps it is only a greater awareness of the corrupt ways of this world ever since I've joined Bourn's management team at Empire Mine. Yet, the more I've prayed, the stronger I feel it." Something about his father's voice shifted then. It was as if it wasn't even his father talking. "Only God knows the full purpose of the week at hand—and His intentions will rise above your own plans."

Dylan hesitated at the gate, flicking the hinge with his fingers and trying to ignore his sweaty palms. Why was his father saying all this now? They had less than an hour before they were to board the train.

"Father?" He waited until they made eye contact. The women only steps away, all Dylan could do was search his father's eyes for a moment.

Andrew Prescot squeezed Dylan's shoulder hard and then patted his back. With pursed lips and a nod, he said, "Do not fear, my son. The Lord will be with you."

Dylan's thoughts from moments earlier repeated in his mind. Was he prepared to accept the outcome of the coming week—even if things did not go as he planned?

TWENTY-THREE

En Route to San Francisco

With a faint lump in her throat, Lydia picked at her meal on the train. During their train ride from Grass Valley to Sacramento, she had planned to ward off her worries enough to enjoy the scenery before descending below the mountain and into the city. But the more the train jumbled across the tracks, the more the hint of nausea from her last train ride attempted to return.

Swallowing, she took a deep breath. Determined to enjoy every moment they would share together in the coming week, Lydia looped her arm through her husband's.

He cupped her face with his free hand and mouthed the words, "I love you." After a brief kiss, they both silently watched the scenery pass by.

At first, Lydia's thoughts streamed along with the view. So many houses, orchards, empty hillsides and expansive fields—each representing a family, a farmer, or a part of creation only God's hand had touched. It was overwhelming and exhilarating at the same time. When her mother and father had fled San Francisco to escape judgment from Mr. Sinclair over twenty years earlier, they probably had no idea they'd never return below the mountain again. Nor could they have imagined the circumstances that would one day take their daughter back to the city where it all began.

And now Lydia and Dylan had the judgment of another parent to overcome. Jaina could put it any way she wanted, but Lydia knew the root of her pleas—Jaina feared judgment now that she was once again a part of an affluent community. Why else would she go to such lengths to ensure Lydia became pregnant soon?

A part of Lydia felt desperate enough to resolve this pregnancy issue once and for all. What if what Jaina said was true? Though Lydia had never been deathly ill and, according to Hattie, her *monthly* had arrived at the normal age, it wasn't impossible that somewhere along the way, something in their life could have affected her ability to bear children. Still, her limited knowledge of the subject left her dumbfounded.

If only she could control her waves of emotions—which seemed to have multiplied in recent weeks. One moment she would feel happy and peaceful. The next, she questioned everything. She couldn't get to San Francisco fast enough. The city would serve as a great distraction and hopefully calm her emotions and deter her unyielding thoughts.

After a while, Dylan's continued silence and her gloomy thoughts forced her to begin a happier tone to their travels.

"I'm so thrilled you thought of bringing one of my dresses to show Uncle Moses and the other tailor. Do you really think it's possible for me to sell dresses to the upper-class women of San Francisco?"

Dylan turned, a wide grin revealing the dimples that always made her stomach flip. "Absolutely!"

Orchards streamed behind him in a blur of white and pale pink blossoms clustered between tangled branches against a pale blue sky. He squeezed her hands, but then his smile faded with a flicker in his gaze.

"What's wrong? You've been so quiet. I thought you'd be busting at the seams to tell me all about your plans for the week ahead." Lydia drew excitement from deep within, hoping it would transfer to her husband.

He pulled her close enough, their bodies only took up half of the gold and red embroidered bench they shared. "I'm only saving my energy. We need to catch up on our sleep this evening so that we can fully enjoy the rest of our time in the city."

"You're not going to tell me of any more plans besides the opera, are you?"

His grin returned and he winked.

"All right then. I want to talk about when we return." She wanted to take the words back the moment she spoke them.

The train entered a tunnel, cloaking them in temporary darkness. But Dylan's silence unsettled her heart.

Back in the daylight, they were now nestled between two rolling hillsides scattered with oak trees bursting with baby green leaves. Sunlight and shadows chased each other across Dylan's face—making his frown even more daunting.

"What is it? Tell me so we can start tomorrow without a single thing coming between us." She resolved she would tell him about the vial as well. Then they would decide together if they should continue to trust God or use this tonic to help them along.

Dylan squeezed Lydia's hand hard enough to make it hurt, but she sensed it was for his own comfort. She searched his eyes while he shook his head, hesitating.

"Lord, forgive me if I'm wrong," he whispered with a glance at the ceiling. "Lydia, I need to tell you what I saw yesterday. Then I need to ask you to be honest."

Heart straight to her stomach, Lydia heard a sob escape her lips. She swallowed hard and fought the urge to shift her eyes back outside.

She knew exactly what he meant. He'd seen the moment of intimacy between her and Pete as they stood closer than they should have outside of the barn.

She put a hand to her throat, as if it would keep her thumping heart from escaping.

Nodding, she began her confession. "You don't need to tell me anything. It is I that need to tell— to confess." She bit her lip, hoping the tears burning her eyes and nose would hold back long enough for her to tell him everything.

Dylan sat silent again, his jaw, lips, and fists clenched. He nodded and shook his head as Lydia told him about every moment alone that she and Pete experienced and how the moments had made her emotions sway.

Dylan's throat bobbed with a hard swallow when she said she was done.

Thankfully, the clunk and grind of the train tracks echoing off the mountainside would keep anyone within earshot of hearing their conversation.

"I'm sorry, Dylan. I can see that I was wrong now—even letting myself believe thoughts alone could do no harm. Violet knows, but she's the one who told me what all this was—."

Dylan raised his hand and Lydia pulled back. "No, I'm . . ." He pulled her into an embrace. With his mouth against her neck, he whispered. "It's my fault, my sweet Lydia. I've seen the signs for weeks and done nothing about it. I've been a coward and failed to take a stand for your honor and our marriage. Forgive me."

Lydia's heart pounded now, but for different reasons. Dylan was apologizing. He was taking responsibility and not blaming her at all.

She pulled back enough to look him in the eyes. There was something strong yet weak about him, and it made her love him more deeply. She believed he needed her affirmation more than he needed to hear of his mother's schemes.

"Of course, I forgive you. But you've never been a failure or a coward in my eyes."

He took her face between his palms and looked at her as if they were the only two people on the train. "I love you Lydia Sinclair Prescot—and the thought of losing you to another man paralyzed me. From this moment forward, you have nothing to fear. No temptation. No circumstance that will prevent me from standing for your honor and protecting you from whatever challenges we face."

He pulled her even closer, kissing her until she fell limp in his embrace.

She would tell him of the vial later. For now, she felt assured that their love was strong enough to endure. Compared to the turmoil Pete had brought upon them, Jaina's tactics felt futile.

That evening, as they settled into the boarding house in Sacramento, the silence between them was filled with expectation. Their conversation was light over dinner. Every now and then Dylan would wink and smile and glance toward the staircase that led to their room.

Butterflies awoke in Lydia's belly while they ascended the steps and entered their room. A wide bed, bureau, and nightstand took up most of the room and fit snuggly between walls filled with repeated images of horse drawn carriages. With her back to Dylan at the bed, she took a moment to wash off the grime from their travels using the cloth and bowl of tepid water on the bureau.

After a few moments, Dylan became unusually silent, not even the sound of his garments rustling against the bedspread. When she turned, Dylan's rhythmic snores told her why.

She finished preparing for bed and then removed her husband's shoes, overcoat, and suspenders. Doing her best to wiggle the bedspread out from beneath him, she snuggled up to his side, reveling how perfect the curves of her body fit around his. She nuzzled her chin into the base of his neck and kissed him soft enough not to wake him.

His snores only grew louder.

Lydia giggled, turned out the light, and pulled the blankets up and around their shoulders.

The sound of the rushing river outside the cracked window soon lulled her to sleep.

TWENTY-FOUR

Monday April 16, 1906 - Ferry Building,

San Francisco

During the ferry ride across the Bay, Lydia hardly spoke. But this time it was because Dylan filled their journey with one story after another about his childhood. Lydia felt like a child once again listening to one of Mama's stories, but Dylan's boyish grin and flailing hands made his stories even more entertaining.

The passing oceanic scenery and crowds of people had all faded into the background as Lydia sat entranced with Dylan's tale. From spooking horses, to swiping pies, Dylan and Dan had many adventures growing up in French Corral. She hadn't even noticed they were about to dock until the horn blared.

In an instant, memories of Lydia's grandfather surged, and her stomach sunk. The desire for reconciliation with him grew stronger. Something within her suggested that her grandfather might need to feel loved himself. Her stomach churned with a sick feeling as she relived her meeting with him during their trip to San Francisco the previous spring.

He'd been outwardly dismissive to the point of cruelty—not even caring that she'd passed out. At the Inn in French Corral, many men had come through talking of striking it rich to find unending happiness. But her grandfather's riches only made him more miserable in her eyes. Lydia would never understand how some people thought happiness could be bought like one of Mrs. O'Shea's pies. Only they expected it to sustain them long after the final crumb was wiped clean.

Hopefully, Dylan would assist her in contacting Uncle Frank while they were there. But she reminded herself, the point of this trip was to rest and enjoy the company of her husband. Yes, she would have a day with her other uncle. Aside from that, six more days were to be spent without concern for the past or the future.

Lydia recognized the man standing before a white, topless carriage without horses. He was Dylan's grandfather's coachman. Yet, she faltered to recall his name, annoyed at how distracted she'd been with meeting her grandfather the previous summer, that the details of Dylan's family and home remained a blur.

"Cecyl!" Dylan boomed and grabbed the coachman's hand, giving it a hearty shake.

Lydia exhaled in relief, making eye contact before extending her gloved hand with a curtsy. "How wonderful to see you again, Cecyl."

Cecyl nodded with a slight grin, and then assisted Lydia to her seat before loading their luggage into a rear storage compartment. Dylan climbed aboard a moment later, joy spread across his face from heart-fluttering dimples to sparkling willow-green eyes. How could such a simple moment seem to expand her love for him so much more?

The carriage rode smoothly compared to the buggy they'd taken during their initial visit, though the speed felt unsettling when they came alongside other carriages. Smooth, red cushions exaggerated the white frame, making Lydia feel like one of the royals in the stories Jaina had read. As they rode past, people turned their heads and stared.

Cecyl announced their arrival at the Palace Hotel, and Lydia gasped when she thought he was driving directly inside. Huge pillars connecting white, ornate arches sat at either end of a circular entrance large enough to fit their Penn Valley home. Lydia arched her neck, straining to look high enough to the top of the courtyard to see a dome of glass windows that reminded her of the ceiling inside the Sutro Baths.

Dylan held out his elbow and reached for her hand with his and helped her down. Her eyes stuck on the enormous and beautiful hotel. She didn't even look down as she stepped out of the carriage.

Like a dream, they entered and were engulfed in an array of elaborate upholstered furniture, oriental rugs, enormous plants with long, narrow leaves, and chandeliers hanging every few feet, throwing light in all directions, reflecting from mirrored walls and slick, glossy flooring. A curved staircase wide enough to hold at least two carriages across climbed upward to a large landing, which led to more staircases at each end.

Lydia had to remember to breathe. Rich shades of red furniture and green trees, exotic clouds of cigar smoke emanating from the bar, accompanied gloriously dressed women and men who paraded about the hotel with gleaming smiles of arrogance.

Lydia grinned, attempting to mimic a woman prancing toward the bar. Chin raised and shoulders back, her confidence surged, and she eagerly followed her husband up the stairs. All she desired was her husband at her side, the luxury of fine clothes against her skin, and the world at her fingertips.

Only days earlier she'd knelt in soiled hay, covered in blood after cutting out a lamb from its dead mother.

The idea made this moment that much sweeter, knowing how well her attire, her hair, and her handsome husband hid any hint of the life they had left behind for the week. Though she knew it was temporary, she felt a glimmer of satisfaction knowing she felt comfortable living in either world.

Their suite was also extravagant, but once Lydia lay down atop the rose-patterned quilt, her eyes grew heavy.

"Darling, go ahead and rest," Dylan's voice sounded distant. "I've no plans for us until this evening for that exact purpose."

Sometime later, a knock at the door woke Lydia. She'd no idea how long she had slept, but she felt she'd slept deep enough to find energy for whatever her husband had planned for their first night in the city.

Lydia sat up, seeing Dylan also asleep on the settee in the corner of the room. He didn't appear to have heard the knock, so Lydia went to answer the door.

Miss Gracie, Grandfather Prescot's housemaid, stood in the hall outside of their room, with a wrapped gown draped across her arms. She smiled and curtsied. "Mr. Prescot asked me to bring this and help you dress this evening Mrs. Prescot."

The familiar impression of Dylan's hands on Lydia's hips made her belly flutter as he whispered from behind. "I'll be keeping you close tonight, Darling. But I am sure you'll still turn heads while I go unnoticed."

Still weary from her nap, Lydia didn't know how to respond.

Dylan chuckled and patted the small of Lydia's back. "I'll disappear into the dressing room to change myself. Let me know when you're ready and I'll come back out." He winked and kissed Lydia's cheek.

Miss Gracie entered and lay the gown across the bed. Dusty blue with strewn lapis and silver strands embroidered on the bodice and skirt, the gown was sleeveless and was accompanied by a coordinating silk shawl and gloves. White, satin shoes and white stockings completed the ensemble, making Lydia feel like an angel from head to toe. Still amazed at how a gown of the same material she had sewn and held time and again for other women, felt completely different when she was wearing it herself.

Dylan looked dashing in his bow tie, waist coat and vest in the same shade of powder blue as Lydia's gown.

They traveled several blocks to eat at *Fior d'Italia* on Broadway.

"We'll dine at the Palace Hotel before the Opera tomorrow evening," Dylan said with a wink after they were seated in a dim and cozy corner. "Besides, you haven't had Italian cuisine before."

The city was alive with energy and full of the strangest and most amazing array of sights, sounds, and people Lydia had ever seen.

Next, they attended the musical *Babes in Toyland* at the Columbia Theatre. Lydia delighted in both the show and the spectacular crafting of detail throughout the theatre. The ceiling alone was something she could stare at for hours. Small cherubs in bronze, detailed flowers that looked real enough to touch. The seats came with individual heaters, which pushed up warm spouts of air which kept people from freezing in the balcony seats. The music, dancing and a dramatic storyline left Lydia in a daze for at least an hour after the show.

Outside, the brisk and pungent air revived her somewhat but the lights and rush of people prancing throughout the streets felt surreal amid her exhaustion. Could this be real? Her shoes soon turned a dark bluish brown from the mud and getting splashed with sewage coming from the gutter when a wagon or motorcar came too close to the sidewalk. But she only laughed.

Dylan at her side, a grin and twinkle in his eye, told her none of it mattered. "Our worries are gone for the next week. I'm determined to make sure that nothing prevents us from enjoying all the city can offer. No work, no pressure . . . just fun and abandon."

Dylan got more entertainment from watching Lydia than he did from the show or any of the array of characters walking the streets of San Francisco. Seeing the city through her eyes ignited a passion in him—like watching a child in a toy store. Things that others took for granted as normal, as routine, Lydia stared at wide-eyed and intrigued. Even some people and their customs made her laugh until

Dylan grimaced to indicate she should keep certain reactions to herself.

He loved how she hadn't a single ounce of judgment within her—only curiosity and amazement at the variety of people and personalities one city could hold. Sensing her exhaustion at one point, Dylan took her around a corner toward a less busy part of town. A quiet street allowed them to catch their breaths. If Dylan felt over stimulated, then she must.

Then around another corner, the mellow, relaxing tunes of a street musician playing a violin beckoned. Realizing Lydia had probably never heard this instrument apart from the orchestra they'd heard at the theatre, he guided his wife to a bench so they could listen and rest their feet before heading back to the hotel.

"It is lovely . . . like someone singing in a very high voice." Lydia hummed along off tune but seemed to enjoy it all the same.

People walked in and out of the establishments lining the block—mostly couples too immersed in each other to notice the world around them. There was a lone man with graying hair and a limp whispering something to himself and then laughing. Then another man approached, tall with a trench coat and a cigarette between his fingers. Dylan wasn't sure if he was going to the bar or to the bench until the man stopped in front of them.

"Excuse me, sir," the man said in a pleasant yet thick voice with Irish overtones. "Would you have a light?"

"No, sir, I do not." Dylan nodded at the bar entrance.

Then the man looked at Lydia. More than a glance, he stared at her until his small smile turned into a large, creepy grin.

Dylan's heart began to race. He didn't want to alarm Lydia by assuming too much. But this strange man was looking a little too long—*longingly*—at his wife.

Dylan cleared his throat.

Lydia looked back at the man, a curious look on her face, and obviously just as intrigued.

Dylan cleared his throat again and stood.

He grabbed Lydia's arm to motion her to stand as well, but she didn't break eye contact with the man.

"Hello, Ma'am." The man tipped his hat, bowed, and then winked.

The nerve! "Sir, my *wife* and I will be going now." Dylan said each word with firm fervor.

Lydia giggled. "Goodbye, sir." She pressed her lips together and followed Dylan's lead up the street.

Lydia could not understand what the rush was. Didn't Dylan recognize that man from the play? It took her a moment as well, and then she froze—captivated by his interest in her and thinking of the role he'd played of the villain and how charming he appeared up close.

Why did Dylan have to make them leave? He could have introduced them and congratulated him on an excellent performance. She huffed for a moment but decided to keep quiet. As they walked, more than a few men gazed at her—looking closely like that man did. Most, if not all of them, came across as kind and even handsome.

What was wrong again with looking, talking? She felt she would only understand this world by interacting with more people. Yet, in an instant, Dylan wanted to prevent her from doing so. Didn't he know she loved him above all else? She only wanted to experience the variety she was now observing, have a conversation with people who talked differently, came from other parts of the country and the world.

"Are we going back to the hotel now?" Breathless in her attempt to keep up with his pace, Lydia felt exhausted again.

"Yes, it's late. And when the hour gets much later, unpredictable types of people emerge on these streets . . . people who are like the ones I warned you about when I first told you about the city."

Lydia had forgotten the warnings, forgotten about the evil Dylan had explained could be present in a city of this size. She didn't sense evil in any way. Just different. This city was different and exciting around every corner.

How could she feel so torn between two worlds? After being in Grass Valley, she'd longed to be back home, working in the garden and sewing in the tranquility of her home with God's creation all around. Yet, now that she was in the city, its lights and activities drew her in as well. Was it wrong?

They boarded a carriage in silence.

TWENTY-FIVE

You cannot do that again." Dylan withheld as much anger as he could, but his voice boomed.

"What?" Lydia crossed her arms and glared.

"You cannot give your full attention to a strange man like that. It gives the wrong . . . impression."

"Wrong impression? Dylan, he was from the play. I was stunned at first and didn't know what to say. He was marvelous in his performance—don't you think?"

"It doesn't matter, Lydia. The way you were looking at him . . . it appeared . . . seductive. And he soaked in every bit of it—"

"*Seductive?* I don't know what you mean. I was only making sure he was who I thought he was. I was about to compliment him on his performance when you stood up and pulled me away."

Dylan clenched his fists. She had no idea what her mere presence could do to a man.

"Lydia . . . sweetheart." He took a deep breath to avoid barking at her. "You are a beautiful young woman. Have you not noticed how men stare and tip their hats at you this evening? It is not your dress they're gawking at."

"What is wrong with being beautiful? It feels nice to be noticed. This dress feels amazing and I am glad people see me. Would you rather I dressed as the mountain mole you met and make other men have pity on both of us while we prance around the city?"

"No . . . Lydia. You're getting that tone with me again," Dylan whispered and nodded at the carriage driver.

The carriage moved at a slow pace up the crowded street. Every few seconds the clamor of hooves and wheels over stone and earth halted, causing the couple to lurch forward. Even Dylan was amazed at how they'd come close yet never collide with a group of pedestrians or another carriage careening across the road.

Lydia shrunk down in her seat and scooted further from Dylan. When the carriage lurched, she pulled her hand to her throat and grimaced, but kept from meeting Dylan's gaze. She faced away from him and acted more interested in passersby than she did in her husband's rage.

Dylan reached for her shoulder to turn her face back toward him.

She pulled away and crossed her arms. "You bring me here for a night of fun and excitement and when I finally start to enjoy myself . . ." Her words faded, voice cracking.

Dylan felt his temper rise. How could he control her, really? Not without getting harsh with her. And he didn't want to be harsh—he only wanted to protect her.

He folded his arms across his chest and looked out his side of the carriage. They would be back to the hotel soon, and he would hopefully figure out how to resolve this matter by the time they got to their room.

So much for a romantic evening.

As the carriage pulled up to the hotel, Lydia's stomach began to turn. She didn't want Dylan angry with her. She wanted to learn about life by experiencing it, even those experiences that could be harmful. If he was with her, she felt safe to explore and experiment.

He quickly lifted her from the carriage, losing his grasp of her waist as soon as her shoes hit the sidewalk. Then he turned away and started for the hotel doors without even offering his arm.

Suddenly, a lump grew in Lydia's throat and her mouth filled with sour saliva. The bush at the entrance her only option, she lurched for the edge and vomited, holding herself up with her palm against the outside of the hotel wall.

Her feathered hat fell onto the ground, the edge soaking up what she had expelled. Tears burned her eyes and she began to shake so badly, she had to kneel or fall over.

A hand rested firmly on her hip, another on her arm. A man's voice not belonging to her husband spoke. "Are you all right, Miss?"

For a moment, the hand left her arm and then a clean handkerchief dangled in front of her eyes. Hand shaking, she grasped the hanky and wiped her mouth and eyes before turning toward the stranger.

Deep blue eyes and thick eyebrows set below black slicked hair. The man smiled, his beard and mustache hiding most of his face.

Lydia attempted to stand, but her legs were too weak. The man gently lifted her, not letting go of her elbows.

"Thank you." She swallowed and glanced back behind his shoulder, thinking Dylan would appear any moment.

"Allow me to walk you into the foyer to sit."

Afraid she would topple over if he let go, she didn't protest. Wherever her husband went, he wasn't here to protect her now.

The man led Lydia to a chaise beneath a large palm tree. She sat, finding it difficult to stray from gazing into his blue eyes. What was it about the men in this city? Handsome, charming, mesmerizing.

"Allow me to get you some water. Are you here with anyone? Do you need help up to your room?"

A wave of nausea filled her throat again, but she managed to keep it to a gag in the handkerchief.

"I will be right back. Here is another handkerchief if you need one…and that planter there could use a little nourishment just in case." He winked, seemingly undeterred by her unbecoming eruptions.

"Thank . . . you," she whispered. It took all she had in her to keep herself from throwing up again.

Where was Dylan?

She couldn't see much beyond the large leaves of the trees surrounding her. The stairs were out of view and looking around too much caused her head to spin. She hadn't had any wine with dinner, so that couldn't be making her ill.

Tears welled. One more thing to ruin their evening. If she admitted it, she didn't feel that interested in being close to her husband now anyway.

Blue Eyes returned swiftly, holding a tall glass of water and a small bowl of some sort. He sat next to her, displaying no hesitation in brushing his leg up against hers and wrapping his arm around her shoulder to help her sip her drink.

He didn't seem like a threat to her—especially in the public setting of an extravagant hotel. The cold water felt nice in her mouth and down her throat. This gentleman had provided her relief to an otherwise awkward moment. Wherever Dylan was, he apparently hadn't noticed she was no longer near him. After their argument in the carriage, it made little sense that he wouldn't be with her.

"Miss." The man held out his hand. Thick, smooth fingers with evenly trimmed nails gestured a handshake. "I am Bradford Hilton."

Lydia reached for his hand, placing hers beneath his extended fingers in as delicate-a-lady fashion as she could despite her hand shaking. "Lydia . . . Lydia Sinclair . . . er . . . Prescot."

"It is a pleasure to meet you, Miss Sinclair? Any relation to Frank Sinclair?"

She didn't know if she was supposed to reveal her maiden name to a stranger, but it was out now. And her error had apparently revealed his connection to her uncle. Her stomach settled instantly at the possibility.

"Yes, yes I am." She felt a smile emerge as she turned toward this kind gentleman.

"How's that? Frank and I go way back," Bradford chuckled and squeezed Lydia's shoulder slightly.

"He's my . . . my uncle on my father's side." She couldn't believe it. Perhaps this accidental encounter could finally lead her to contact Uncle Frank.

"Uncle? Frank's sister didn't have children before she died." Bradford's thick eyebrows knit together, and he tilted his head to the side.

Lydia shook her head. "My father was Charles Sinclair."

"Charles?"

"Frank's older brother, Charles. Do you know him as well?"

"I never met Charles. He was long gone by the time I met Frank. He spoke little of him, I assumed he was dead, or they'd had a falling out, so I didn't press the issue."

Suddenly, Dylan's voice echoed behind them. "Lydia? Lydia, are you here?"

Lydia caught a glimmer of Dylan's blue vest between the palm tree branches. She stood to spread them open. "Here, Dylan! I'm right here."

Dylan's eyes grew wide, then he pressed his lips together and shook his head. "Don't move!"

A second later, he'd made his way around the various potted trees, couches and chair that stood between them. In that flash of time, Bradford had removed his arm from Lydia and now stood to the side of the chaise lounge where she lay.

Immediately, Bradford thrust his hand out to Dylan, a small smile and direct eye contact complementing his sure posture. "Bradford Hilton."

Dylan took his hand, shaking it firmly while his forehead wrinkled, and he forced a smile past his frown. "Dylan Prescot. I see you have met my *wife,* Lydia. Darling, what happened to you?" Dylan was on his knees before her, obviously uninterested in further engaging with Bradford.

"I felt ill as soon as you entered the hotel. I dashed to a potted bush outside and Bradford here must have seen so he—"

"Ill?" Dylan reached for her forehead. "You don't feel ill, though you look a bit pale. Maybe this rich city food isn't for you?"

Dylan didn't look well himself. His skin pallor and beads of sweat moistening his collar.

"What happened to you?" The shrill tone of her own voice surprised Lydia at first. She sounded more upset than concerned. But she should be upset with him for leaving her alone for so long.

"Right after I walked in, a footman handed me this telegram." Dylan held up a square of paper, squeezing it in his palm until it crinkled.

Lydia's heart fell and she knew the message carried bad news. Her hand fluttered to her throat as she prepared for the worst.

Dylan cleared his throat before continuing. "I thought you were right behind me . . . I was halfway to our room when I realized you weren't. The telegram says . . ." his voice cracked, his eyes peering into the soil in the planter.

"Bad news?" Lydia held her breath.

"It's my grandfather. He . . . he passed away only hours ago." Dylan's throat bobbed with a hard swallow.

Lydia's thoughts swarmed. She'd been selfish again. Her husband needed her now more than she needed to experience adventure in the city. "Oh, Dylan. I'm so sorry," she clutched his arm. "So sorry."

Bradford cleared his throat. "Pardon me, Mr. and Mrs. Prescot . . . I would leave the two of you alone, but I sensed an urgency Mrs. Prescot, regarding your Uncle Frank?"

"Yes," Lydia said and then faced her husband. "Dylan . . . I know you have other things on your mind, more important things, but Bradford knows Frank—my Uncle Frank. Our meeting here this evening can't be by chance."

Afraid his gamut of emotions would erupt in an outburst toward Lydia, Dylan inhaled, allowing the details of the previous several minutes to take hold. His grandfather was gone. He'd allowed yet another strange man to provide not only attention, but conversation, to his wife. Yet, he couldn't deny the possibilities of Divine intervention.

What were the chances of him and Lydia happening upon an acquaintance of Frank Sinclair in this vast city? Especially during a week like this with the Opera in town and many on holiday for the Easter week. They'd been writing Frank for nearly a year to seek resolution with Lydia's grandfather, but without a reply.

Dylan made quick arrangements to meet with Bradford later in the week and they exchanged address and telephone details. Maintaining eye contact to offset this man's potential intentions toward his wife, he hesitated but then provided their room number so that Frank could contact them before they left the city.

TWENTY-SIX

Lydia steadfast at Dylan's side, they ascended the stairs to their room in relative silence. If Lydia spoke, her words didn't register beyond the sound of her voice floating past his ear. He had only a few moments while they walked down the wide, gleaming, and echoing hallway to accept the change in plans.

Notions of escaping their troubles with a romantic weekend in the city ending in a family reunion with Lydia's mother's Uncle Moses lingered no longer than the cigar smoke hovering in the hallway. As soon as a door opened or a serviceman swept past, the smoke would scurry away with the draft.

With the side-issues of Lydia's curiosity and hope to contact her father's brother handled for the moment, Dylan considered more pressing matters. His grandfather had passed. A moment he'd been prepared for, but not now. He hadn't had the chance to request the additional funds he would need to sustain the ranch through spring. As if he'd knocked over a bees' nest, a series of worries stung him like angry wasps coming from every direction.

He'd lost his grandfather as well as the hope for a financial back up plan. The only glimmer of a chance they had to keep from selling the farm, would be if Lydia could indeed bring in additional income from her sewing orders. But then he would have to tell her that he'd once again kept information from her. She knew their finances were not in ideal order, but she didn't know things were bad enough she may not have a choice but to earn extra income from dressmaking for their survival.

Eventually, she would learn that he couldn't tell her everything all the time. There were things a husband could keep from his wife after all. The details and pressures of providing for their financial stability did not need to be her concern.

However, any thoughts he had about paying Pete for his labor upon their return and then dismissing him, seemed unwise. They would need Pete and Albert and several more farm hands to avoid accumulating more debt than they could pay back in a reasonable amount of time. How would he manage to gain that many workers on a promise to pay later? Only so many capable workers were desperate enough to work for room and board on a ranch when mining opportunities and profits were still so plentiful in the Sierras.

Then there was the matter of Lydia, in the same home, with all these strange men. Dylan hadn't been prepared for the attention her beauty would bring. He'd assumed men would have more discretion, especially the ones who knew she was married.

Yet, the innocence of this incredible young woman who helped him see the world in a whole new way, was now the one reason he had failed to protect her. Well, he supposed, she hadn't chosen him as much as he'd chosen her. He was the only eligible man around at the time. He hadn't considered she would want to choose another if given the opportunity. Would she ever doubt her choice for him as her husband if a more capable man entered her life?

He patted her hand on his arm as they approached the door to their hotel suite. She turned toward him, and tilted her head, her expression plain and pure. Full lips rested one atop the other, the tip of her pale pink nose below round glassy blue eyes asking things without words that he couldn't answer anyway.

He reached for the door handle, trying to keep hold of her gaze, but he fumbled. Lydia snickered softly. Dylan shook his head. There were more crucial matters at stake. He needed to focus on the next 24 hours. When they entered the room, he resisted the urge to gather his wife in his arms.

Lydia didn't give him a chance anyway. "I should change out of this soiled gown." She pinched the edge of her skirt and glanced toward the powder room.

Dylan nodded, and then contacted the front desk from their room phone extension to arrange for a carriage first thing in the morning. Was it presumptuous to assume Lydia would be welcomed at her Uncle Moses' tailor shop several days sooner than planned?

Although she could accompany him to his grandfather's house, he'd have no choice but to leave her alone so he could handle all the many responsibilities awaiting upon his arrival. Obviously, leaving her alone at the hotel was not even an option.

Especially since he'd given their room number to Bradford Hilton.

"Dylan," Lydia whispered the moment Dylan cradled the phone receiver.

He could tell she was sobbing before he even turned around. He nestled her cheeks, warm with tears, between his palms. "What's the matter?"

"I'm sorry about this evening . . ." her chest shook as she inhaled. ". . . sorry about not letting you protect me . . . sorry that you didn't get to say good-bye to your grandfather . . ."

He couldn't stand to see her carry the burden that belonged to him—*no*—that belonged to God. He sighed and kissed away her tears. "Don't worry about any of that, my sweet Lydia. It's been a long day for the both of us. Thankfully, God's mercies are new every morning, right?"

The corners of Lydia's mouth curved up for a moment. She nodded and dabbed the damp part of her chin where tears had trailed.

The rest of the evening, the couple kept busy with random tasks about the hotel room. They packed the bags they would need for the following night when they would be separated between the Prescot home and Uncle Moses. Dylan knew estate dealings would probably take a day or two, but they'd keep their room at the hotel through the end of the week anyway.

Thinking Lydia was finished transferring her day clothes from the larger suitcase on the bed, Dylan scooped up the strap, not realizing it wasn't latched. Clothing toppled to the floor followed by a strange glass vial that rolled beneath the bed.

Dylan glanced at Lydia, who stood frozen at the vanity table, a fistful of stray strands of hair she'd removed from her hairbrush. Her eyes darted from his face to the floor near the bed, and then back to his face again.

"What was that?" He stepped toward her, fighting to keep her eyes on his.

She shook her head. "Nothing. It's not anything at all."

"If it's not anything, why do you look like you just got caught with your hand in the cookie jar?"

"What?" Her forehead crinkled indicating that she didn't understand what he meant.

"As if you got caught doing something wrong." He was too exhausted to control the frustration saturating his voice.

"It wasn't me. It was your mother." Lydia let the strands of hair in her hand float to the floor as she set the brush into her toiletries bag. Her jaw quivered and he realized she didn't have the words to explain.

He dropped to his knees and reached under the bed until he felt the cool, smooth sides of glass roll against his fingertips. With a nudge, the container slid into his palm.

"This is not nothing. Did my mother give this to you? What's in it? What's it for?" His voice raised in volume with each question. He wasn't as angry with his wife as he was with his mother.

How did they get into a cycle of hiding things from each other over the past few months?

Lydia waved her hands and tears burst forth once again. "It's to help me . . . help us. . . to conceive."

Dylan threw the vial at the drapes on the other side of the room, hoping to throw the rage boiling inside away with it. But he missed, and the glass shattered against the window frame.

With a loud cry, Lydia rushed past him and flung herself beneath the covers of the bed.

While she buried her sobs in the pillow, Dylan stepped out into the hallway. A maid skittered around the corner at the far end, too far away to have heard the voices or clamor from their room. Though faint as it was, he thought he heard a man singing on the floor above. The sound distracted him long enough to temper his heart and mind. Why would someone be singing at this hour? Then he realized it must have been Enrico Cariso, the opera singer. Dylan raked fingers through his hair. He'd forgotten all about their plans to attend the opera the following evening.

Nothing he could do about it now. He'd make it up somehow. He had to.

Lydia lay still and silent when he returned to the room. Coming around her side of the bed, he rested his hand on the back of her shoulder. She breathed steady and shallow.

He sighed, turned the room lights down and slid under the covers, careful not to wake his wife. As much as he didn't like the idea of going to sleep angry at himself or anyone else—exhaustion took over before his mind could contemplate another solution.

TWENTY-SEVEN

Tuesday April 17, 1906 9am – Palace

Hotel, San Francisco

The room bell rang before dawn. Room service brought up a light breakfast. Weary from the evening before, Lydia didn't bother making conversation with her pensive husband. They exited the hotel with few words passing between them.

"Does Uncle Moses know I'll be arriving so early?" Lydia broke the silence once the carriage began careening at a steady pace toward Folsom Street.

"He knows you will be there today, but not at this hour. Let's pray tailors rise early." Dylan clenched his jaw. He wanted to apologize but feared the gesture would only lead to another argument.

"I'm nervous, and my stomach feels unsettled again."

Her hands shook.

Dylan took her hands in his and squeezed slightly, hoping the gesture was enough of an apology for now. "You're awfully pale. You can nap on my shoulder if you need to."

Lydia looked at him, smiling with closed lips before swallowing the sour taste in her mouth.

They pulled up to the tailor shop, lantern light illuminated every window. The sounds of children permeated the silent street.

Lydia had a thousand words to tell her husband, but she feared opening her mouth would also expel her breakfast. Oh, why did her body react so violently to her nervous spells? Hands shaking. Nausea. Would it ever stop?

She'd thought that if she pressed forward and faced everything she feared repeatedly that soon her nerves would calm. It was the unknown that shook her up—never knowing how something would turn out due to her lack of experience with people and new circumstances.

This is what Dylan didn't understand. She knew her actions could result in unseen consequences. On the other hand, she couldn't avoid experiencing the world in case things didn't work out.

And now, she would have a chance to experience a little of life in the city without Dylan's constant eye on her. In the safety—she hoped—of her uncle's presence. With his lack of knowing exactly how isolated she'd been, she secretly hoped for a few more opportunities to explore over the next day.

Of course, first, she wanted to learn all she could about Mama. This was her main reason for meeting and visiting with her uncle. She hoped Uncle Moses could fill in the many unanswered questions about her mama's past.

Lydia took Dylan's hand as he helped her down and grabbed her suitcase with his other hand.

She tried to search his eyes, but they swirled with emotions she didn't recognize. He had known his grandfather's illness would eventually be terminal. She didn't think she saw mourning as much as she detected uncertainty. Hopefully having a day apart would provide a bit of healing, even if they hadn't resolved the tension caused by the combination of other men's attentions and Jaina's interventions.

They approached the tailor shop door. The shop downstairs was closed but Dylan knocked anyway, then he saw a string and bell at the side of the door. He pulled the string, and a clamor came from the upper floor.

The noise of children and adults flooded the air following the squeak of the window sliding open.

"Hello!"

Lydia looked toward the sounds to see a man leaning out the window, his long beard grazing the edge of the windowsill. He smiled and waved.

"I'll be right down." With the words, he re-entered the house and disappeared.

Moments later, the glow of a lantern bobbed back and forth inside the dark tailor shop. As it came near the door, the man's face came into view.

After a warm greeting and a tight hug, Uncle Moses led Dylan and Lydia through the shop and up a narrow and steep stairwell.

Any ideas about plans for the next day vanished upon meeting Samuel and Minnie, who helped run the tailor shop with Moses, and their four children. Chaos abounded for nearly an hour.

Dylan wrapped a gentle arm around Lydia's waist and whispered in her ear. "I must leave now. Will you walk me back down?"

Her stomach fluttered. She closed her eyes and nodded.

Back before the carriage, the hustle and bustle of a city morning surrounded them. Dylan took her hands and gazed into her eyes—again showing emotions Lydia could not decipher.

"Have a wonderful time visiting your uncle. Don't concern yourself with anything else." He cupped a hand along her cheek.

She grasped his wrist, clutched his hand against her face and discretely fought off another wave of nausea, not wanting him to feel he needed to stay. She swallowed and took a breath of what she hoped was mostly fresh, fogged-filled air.

It wasn't. Stench from the alley wafted into her throat and she bit her lip, unable to hold back a grimace.

"What is wrong?" Dylan's other hand wrapped around the small of her back.

She shook her head, exhaled, and attempted to speak. "Nothing is wrong," she whispered and then found her voice. "I'm still getting used to the smells of the city, that's all."

He drew her closer, pulling her with both hands now.

"I love you." He hovered before her, mouth straight, eyes serious.

"I love you," she repeated, a twinge in her gut trying to convince her the words were not true as Pete's face flashed through her mind.

A cable car screeched past, the passengers yelling and an infant screaming on board.

Lydia's heart skipped and she glanced behind Dylan to watch the commotion. As she turned her gaze away from him, his lips reached her cheek.

He stepped back.

She had not meant to turn away from his kiss.

"I better be on my way. I will return by noon tomorrow. I should be able to handle the paperwork and funeral arrangements by then. If not, I'll send a telegram to the tailor shop."

He was not going to attempt another kiss.

And she felt too weak and nauseated to try herself. She could use a nap, but she doubted that would happen in that loud room upstairs.

Instead, she reached for his hand and squeezed hard. "I am sorry about your grandfather. I will be praying for you and that there are no problems with handling all the responsibilities and choices you'll face."

He let go of her grasp and turned toward the carriage with the tip of his hat.

TWENTY-EIGHT

Lydia turned toward the tailor shop door. But before she could grasp the handle, her mouth filled with saliva again and she pivoted to the alley. What she expelled could not make the filth polluting the street any worse.

But with her breakfast gone, she shuddered. This time, no man came to her rescue. Slowly, she leaned against the wall and door frame, praying for strength to get her up the stairs and that Moses, Samuel, Minnie and the children would not notice her dire state.

No such luck. Minnie immediately came to her aid, bringing her to rest on the armchair in the snuggly arranged living room area. A toddler hopped up on Lydia's lap, a ragged red book in her hand.

"Miss Lydia . . . read me a story!" The little one's brown curls bounced on her shoulders.

"Miss Lydia needs to rest, Abby." Minnie scolded.

"No, it's fine . . . I have actually been wanting to read more books for children."

"Are you sure it was the fumes from the alley?"

"Yes, it happened the last time I was in the city. My nerves get the better of me with all the noise and sights. I'm sure I will be fine in a minute or two."

"Read, Miss Lydia, read it!"

Though her stomach continued to feel weak, it wasn't long before the children and Minnie could distract Lydia. She was amazed at how orderly everything was for so many people living in such a small space. Samuel and Moses had to open the shop, but Moses assured Lydia he would be back upstairs shortly.

By the time the sunlight had fizzled away the morning fog, Minnie had the children settled with their studies and the upstairs grew nearly quiet besides the rattle of carriages and street cars outside.

"That dress you are wearing, Lydia . . . where did you buy it?" Minnie asked after she served up tea.

Lydia took her tea, breathing in refreshing mint and sipping lightly. "I made it, actually."

Minnie's eyes raised as she examined the seams and pulled out the ends of the skirt. "This is masterful work, Lydia. Emelyn taught you to sew?"

"Yes, Mama and I used to sew dresses for the angels—uh—townsfolk at French Corral. But we didn't have a sewing machine. I recently learned how to use the machine and Dylan bought me my own to fill a dress order for Sacramento before we came here."

"Dress order? I am impressed! But not surprised. It seems sewing talent runs in the family. Moses has been quite an asset to our shop, providing suits and coats to the councilmen and officials for several years now. We could have expanded had Noah and Eva not perished in that fire many years ago."

Uncle Moses entered the room, rubbing his hands together and smiling.

Minnie flattened the wrinkles on her tattered, cream-colored apron. "There is tea here for you as well, Moses. I will leave the two of you to catch up while I tend to meals for the day."

Moses took a seat with Lydia. His smile warmed her and she imagined what a difference it would have made had her grandfather been as inviting.

"From the letters you and Dylan wrote, I was surprised to learn that Emelyn never mentioned me. I was in the process of planning a trip. We only had to get through spring orders." He crossed pleated pant legs, and folded dry cracked hands over one knee.

Lydia couldn't quite pinpoint the source of earth-tinged aroma emanating from her uncle in bursts whenever his movements pushed air in her direction. The combination reminded her of the scent of the forest along the Valley's edge—the scent that represented God due to its power and mysterious origins. Even if she couldn't determine what combination of flora and fauna it came from, it brought her comfort and made her feel at home.

"Mama never told me much about her family. I guess I will never understand why."

Moses nodded. "I didn't know your mother very well. She was only a toddler when her parents left Bremen for America."

Lydia recalled the letters Dylan had read to her. Aside from learning that Moses had arrived in San Francisco a few weeks after Emelyn and Charles had relocated to French Corral, the letters contained little else besides sewing strategies. Moses

had supplied Mama with the latest fashion patterns—a mystery solved about how she'd come up
with them.

Lydia continued her line of questioning. "What
about before you came here . . . anything from her
parents about their life here? About why she would
have felt the need to leave and not wait for you to
arrive?"

Moses shook his head, then his eyes widened.
"There was something left behind from the fire.
The owner of the general store down the block had
recovered it. At one time, I tried to tell Emelyn
about it, but she said to leave anything about her
past here. She had no need for it."

"What was it?" Lydia felt a surge of excitement.

"A metal box. But it was locked and I never
found the key."

Could they key from Mama's music box be a
match?

Lydia sat up straight, her tea sloshed around and
spilled onto her dress. "I have the key . . . I think."

"You do? But how?"

"It was in a music box I found under Mama's
bed. Dylan and I searched for clues as to where it
belonged but found nothing. I don't remember him
reading anything about a box in the letters."

"The box is somewhere in the attic. It might take
some time to locate. But I will get it to you before
you head back up the mountain."

Lydia couldn't contain herself. Her giddiness
overflowed to her Uncle, who also beamed.

"This is wonderful . . . thank you!" She set her
cup down and leaned in to hug her uncle.

His arms around her brought tears. It was the closest thing she'd felt to ever being held by her father.

More frustrated than sad, Dylan said a belated and final goodbye to his grandfather back at the Prescot estate. Then he sent word to his father and mother in Grass Valley.

He ignored the pang of regret for not attempting to kiss Lydia again. Once he entered the Prescot estate he had no room for stray thoughts about his wife on the other side of the city.

A long list of items and a surge of servants, lawyers, associates, and extended family demanded every bit of Dylan's attention. He had to leave his marriage in God's hands for the next 24 hours.

By the time night settled in, he was physically and mentally spent. He'd accomplished what he needed for his grandfather's affairs. In the process, the truth about the Prescot financial state came to light.

There was no money to borrow. Grandfather's illness had exhausted all business profits. And his father had relinquished further profits in exchange for the one-time lump sum he took to relocate Andrew and Jaina to Grass Valley and assist Dylan in purchasing Rolling Oaks Ranch.

A part of him considered there might be a better man out their suited for the job of Lydia's husband.

At the time he believed that God had brought them together for a purpose. But that purpose was getting diluted more each day as they drowned in their immediate problems.

Oh, Lord will you have some mercy here?

He knew that leaving the city was the best plan. But then going home meant confronting Pete, and Dylan didn't have the strength to manage that now.

Lydia obviously did not understand the danger of her treading—her attempting to know and understand another man. And then that moment under the tree when he'd watched her caress his arm in such an intimate way. What was that all about? The moment kept running through his mind. Had Lydia told him everything back on the train?

Time to practice my faith, eh Lord?

In bed that evening, the vision of his wife, laying by his side with the moonlight streaming across her face lulled him to sleep.

Later that evening, Lydia pressed back thoughts about the possible contents of Mama's box. Happy to have simply met a relative and been welcomed with open and accepting arms, answers about her mother's past didn't matter so much anymore.

City sounds and the commotion of children settling into their beds, prayers, and finally, the low hum of conversation between Moses and Samuel in the kitchen, eased Lydia into sleep. She recalled the pleasant day, sad Dylan hadn't been there to share it. Minnie had served the most amazing dinner full of flavors Lydia had never experienced.

Before she felt herself drifting deep enough to forget where she lay, she said a silent prayer for her husband and marriage.

Lord, show Dylan that my love for him prevails above all else. Show me how to prove it.

Yet, as her mind thought the words, the image of Pete's sorrowful face beneath the oak tree dominated. The warmth from the stove hovered over her cheeks while a slight breeze came in through the cracked window at her feet.

Then she stood again with Pete below the oak tree. But this time, she brought her lips to his cheek, feeling the bristle of his unshaven jaw prick her lips.

TWENTY-NINE

April 18 5:12am - Prescot Estate

Dylan awoke with a start. The bed shook and rocked. The walls creaked and groaned. His weary eyes pried open to see the bureau bobbing toward the bed. The vase of fresh flowers on top of it slid to-and-fro until it toppled over the side, landing with a crash. The bureau banged into the foot board and tilted toward Dylan's feet before leaning back to a standstill.

Dylan scrambled to his feet, digging them into the end of the mattress as he braced himself against the wall.

Earthquake?

He stood still, waiting for the bed to stop moving. Items on the bookshelf and his bedside table rattled.

Sighing, he fell to his knees and stared out the window. Still dark outside.

A rap at the door brought a shudder to Dylan's chest. For a moment, he thought another quake was beginning.

"Yes?"

Miss Gracie entered. "Mr. Prescot, Sir. There has been an earthquake."

"I felt it, Miss Gracie. A mild one . . . nothing to concern yourself with."

"No, Mr. Prescot—only here it was not too bad. But if you look out the balcony—sir . . . where did you say Miss Lydia was?"

Dylan jumped out of the covers and bound to the window, throwing back the drapes so quickly the rod toppled to the floor. He flung open the balcony doors and stepped outside.

Far below, at the edges of the city, he hardly recognized the view he'd had the day before amid what was major devastation. Jagged, black cracks divided streets and buildings lay on their sides. Clouds of dust swirled.

Then he smelled smoke.

An eerie silence fell across the city. He strained to listen for a scream, a wagon jumbling. Nothing.

Dylan couldn't tell where the smoke came from. Gaining his sense of the city without the normal markers, he scanned from left to right, trying to locate the vicinity of Folsom Street and where Uncle Moses' tailor shop would be standing.

But the rubble, dust, and smoke hindered his view. He wouldn't know if Lydia was safe or if the quake destroyed the tailor shop unless he went there himself.

A heaviness crept into his gut.

Lydia . . . an earthquake.

Had he ever even told her about earthquakes? She probably had no clue what was happening.

Lord, let her be okay . . . far from harm. Protect her, oh God, protect her until I can.

5:12am - Folsom Street Tailor Shop

Pete grabbed Lydia's shoulders, and he pushed her back enough to display dark eyes that did not resemble the deep blue she knew. He moved forward and she thought he was about to kiss her when he stopped short, his breath so heavy on her face, it suffocated her.

Branches shook as if the very roots of the tree were coming up from the ground. Pete rattled her shoulders as if he were angry at her, but he didn't say a word.

Back and forth he shook while the tree roots flung around her ankles, twisting hard and pulling her to the ground.

A piercing pain ran through her temple followed by a searing stab across her shin. Pete disappeared and darkness filled the void.

She opened her eyes abruptly to blinding dust that blurred her view and filled her nostrils. A series of sneezes and a forced cough gave her enough relief to take in a shallow, yet guarded breath.

Shrill screams grew louder and louder. Then she fully awoke and remembered she was in San Francisco at her Uncle Moses' tailor shop.

Not a moment later, it was as if the sofa beneath her had come alive, jolting her off like a spooked horse. But the floor continued to shake and roll, forcing the feet of furniture to bounce across the floor. Paralyzed from the pain in her leg, she could only see as far as the gap under the couch would allow.

Something smacked into her face. Then dust filled her nose again and covered her eyes. She couldn't open them without risking the dust blinding her.

She could only listen to try to understand what was happening. With only one free arm to feel about, Lydia tried to determine where she lay in vicinity to the couch.

Voices mingled with rumbles and roaring out the window that sounded like waves crashing along the cliffs. But the tailor shop was too far away from the shoreline for her to hear waves, wasn't it?

"Lydia, you've got to get up," Minnie wailed while one of the children sobbed wildly.

"I've got her," Uncle Moses yelled. "Get the children to safety."

Feet scampered, and children's cries echoed from the stairwell.

Feeling hopeful, Lydia waited in anticipation of Uncle Moses lifting her into his arms and following Samuel and Minnie down the stairs.

But it wasn't Uncle Moses that lifted her up—it was the entire apartment. Her body raised up with the floor, pain shooting through her leg while she pressed into the floorboards to keep from flying across the room.

"Stay there Lydia, don't move." Uncle Moses' voice sounded strained, as if he were lifting something heavy.

Then, like a tree branch breaking from its trunk, a loud crack came from the direction of the front of the building.

Uncle Moses grunted against a creak turned into a clatter and crash.

A weak whispered uttered, "Keep her safe, Lord—"

Then silence.

Nothing.

She tried to move, but the pain in her leg paralyzed her.

She blew hard, spitting out what tasted like a mixture of ashes and bitter dirt. She turned her head to the side and managed to pull her hand out from the hard metal object pinning it down. Her wrist throbbed but she could still move it. Feeling around some more she grabbed a cloth that felt like the edge of the quilt. Shaking it best as she could with only moving her arm, she hoped whatever the dust or dirt that clung to it would fly off enough that she could use it to wipe away the debris on her face and eyes.

Carefully, she whisked the blanket edge across her face and then slowly opened her eyes.

Russian Hill

A second wave jolted the upstairs while Dylan dressed. Once it subsided, he jogged downstairs to find Miss Gracie putting together a picnic breakfast while skirting around the buffet that had scooted across the kitchen floor, dumping china and serving platters along its path.

"You're a sweetheart, Miss Gracie." Dylan squeezed her shoulders and kissed her cheek. "But it's not necessary. I hate to ask you to stay here . . . but just in case Lydia—"

"Of course, Mr. Prescot." Miss Gracie bit her lip and nodded. "I've nowhere else to go anyway."

The evening before, everyone else had gone home. Only his grandfather's body lie, cold, in the backroom. He had even dismissed Cecyl for the night, planning on resting into late morning before leaving to pick up Lydia.

"Thank you doesn't seem like a sufficient response, but I need to find a way to her . . . I need to find my wife." He placed a sheet of paper into her palm. "This has the address of the Tailor Shop on Folsom Street, our room details at The Palace Hotel, and what I know about how to contact Frank Sinclair and Bradford Hilton, an acquaintance of his. Should Lydia somehow make it here before I find her, please do what you can to contact every person and place on this list to find me."

Gracie nodded again, tears pooling her eyes.

Folsom Street

Against the pain, Lydia sat up enough to rest on the back of her elbows. There was no sign of Samuel, Minnie, or their children. Unsure as to where Uncle Moses would have been sleeping, she scanned the room. A pile of debris, a broken window in the sink, the bookshelf toppled over the settee.

The settee! Was that a hand she saw covered in dust beneath the edge of the shelf.

She leaned forward, but blinding pain shot through her leg.

She had to get the chaise off her leg somehow.

She frantically swept her hands through the pile of books at her side, the broken tea pot in shards atop the splinters that had been a coffee table.

She reached for a table leg. It broke off easily. Leveraging it between the floor and wall, she nudged it under the edge of the chaise. Then, she leaned down with all her weight, lifting it for a split second. Without considering the pain that would result, she grabbed the inside of her thigh and forced her leg out from beneath it.

Pain shot through her temples again and blackness surrounded her.

THIRTY

Smoke woke Lydia, causing her to cough violently enough that she vomited. Prying her eyes open, she realized this was happening. What—she had no idea. But she lay in the upstairs house, which seemed to be leaning to the side, though she didn't know if that was her nausea or not. Broken, shattered furniture lay all around her. Her leg throbbed with indescribable pain, her head pounded, and her stomach lurched.

She was alone, reliving the nightmare from moments earlier.

Her priority was to somehow dull the pain in her leg. She looked at it, now that the chaise no longer crushed it. Blood soaked through the edge of her nightgown and her stockings. Along her shin, something poked through her stocking. Was it a large splinter causing her pain? She reached for it, but the slightest touch shot a stab of pain up her leg. It wasn't a splinter.

It was her bone.

Swallowing hard against a dry heave, she took in a deep breath. Choking past the dust and smoke coming through the window, she wiped snot and slobber away from her face and bit her lip.

Be strong. I must be strong. I can't die here! Not alone . . . not without Dylan at my side.

Staring at her nightgown, she recalled how Mama had once bound a horse's leg after it fell. She ripped off her nightgown and, using her teeth to cut the seams, made shreds of cloth from the garment.

Then, wincing against the pain, she wrapped the shreds of nightgown around the top of her leg, above the break, and then below it. This alleviated the pain some, but she still needed to keep it from moving. Then she pulled an already broken coffee table leg from the debris surrounding her and lined it up with the side of her leg. Over and over, she wrapped the wooden leg secure to her leg, imagining she was mending a leg that wasn't her own. She still dry-heaved when the pain became too intense.

Once her leg was secured, she used what strength she had in her arms to crawl backward until she leaned against the wall. She avoided the puddle of puke in her path, but she still dragged the toe of her uninjured foot through it.

She looked at the ceiling to gain her balance. Thinking her vision was failing, she blinked when the ceiling blurred. Then the rumble began again. From the edge of the back wall, a crack appeared and climbed up and then across the ceiling above her.

She sprung back toward the kitchen as the front half of the apartment fell away from the floor, crashing into the street below. The clanging of bells reeled outside, the noise enough to continue ringing in her ears long after the echoes of horse hooves clattering across the cobblestones faded.

She gripped the stove pipe with all her strength to avoid falling to the ground below. Her good leg dangled from the edge of the broken floorboards like a leaf about to float from a tree branch in late autumn.

"Help," she gagged . . . no sound coming from her throat. "Hel—help!" She managed to scream past the dust clogging her throat.

Nobody below seemed to hear her. She scanned what was left of the apartment behind her. The shaking had rolled the bookshelf off the settee along the back wall—her Uncle Moses now lie on top of it, lifeless under a cloud of white and gray dust.

If she tried to breathe too hard, she coughed and the gyration only amplified the pain in her leg. Somehow, she had to get down to the ground. She had to find a way to help, someone—anyone who could help her get to Dylan.

Crawling with only her arms, she managed to find relative security on the other side of the kitchen floor. It was then she realized she was only in her undergarments, having used her nightgown to secure her leg. She scanned the room for a sign of clothing, trying to think where her suitcase could be in the piles. Then her eyes landed on a brown bottle that had rolled beneath the cupboard.

She scooted over to it, and realizing it was a form of cooking alcohol, uttered a prayer of praise, and took a swig. She'd heard that strong alcohol could numb the pain when nothing else was around. But nausea emerged and she threw it right up. Not sure if it would even work, she poured the liquid over her leg. It burned, causing her to shriek from the pain, but then it numbed it enough that she could pull herself up to stand.

With a better view from a standing position, Lydia saw a crude pile of rubble descending like jagged stairs toward the street. Like random river rocks making a path to the shore, she traversed one pile of ruins at a time, slowly climbing down to the security of the street below. Briefly she thought of Minnie and the children and prayed they'd found safety. But finding Dylan and staying alive were Lydia's priorities—nothing else.

Flames roared and flickered from the building next door. Heat emanating, and ash floating through the sky like snowflakes, she hobbled in the opposite direction of the entire city block engulfed in a burning blaze that reached the sky.

The slightest pressure on her broken leg shot searing pain into her hip, but she soon ignored it, knowing it was her only way out. Not sure at all which direction led to Dylan's grandfather, she followed a group of people marching a couple of blocks ahead of her. They had to know better than she which way to go for help. But their pace quickened, and Lydia found herself too far behind them to holler for them to wait or help.

She rounded a corner, a slight breeze temporarily relieving her of the soot and smoke. Feet ahead, the group she'd been following had stopped, many of them shouting and reaching into the ruins of a building that had fallen partially into the street.

The pain in her leg intensified with her racing heart, and she found a stable place to sit on the edge of the chaos.

Had God's wrath ravaged this city from the ground up? Had he no mercy on a single soul here—not even herself or her husband—if he had even survived?

Lord, where are you in this?

It was the first moment God had entered her mind since the earth rumbled and shook her life in this rubble she sat on.

She coughed and expelled a conjuration of saliva and grayish mud from her throat. She was sitting on the corner of a large sign. Feeling another dry heave coming up, she leaned over, ready for the burning and whatever else remained in her stomach to shoot through her mouth.

She wiped her face with her sleeve, undaunted that she'd forgotten about locating a dress before she climbed down from the room above the tailor shop.

She recognized the sign as a hotel Dylan pointed out before they arrived at the tailor shop.

"*Val . . . en . . . sia . . .*" Her voice echoed and then dissolved into the shouts coming from the other side.

"The water main's busted!"

"They're drowning!"

Shrieks and groans pierced Lydia's ears. People were dying inside the fallen hotel and those outside couldn't stop it.

Her lower lip trembled.

Dylan . . . she should have stayed with him and waited to meet her uncle at another time. Although now, that would probably never have happened.

She rubbed her eyes and leaned forward on one knee, face in her hands.

She allowed her own sobs to shield out the horror surrounding her. Finding Dylan, nothing else, was her only hope . . . the only way through this now.

Slipping onto the ground beside the sign, she crumbled, prostrating herself the best she could without amplifying the discomfort in her injured leg. Leaning to one side, she raised her hands into the air.

Though my enemy seeks destruction, I will praise thee.

Somehow, from the depths of her memory, she recalled the concept of a Psalm of David. David continually praised the Lord in times of trouble. And every time, the Lord came through and rescued his servant.

Lydia felt more futile than David facing a giant, but she could not release herself from the thought—the urge—to simply praise God.

She kept her hands raised, her fingers crooked and shaking as she reached beyond dust and ashes to the invisible God, that with every ounce of life left in her, she believed could save her and guide her next step.

A fire wagon clanged passed without slowing down.

She closed her eyes, and began to sing, first in a whisper and then as a hum, until finally a single word uttered from her lips again and again.

"Hall . . . elujah . . . hall . . . elujah . . . hallelujah . . ."

Each word brought a flash of memory to her mind.

Mama and her in the garden . . . *hallelujah*—

Picking wildflowers . . . *hallelujah*—

Sewing by candlelight . . . *hallelujah*—

Riding Jasper across the Valley . . . *hallelujah*—

Dylan's willow-green eyes, his dimples and smile . . . *hallelujah*—

His strong, assuring arms embracing her and his lips nuzzling her neck *hallelujah*—

Then she thought she heard a lamb bleating. Then another whine.

She opened her eyes. That was not a lamb. It was a baby crying!

Lydia spun her head from side to side. Where was it coming from? And how had she heard it despite the screams and shouts from those on the other side of the rubble? The cries grew louder. Lydia pressed into the side of the sign and leaned up to stand.

The cries were coming from an opened window of the floor of the hotel still above ground.

She looked for someone to notice her waving and yelling, anyone who could help—anyone else who could hear the crying.

THIRTY-ONE

Hyde Street

Smoke and flames billowed from dozens of buildings to the west near the Bay. Though still quite a distance away from where Dylan was on Hyde Street, he watched the Palace Hotel sink along with his heart. He and Lydia could have been there, possibly buried within moments. Instead, the Lord had strategically place Dylan out of relative harm. Would Lydia also somehow have survived the quake at the tailor shop?

As if the city were a forest being chopped down by invisible, giant axes, building after building crashed to the ground near and far. They toppled over like timbers, crackling and rumbling in horrifying echoes. If he continued by foot, it would take hours, maybe even half a day to walk the dozen or so blocks to Uncle Moses' shop. With buildings crumbling and bursting into flames without notice, he would need to dodge disaster at any moment. A straight path without a detour was very unlikely.

Hand to his forehead, Dylan peered toward Folsom Street, but it was impossible to tell how close the clouds of smoke were to Lydia's location.

Heart wrenching, he put one foot in front of the other and tried to ignore the devastation surrounding him. Other displaced citizens surrounded him, each trekking along in a different manner, seemingly oblivious to the crowd of strangers they accompanied. Many were quiet, only the sound of their stockinged feet or untied shoes thumping or crunching along uneven cobblestones or over shards of wood, brick or glass. Others wailed or spoke gibberish. Men cried. Women cursed. Was there any hope left in this city on the Bay?

A group of men, including a police officer, joined the group of earthquake survivors at Washington Street. Faces washed in soot and streaked in either tears or sweat, each stared at the ground in obvious sorrow.

"We'd all have perished if we kept trying to save them." The officer said, voice strained.

"But to watch them burn alive with nothing we could do . . ."

Another man from the group pulled at his cheeks with bloodied fingers and howled. "At least you didn't kill a man!" He shrieked. "Even if he was begging someone to take him from the pain of being crushed by that building . . ."

Dylan listened, speechless at the events that had transpired in mere hours. He walked several paces behind, trying to absorb the reality of a city in ruins and all those who'd already lost their lives. Like ants, they marched on, stopping to pull men, women, and even children from fallen homes and businesses along the way, working to save as many as they could before each home or business collapsed.

After several blocks, the survivors and city officials blended together with smoke, ash floating southeast of Market Street. A muted orange glow emanated off the horizon.

Heart sinking against hope, Dylan sped his steps and prayed.

He was near certain that the tailor shop had not escaped the flames.

As the group approached Market Street, droves of people walked in the direction of Golden Gate Park. If Lydia was able, would she have followed those people? Would Moses' family ensure Lydia was safe or would they be too concerned about their children to realize Lydia would need as much help as the little ones?

Every possible scenario crossed his mind. His beautiful, innocent wife wandered the city alone. Would she know the difference between an angel of mercy and the devil in disguise? He couldn't let his thoughts explore the possibilities.

He had to believe she would be fine. God would protect her. He had to. She was all Dylan had to live for. He was all she had left in the world.

No. NO! God would not bring them this far for Lydia to face an evil fate. Would He?

If he even learned of a man touching his wife in a manner unbecoming of a gentleman—Dylan would be guilty of murder if he caught the weasel. The thoughts pushed his pace into a near run. He didn't care if exhaustion tried to overcome him. He needed to find his wife—now.

Then a group of police officers stopped the men in their tracks.

"We need men to dig."

"I've got to find my wife—"

"That is not a suggestion, sir." He pushed a shovel into Dylan's hand.

"I will come back—"

The officer pulled his gun from the holster. "Anyone not willing to cooperate will be shot on site!"

Dylan uttered a prayer and took the shovel.

She's in your hands now . . . Lord, I beg of you to keep her from harm.

The rest of the day evaporated, and the panic of impending dusk settled into Dylan's chest and stomach. Reddish clouds burned along the horizon making it impossible to tell the difference between flames coming from buildings and the setting sun.

There were no phone lines, no running water. Explosions had replaced aftershocks in a meager effort to deter the fires from spreading further—or so Dylan heard among the chatter of policeman and others in charge of attempting so-called "order' in the city. They had blocked off most routes through the city, forcing hundreds of thousands from their homes regardless of the damage. Any man not injured was put to work on the street, digging fire lines. Only those fortunate enough to be with their families at Golden Gate Park had escaped this forced labor. Dylan would have been more willing to help if he knew his wife was safe.

A strange sensation crept across Lydia's leg and she found the strength to climb over the hotel sign and remove the debris that blocked the window opening. She could barely decipher the border of a window and inside it, the remains of a mostly intact room, save for the fact it was several floors closer the ground than it had been prior to the rumble.

Careful not lose her footing yet rushing without knowing how long her leg would feel numb enough to allow her to place weight on it, she pulled the front half of her body into the window. Looking down, she saw the arm of a rocking chair. To the side of it, a man's arm cradled a swath of blanket. His other arm, clutching to a beam, blocking the blankets in his arm from the pile of ceiling that appeared to have landed on his head.

The blanket moved. A high-pitched wail, Lydia now knew came from an infant, pealed from the fabric and a small hand peeked through the folds.

Lydia gasped, and made a quick assessment of the room.

She had no choice.

Dangling head down, she hung from her hips and stretched as far as she could into the room. She slipped her hands beneath the blankets, pulling the corners up in a way that would hopefully ensure the infant would stay nestled inside and swung the bundle toward her chest. Then, with one hand holding the blanket against herself, she grabbed the windowsill and inched herself up and out of the window and onto the outer wall.

The infant squirmed and squealed as Lydia maneuvered them both. The noise assuring Lydia the child could still breathe.

Rolling onto her back, she struggled for air until her quickened breaths slowed to sighs.

Without realizing it, she had started patting the back of the babe on her chest. The cries turned into grunts. She pulled back the blanket, craning her neck to get a glimpse of this orphan from the ashes.

She caught her breath. The child could not have been more than a few weeks old. Either that or it was highly undernourished. If that had been its father holding it, where was the mother? Was she too, buried somewhere in the hotel room?

Before Lydia finished the thought the wall shook beneath her, rocked to one side and then collapsed. Staying parallel to the ground, Lydia and the bundle in her arms plummeted several feet downward, then stopped. The crumble jarred her head, but nothing more. The room on the other side of the wall now lay level with the street.

If the child's mother had been in there, she had not survived.

The infant's eyes closed, its lips rooting for something to suckle.

Lydia sighed. The child needed its mother's milk.

"Ma'am! Down here, we've got a wagon taking people to the park."

She nodded and pulled the infant closer to her. "Thank you . . . I have . . . I've a broken leg."

"Wait there . . . we'll be right up with a bed."

The next few minutes were a blur. The pain in her leg returned as the men helped her onto a gurney and wrapped her and the infant in layers of wool blankets. Then, they transported her into the back of a wagon.

Soon, she fell in and out of sleep and waves of nausea continued with the rock and tumble of the wagon as it went over piles of rubble and turned corners.

To pacify the infant temporarily, Lydia licked her finger to remove as much dirt and dust as she could, then place it at the end of the child's lips. Instantly, its mouth pulled her finger in and began to suckle, the familiar grunts like music to Lydia's ears. She recognized the sound from when Brian used to nurse from Hattie.

Within minutes, the child had resumed deep breathing and seemed to nestle perfectly in the crook of Lydia's neck and elbow.

How long would the child be able to be satisfied by suckling alone? It would need milk soon.

But pain and weariness soon took over Lydia's concerns. They both slept for the remainder of the journey to the park.

Dylan was forced to detour toward Valencia Street, in the opposite direction of the tailor shop, when the digging crew lost the race with the blaze that consumed the lower half of the city. What had been the four-story high Valencia Street Hotel, was now a single floor that lay partially in what remained of the street.

"The flames are getting too close!" Several yelled.

Cries laces with final breaths stung the air.

"We're drowning!"

Compassion shifted to opportunity when Dylan saw the militia men distracted with the rescue efforts. He risked his life whether he escaped or stayed.

Taking several slow steps back, he waited to see if any officers noticed his departure. When nobody paid mind to his growing distance from the hotel, he shuffled toward Mission Street.

By now, most of the main streets were empty of people. By wagon or foot, the refugees had made it to shelter for the night. Sleep a luxury, he kept walking as if an invisible thread connected him to his beloved. Bodies and rubble in every direction, he tried not to think of the lives lost. If only he could find a loose horse somewhere. But he was positive any horses in the city were attached to a firetruck that was closer to the flames than he needed to be.

Block after block he strode, having to regain his sense of location at every corner.

It was nearly impossible to decipher where the cityscape ended and the horizon began. A smoky, darkening orange sky grew in every direction he could see from below the remaining buildings.

After several blocks, he regained his sense of place by shattered landmarks and realized he was not as far from the tailor shop as he'd first thought. The city in shambles and his minimal experience perusing the streets without a carriage or other type of transport made it hard to calculate walking time.

Taking a deep breath, he willed his legs to move faster. They throbbed and his feet ached. His throat burned, a layer of soot and ash in his mouth forcing him to spit mud every few feet. He needed water, anything to drink. Darkness giving way to light from flickering flames caused him to trip more than once over rubble and holes in the streets.

But Dylan probably looked like a bum too. The more he descended the hill, the worse the buildings looked. His hope dampened. Charred structures lined an entire block.

Sparse folks wandered the streets now, looking mostly like bums, but putting Dylan on guard in case any presented a threat. Along the way, he'd placed a few pocket-sized broken brick pieces in his pockets and held a splintered portion of doorframe for defense if needed.

When a man the height and breadth of Pete stepped out of a shadow toward him, Dylan shot the stick forward, arm shaking.

The man placed a controlled palm down on the tip, bits of a reflecting orange sky revealing kind eyes and a soft smile. "I'm about to offer you shelter, sir. I've a space far from the fires and out of sight in that abandoned building over there."

Godsend or a deathtrap, cooperating gave him a better chance at survival either way. He lowered his stick.

"Name's Gabriel." The man reached his open hand toward Dylan.

Dylan cleared his throat and shook firmly. "Dylan . . . Dylan Prescot."

THIRTY-TWO

April 18 - late evening, Golden Gate

Park refugee camp

a'am?" A hand gently rocked Lydia's shoulder. "Ma'am, wake up."

Lydia opened her eyes and tried to move. Sheer pain emanated her leg from knee to toe and she yelped. An infant's cries filled the room.

"Don't move . . . I'm Lucy, one of your nurses here tend to your leg. Your baby is with Nurse Mary. She's changing him and getting him good and hungry for when you are ready to feed him."

Baby? Feed him? Lydia turned her head, the bright lights inside the tent blinded her momentarily. Her vision blurred, her head fuzzy. She focused enough to see a woman in the corner attending to a small infant on a make-shift table. He screamed, arms and legs flailing out stiffly in four directions.

"What's his name?" The nurse asked.

"Huh . . . his name?" Lydia's mind spun. She felt a tear streak down her cheek and into her ear.

The baby she'd saved from the rubble.

This nurse thought he was her child. What should she do? What could she do?

Nurse Lucy held up an auricular object, taking Lydia a moment to realize is was a large needle. "Your baby's name? He might calm down a little if he hears his mama's voice. Go ahead and talk to him for a minute. This will pinch a bit, but after a moment, it will dull the pain for surgery."

Lydia sucked in and swallowed hard. The baby continued to wail. She knew he needed milk . . . how could she deny him this need for life? *He* . . . they said it was a boy.

"Moses. His name is Moses." As she said the words, something in her switched and her fearfulness disappeared. This child needed her as much as she needed him.

Recalling the moment before she'd heard his cries inside the hotel, it was clear—God had answered her prayer! In her despair, and amidst the thousands of others needing Divine attention, he'd given her a reason to go on and not yield to the ashes and smoke that threatened to take her life.

"Moses. A beautiful and strong name for such a determined young boy," Nurse Mary brought the baby over to Lydia. "He's been rooting for at least twenty minutes." His lips curled to the side, tongue protruding and mouth open toward the edge of the blanket that swaddled him.

Lydia tried to recall Hattie's method. Perhaps the nurse would help, and not question her fumbling, given the circumstances.

"I think I need help . . ." she whimpered, attempting to reveal her weariness and lack of strength obvious in her voice. "He has . . . trouble sometimes." She'd heard of newborns not latching right away . . . even some moms had ended up needing to feed goat's milk to some when their milk was not sufficient. Lydia assumed she'd be dry and then the nurses would find alternative nourishment. But how would she explain the child wasn't hers?

"Here you go." Mary lifted the wool blanket and nudged Lydia over enough for the baby to cradle inside her arm on the edge of the gurney.

Lydia couldn't bear seeing him suffer any longer. With her free hand, she pulled the sleeve of her slip down, exposing her small breast and thinking surely the nurses would know she hadn't fed a baby before. But Mary didn't appear concerned.

And neither did Moses. His little hand reached up through the blanket and rested on the top of her breast as his mouth opened, his tongue thrust forth and the nurse pressed his nose toward her nipple. In a split second, he was suckling and sighing between empty gulps.

Though the sensation was unlike anything she'd experienced, the action itself felt oddly normal. His mouth fit perfectly, and he wasn't deterred when no milk came. At least not at first.

Then he sucked harder, more aggressively, his little fingernails opening and closing as they made miniature scratches on Lydia's chest.

After a few more minutes, a tingling filled her bosom. Faintly at first and then stronger. Then Moses seemed to calm and relax. His efforts slowed until he nursed at a steady rhythm. Then he stopped, released, and fell asleep.

Once Nurse Mary saw that he was asleep, she gathered him up, placed him on her chest, and patted his back.

"You're both very fortunate. Many mothers' milk dried up from the stress of the quake. We've been running low on clean milk and bottles while we wait for water supplies."

A moment later, the doctor came into the tent to tend to Lydia's leg.

"I'm Jim, a surgeon with the Red Cross. The Presidio is overflowed with more urgent cases. I apologize for nonstandard surroundings, but it's all we've got to work with. We want to make sure your bone is aligned and we've minimized the chance of infection before closing up the injury."

"Moses will be fine for the time that we need to put you out." Lucy held a gray mask in her hand. Before Lydia knew what was happening, the nurse put the mask over her nose and mouth, and all went dark.

April 19 - Lower Folsom Street, early morning

A warm breeze woke Dylan. His temporary companion gone, the only evidence of his presence the evening before an unusually clean satchel lay near his head. It contained an unused box of matches, half a loaf of bread, an apple, a thin blanket, a canteen filled with water, and a small, yet sharp knife enclosed in a case with a clip for easy attachment to a pant waist.

Without questioning how, he slung the satchel over his shoulder, spoke aloud a prayer of gratitude and went on his way.

Before long, the sign for Folsom Street, though covered in a layer of ash, peeked through a teetering street pole. Folsom was several blocks long.

With the Bay behind him, he strode up hill, mentally calculating an estimate for how many blocks lie ahead before he'd reach the tailor shop.

Each step lagged, covering less of the sidewalk in front of him the further he went. Finally, he made it to the corner of the block with the tailor shop entrance around the bend. He stopped and took in a breath, holding it before exhaling with a prayer.

"Dear God, please let Lydia be alive." Closing his eyes, he stepped around the corner. Darkness shrouded the street more so than where he had just come from. But the street was gone.

The entire side of the tailor shop building lay where the street had been. A bed and a bureau topped the pile, broken to pieces. Dylan ran to it, pushing away the possibilities off seeing Lydia's hand or foot, or even her hair strewn within the mess of wall and wire and broken furniture. He pulled off layers of warm rubble, finding nothing but more debris, more ash. Fire had come and gone here, giving little hope for survivors.

He looked up to where the building had stood. A portion of the apartment remained above. The rubble piled in layers, making a crude stair-like path to the upper level. Getting his balance and steadying himself with each step so that the piles would not topple over with his weight, he climbed.

With each ascent, he yelled.

"Lydia!"

"Lydia, I'm coming!"

"Lydia, I'm here!"

Mucus and tears clogged his throat with despair when silence followed each shout.

Maybe Lydia was up there. Maybe she'd grown tired of waiting for someone to rescue her and had fallen asleep. He hoped she was because he did not hear a sound of life coming from the room.

He slipped once, cutting his hand on a metal barb poking out from a wall post. He cursed under his breath, though left the name of the Lord out of it. This wasn't God's fault at all. This was the result of a poorly built city, designed with greed and lust and pure profit in mind—not the safety and security of its citizens.

Nearly out of breath, Dylan made it to the wobbly apartment floor, or what was left of it. But it was too dark to see anything.

He felt around with his shoes, sliding with caution to avoid causing the rest of the building to topple to the ground level. Then he came up to what he thought was a bookshelf on its side. He reached out to the side and felt up and over to the top of it. Somehow, the flames had left this portion unscathed.

Then his finger grazed a clump of hair.

No!

Panic emerged and his heart thumped hard against his chest. Sweat dripping muddy ashes into his eyes, he swiped at his brow. Then, hope dwindling, he shoved both hands forward, and eased his fingers across the strands of hair laying across the topside of the shelf. With hesitation, he patted little by little.

Coarse and frizzy, it was human hair, but it felt nothing like Lydia's silky, straight, strands.

He sighed with relief. But whose hair was it if it wasn't Lydia's? Feeling around a bit more, his hands felt around the side of a face, an ear, and a beard.

Moses! Dylan frowned, but inside he felt a glimmer of glee.

He needed to light the room to see his surroundings better. He tried to recall how the room was arranged when he'd brought Lydia. If the bookshelf was here, an oil lamp had to be nearby. Crouching on his hands and knees he felt around for anything that felt like part of a lamp.

His mind flashed on the night he'd spent in Lydia's cabin before they were married. That night, the wind had blown the door opened, and the candles out. That night, he had kissed Lydia for the first time, in the dark, while they had been searching for a dry match.

He sniffled and swallowed the lump in his throat. He thought he could protect her back then.

He thought he was all she needed.

Then he felt it. The narrow, rounded curve of a lamp base. It wasn't broken but rolled on its side at the base of the couch. He carefully brought it upright, the scent of lamp oil coming up strong into his nostrils. He felt the wick. Slightly hard at the top and damp along the bottom portion. Now, all he needed was a match.

"Praise God Almighty!" Dylan slid the satchel down his arm and reached for the box of matches.

He lit a match and was about to join the flame to the wick when a loud creak from the kitchen area startled him and he flung back toward the chaise. The stove piping, still imbedded into half a wall, whined and screeched until it clamored into refuse in the street below.

Clang! Clang! Clang!

A cloud of dust flew up, hovering in the sky that used to be the living room for several seconds, then dissipated, extinguishing the match flaming between his fingers.

Dylan remembered to breath and sat carefully on a cushion edge. He lit the lamp wick on the second try. Light illuminated the room that hardly resembled a home. He assessed the condition of the apartment and searched for any sign of Lydia. Moses' body lay lifeless, atop the bookshelf, his face coated in ash except for the few spots Dylan had ran his hands across.

He stood, carefully creeping through the room. It could topple into the street at any moment. There was not a sign of Lydia anywhere. Nor of Samuel, Minnie or their children. Dylan prayed that they'd taken her with them and found shelter with the other refugees. Though it didn't explain why Moses had stayed behind, unless he'd been crushed before the rest of them escaped.

Sighing, Dylan gripped the lantern and climbed back down to semi-level ground. He had to make it to Golden Gate Park.

While he considered his options, he trekked ahead, pushing aside notions that his wife was anything but safe and being cared for by God-ordained angels in disguise. He had to believe in anything rather than giving into despair and desperation. Dylan could afford neither.

THIRTY-THREE

April 19 - Golden Gate Park Refugee

Camp

Lydia awoke to a bright light beaming on her face. Lucy's back stood among the shadows, rocking back and forth and humming a lullaby.

Unsure how long she'd slept, she tried to move but felt a heavy weight on her leg. It still throbbed but the pain was not nearly as severe as it had been.

"Miss . . . nurse . . ." Lydia whispered.

The nurse turned, baby Moses in her arms, wide awake and hands waving in the air.

"Good morning. You know we never did get your name? This child of yours has captivated us all. He is the sweetest thing. Mary and I were thinking we could send someone to pin a note along the wall up at Union Square, now that the fire has passed through there. We've heard many dislocated family members are using it to let loved ones know they are alive. We could alert your husband or other family that you and the baby are safe. We'll need your name then we'll do the rest."

It took several moments for Lydia to understand what the woman meant. But what she needed to know was what exactly happened. What had caused this city's destruction?

"My name is Lydia Sinclair Prescot." A glimmer of hope saturated her heart. If they posted all her names, she thought she'd have a better chance of being found. "But please, can you tell me what's happening? Why is the city in ruins? Where am I exactly?"

The nurse stepped over, handing the baby to Lydia, her forehead wrinkled above a curious smile. "Why, there was an earthquake, Mrs. Prescot. The biggest earthquake this city has seen in decades. After the quaking stopped, fires broke out everywhere. You're in Golden Gate Park among thousands of other refuges. It's the safest place for anyone not tending to the disaster who hasn't already boarded a ferry over to Oakland."

Earthquake? Lydia didn't know such a thing was possible.

Nurse Lucy handed Moses to Lydia. "Where are you from, Mrs. Prescot?"

She took Moses in her arms and nuzzled her nose into his petal-soft cheek. His large, blue eyes looked wide at her, his tongue played with his lips.

"Penn Valley."

"He probably needs to eat again," said the nurse with a soft smile as she patted his wrapped feet. "Penn Valley? Is that near mining territory in the Sierra Foothills?"

Lydia nodded, her thoughts more on the infant in her arms than the nurse's questions. Dainty fingers curled around one another below his chin. Had she fed him last night? It seemed like a dream.

The thought brought the tingling back to her bosom. Fear crept in that this nurse would discover the child was not hers. If she could somehow continue to nurse him—if she could produce milk despite never having been pregnant or nursed a child.

Then she remembered the sheep and the lambs. Although Mama had never needed to give an orphan lamb to a sheep that had not already bore young, Lydia supposed that God could provide such a miracle for humans.

Believing that this was God's plan to unite this child with her—for her to become his mother because of the past week's events—and a love for this babe in her arms filling a void she had not even realized existed, she attempted to feed the child again.

This time, there was no doubt milk flowed from her bosom. How could this be? Joy filled her—she may not be able to bear a child of her own, but she could still sustain this one in need. She felt as if she were participating in a miracle.

The nurse left the two of them alone in the tent. Looking more closely at her surroundings, she was now in the corner in a makeshift bed where she could sit up and lean back. Once Moses was finished feeding, Lydia took the opportunity to get to know him better. She talked and cooed with him, laying him to face her on her legs. She removed his blanket and caressed his smooth arms and tiny toes, counted his toes and rubbed his round, full belly. He gurgled and grunted in response. He seemed to be enjoying the attention.

She swaddled him tightly and held him between her chest and shoulder so that she could rest her lips on his forehead. She repeated prayers over him, over the loss of his parents and that if this was God's will, nothing would hinder her from continuing to care for him.

She closed her eyes, and gently kissed the Moses' cheeks as he drifted off to sleep.

She heard a man's voice outside of the curtain and her thoughts switched to Dylan.

The curtain opened. At first, she didn't recognize the man who stood there.

"Greetings, Lydia."

But when he spoke, she remembered.

"Uncle Frank?" She couldn't believe that he found her.

"'Tis me!" he beamed.

Uncle Frank strode toward Lydia, his smile undeterred by Lydia's disheveled state. She must have looked a fright and she was holding a baby no less!

He had his right arm in a sling but appeared clean-shaven and well rested.

"I see you and Mr. Prescot wasted no time in getting your family started." Frank patted Moses' bottom lightly and gently punched Lydia's other shoulder.

"Uncle Frank? How did you find me . . . us?" Should she keep up the act of pretending to be this child's mother? If the nurses could overhear her, she'd better play it safe.

"Bradford Hilton and I shared a couple drinks the other night. He told me all about your chance meeting at the Palace Hotel, and that you had been trying to reach me for some time. He didn't mention you had a child, however." Frank's smiled diminished.

Lydia cleared her throat. A twinge of nausea threatened to return but her stomach grumbled against it. She couldn't recall the last time she ate. She rocked back and forth, hoping Moses would stay asleep. Perhaps she should avoid answering anything related to the baby.

"Have you heard from Dylan? He left me at my Uncle Moses'—" she held her tongue. How would she explain a baby with the same name when she'd hardly met her uncle? "My grandparent's old tailor shop to tend to his grandfather's funeral."

Frank shook his head. "No, he's not here with you? All I knew was that the two of you were in town and when I heard the hotel had burned, I went searching for you, hoping against all catastrophes, that you'd both survived." Frank continued to glance between Lydia and the sleeping baby.

But she continued to avoid the topic.

"Dylan was at his grandfather's house on Russian Hill. Do you know if those houses were also destroyed?"

"Miracle it is. A large portion of Russian Hill is still standing."

Lydia let out a sigh of relief. Dylan could very well be alive.

"Can you get there? Can you take me to see if Dylan is there?"

Frank pressed his lips together in a deep frown. "Sorry, Lydia but they aren't letting anyone up or down. The fires have continued to spread into Chinatown and toward Telegraph Hill. They evacuated everyone from all homes in the path."

Lydia's shoulders fell. "Where did they have them go? I thought everyone was at the park."

"Dylan could be here . . . but there are thousands of people. It's taken me two days to find you. I'll begin a new search for your husband soon. But first, I have some good news to share with you."

"Good? Anything to give me hope at this point." If he didn't know where Dylan was, what kind of good news would Frank possibly have for her?

"Your grandfather . . . my father . . . would very much like to see you. I'm unsure if his heart changed prior to the earthquake, but ever since our home tumbled to the ground and we scarcely escaped, you are all he's talked about."

What? Tears stung Lydia's eyes. She must be misunderstanding what Frank meant. She felt like she might be sick.

"Whoa there . . . didn't mean to make you white as a ghost." Frank clasped a soft, warm hand over Lydia's shoulder.

She shook her head, squeezing back tears. "No, I've been . . . not feeling too great the whole time we've been here. I think I need food—if I can hold it down."

"Well, then, this can wait. I will alert the nurses to send someone through the line to grab you a plate of food right away." Frank tipped his hat and rushed out of the tent.

Lydia gagged, hoping she would be able to eat something. She needed energy to face this latest information, not to mention the means and time to think of how she would explain this child in her arms.

A few minutes later, Nurse Mary came in with a plate of biscuits and gravy, and a cup of hot tea. She set it on a crate near Lydia's bed, gathered up Moses with one arm, and then placed the tray on Lydia's lap with her free hand.

"Thank you." Lydia's stomach gurgled at the sight of food.

After a few bites, though, her nausea returned with a vengeance. She leaned over, facing the corner away from the nurse, and thankfully expelled her breakfast into a waste bin near the head of her bed.

"Oh dear . . . it might be from the medication," Nurse Mary said, sweeping open the tent curtain. She called to the Nurse Lucy.

"We'll try broth or tea instead. Your stomach is probably weak for various reasons." Mary cleaned up the mess and swapped out the blankets covering Lydia. "I will also locate a few items of clothing for you. There's a donation site on the other end of the park. You aren't the only one who escaped the ruins in only her undergarments."

Frank returned and took a seat on the crate near the bed.

"While your baby is in good hands, are you ready for me to continue about your grandfather?"

Lydia nodded, a sudden chill rushing through her.

"Late Tuesday. Rather, early Wednesday morning, I had arrived back at the house after having drinks with Bradford. Excited at the prospect of contacting you and your husband, I decided to make a bold attempt at approaching Father first thing in the morning. He'd obviously been hiding the letters you'd sent. I decided enough was enough."

Lydia's face felt flustered and the throbbing in her leg suddenly worsened.

"Do you need another blanket? You're shivering, though the temperature in here feels fine to me." Frank stood and then clamped his hand on Lydia's forehead.

"You are rather warm . . . I'll fetch the nurse."
Frank looked concerned, shadows filling his otherwise sparkling eyes.

Lydia must have dozed off the moment he left,
because a cold hand grabbed her arm, startling her
out of darkness. She blinked against the light in the
corner, the silhouette of a nurse's cap all she could
see.

"I'm afraid you have an infection. Your fever
spiked too suddenly for it to be anything else. I'm
re-bandaging your leg and head now. Lie still."

A moment later, that gray mask was over her
face and she fell back into darkness.

In the distance, a baby cried. But Lydia could not
get to him. She was walking along the shore, waves
crashing on her feet and making her toes numb.
Where was the baby? Why couldn't she find him?
*Moses! Moses . . . Mama is here . . . Mama is here looking
for you . . .*

THIRTY-FOUR

April 19 - early evening

Golden-red light outlined the tops of clouds above vacant buildings which barely stood, their crumbled walls and black, windowless boxes only skeletons of what they were a few days earlier. Ash, soot, and filth filled every crevice of open street and sidewalk. The fire burned behind Dylan now, but the entire sky held evidence of this city burning to the ground.

He didn't care about any of it. All he wanted was to hold his wife in his arms, breath in her lavender scent and take her back where she belonged, on the top of the mountain—where God's presence was clear and they could seek His purpose for them unhindered.

Who cares if they had to be in debt for years? He would come clean about the finances and do what he could to encourage her to grow her dress business. Of course, he had imagined a significant source of that income would come from people in this city. But the elite were still the elite—and perhaps the demand for dresses would increase with the loss of belongings and store inventory.

Trekking back down Folsom Street and toward Golden Gate Park, Dylan stopped to help two men digging frantically at the base of a charred, fallen building. Cringing, he climbed over the remains of a fallen horse to get to them. This devastation was no respecter of persons or creatures.

While he did so, he asked if they'd been to Golden Gate Park and if they knew how he'd locate his wife. They informed him they'd heard postings were being placed at Union Square.

Block after block, his mind wandered from past to present to future. He had to stop and cough out smoke-filled lungs from time to time. He must be getting used to it since he had to concentrate now to even smell the smoke.

Up ahead, a family sat at a formally decorated dining room table on the sidewalk.

The man at the table stood and reached a soiled hand toward Dylan. "I'm sensing the good Lord prompting us to offer you a meal. Weariness and worry mark your face more than the ashes across your brow."

Though he felt an intruder, he'd learned long ago not to refuse someone else's obedience to be a blessing. He took a seat on a stack of wagon wheels. Generously and with smiles, the woman and an older girl, filled a metal bowl with stew.

Despite introductions and a prolonged discussion on the city's corruption, lack of consideration for its citizen's safety, and other rants, Dylan retained few details. He stayed only long enough to display his gratitude, then offered farewell and Godspeed to the family.

Before he was on his way, the man's wife loaded a potato bag with rolls and dried jerky for Dylan to take with him.

Now nourished, he quickened his pace. He was sure it could only be mid-day, but darkness enveloped the city as if the sun had decided to shine upon somewhere else that had hope.

At Union Square, dozens of tents littered the lawn, an overflow from the St. Francis Hotel, so he heard among the chatter of the displaced tenants. In the center of the makeshift camp, he found the wall. Scraps of paper, ripped shreds of fabric, thin pieces of wood, and more covered the wall from end to end. Each one contained a note for a loved one or friend that needed to be found or was looking for someone.

His heart fell. So many people had become separated in this disaster! How many of them had been found?

A cluster of people formed behind him. Each one standing silently, eyes dashing back and forth, up and down, pausing on each note for a moment before moving to the next. Dylan searched for one with a child's handwriting—since Lydia hadn't been writing long. He prayed that somehow, someone had told her about this wall, provided her with the chalk or pen and writing material she needed. But if she was hurt, how would she have made it here and then to the park? Again, he forced himself to believe this was in God's hands. Dylan needed to trust the situation and not try to predict how it would work out.

He sighed. There were hundreds of notes. Most he could barely read himself—scratched and scrawled with shaky hands in various languages. He

started to walk away, thinking he might have a better chance heading to the park and describing Lydia
to medical personnel or law enforcement.

Then a note on the bottom corner caught his
eyes. In unfamiliar handwriting, it read "Lydia Sinclair Prescot and child—medical tent 381."

How could that be? The name was correct, but a
child? It must be an error of some kind, but who
else could have the same name? He pulled the note
off. The pin sticking it to the wall fell with a clink
on the cracked cobblestone.

He rushed past, barely noting City Hall in shambles to his right at the intersection of Van Ness and
Market Street. He pounded one heavy foot in front
of the other along what he was sure was McAllister
Street. This path should take him directly to the
park.

Lydia fell in an out of a deep sleep. Frank remained at her side, holding her hand and cradling
Moses when he wasn't eating or needing his cloths
changed. She hardly even woke when a nurse poked
her with a needle at regular intervals.

Thoughts of Dylan flitted in an out. Then visions of Pete came, seemingly out of nowhere. He
stood before her, a golden light outlining his frame
as if he were an angel coming to take her to be with
God.

Deep in her mind, she pondered the idea of
death. Of reuniting with Mama in heaven. Maybe
that would not be so bad. If anything had happened
to Dylan—she'd heard mingling of robberies and
self-appointed police shooting citizens on site—or

worse. What if he'd gotten caught in the fire and died in a blaze of ash and smoke?

Would God allow her to lose both her Mama and husband to fire and flame?

At least she had the baby. She needed to live for him. And although Frank had not fully explained, a glimmer of hope lit her spirit at the possibility that her grandfather had a change of heart.

Thoughts straying further, she reasoned God's methods. If Dylan was dead—God had provided a child and her grandfather's love to replace him.

Pete's faced flashed again and she felt the strength of his arm beneath her hand. Could God have provided this man as a substitute husband, knowing in advance that Dylan would perish here?

Pete had lost his wife and child. Maybe this wasn't about Lydia and Dylan at all. Maybe they had been placed here to meet the need of this widower.

She did not fully embrace the idea—though she admired God for the possibility. Not all was lost. There was hope—even if it meant a life nothing like Lydia had imagined.

THIRTY-FIVE

April 19 – Golden Gate Park

The arm beneath Lydia's hand moved and she began to wake. She was resting her hand on a man's arm. And it felt familiar. Her eyes shot opened. "Dylan?"

He sat at her bedside, his arm on her waist and his head down.

At her voice, he raised his head. Bloodshot eyes and unshaven, she smiled through his tears. "Yes, Sweet Lydia. It is me."

She pulled him toward her by his arm. She had no words, only tears.

He showered her face with gentle kisses and tucked her blanket in snuggly around her before taking Frank's seat at the crate.

"Darling, you have no idea how wonderful it is to see you—here—alive and being cared for." His voice cracked, but he grinned.

The dim lamp light made it hard for her to see his eyes, but his dimples emerged, surrounded by stubble.

"I thought you were . . . you had . . ." She could not say the words.

The door flap of the tent opened, lamp and fire-light filtered through. Frank entered, holding a whining, squirming Moses in his arms. "Someone needs to eat." White teeth and eyes glimmered in the light, while his face remained shadowed.

Dylan turned toward them and stood. "I will take him, Frank. Thanks."

Lydia sat up in the bed, speechless. She had no idea what Dylan knew about the baby—or how long he'd been here.

She waited for Frank to leave before trying to explain. Dylan brought the baby over to the bed and sat back down, though he did not hand the child to Lydia. He set the bundle on his lap and rocked them back and forth. Then he gazed at Lydia, a wry smile across his face.

"Where do I start?" Lydia sighed and looked her husband in the eyes.

"From the beginning." Dylan continued to rock. Moses ceased crying and began cooing.

Seeing Dylan hold this child warmed her heart. Without even knowing how she'd come to acquire him, Dylan had embraced him.

She swallowed a twinge of nausea and began. Managing to contain her tears, she explained about the earthquake and not even knowing what it was. Then she told him how she bandaged her leg and climbed down to the street after discovering her Uncle Moses had died.

When pain and despair tried to take over then she had an undeniable urge to fall to the ground and praise God. Not a moment later, she'd heard this child crying from the inside of a fallen hotel.

Without a doubt in her mind, God had saved them both within seconds of the hotel's final collapse.

"Then, the nurses assumed he was mine and since I wasn't wearing clothing, they assumed I was lower class and had no nursemaid. By then the pain had overtaken my senses and my compassion for the child had grown. He needed me . . . and I needed him." A tear streaked her cheek and she turned away, feeling guilty for considering Dylan was dead and entertaining the notion of her and Pete raising this baby as their own.

"That is amazing . . . a miracle in every way. And you fed him from—" he nodded at her bosom. "I didn't think that was possible." He shrugged. "But I don't know much about that sort of thing."

"Neither did I. Now if I'd already had a child, or was pregnant—"

Dylan's raised his eyebrows.

It had not occurred to her until that moment. Her swinging emotions, her nausea. Could it be true? She thought back through the moon cycles. She had not even realized how long it had been with everything else happening. The few weeks she'd spent in Grass Valley had thrown her off for the whole month.

"Dylan . . . I think I may be . . ."

Dylan stood, gathering the baby to his chest before joining Lydia at the bed. He rested Moses in the crook of Lydia's arm and then kissed her hard and firm on the mouth.

"I should have done that days ago," he breathed and then kissed her again.

She began to laugh, and Moses squirmed, his scream ringing over the sound of Dylan kissing her neck. "We can't know for sure. But it would explain why I have been able to supply milk for this little man here."

Without hesitating, Dylan leaned over and kissed the top of Moses' head as well. "What is his name?"

"I . . . I didn't know so I told the nurses the first one that came to my mind . . . Moses."

The infant wailed louder.

Chuckling, Dylan stood. "There are a million details to consider with all of this, but I can't help but have hope for the best. Praise God!" He shoved fists into the air and smiled. "For now, we will continue to act as his parents. Go on and feed him. I have a few matters to discuss with Frank."

Exploding with joy and amazement, Dylan exited the tent and scanned the dimly lit park for a sign of Frank. A few yards away, Frank stood at a bonfire, smoking a cigar, a metal cup in his other hand. He was laughing with a few other men holding the same.

Dylan rubbed his hands together, trying to decide the best segue. When he first got there, Lydia was still in a deep sleep and her fever had not yet broken. Frank explained how he'd found her and that he had tried to give her the good news about the grandfather, but she was too ill to hear it.

And then Frank talked about the baby he held as if Dylan knew him. Not understanding how, but realizing anything was possible in this city now, he played off being shocked and too shook up to hold the child right then.

Curious about the grandfather, but more concerned about his wife's state of health, her possible pregnancy, and finding a more private place for the members of the family to discuss options, Dylan cut to the chase.

"We have few delicate matters to discuss, Frank." Dylan patted Frank's back. "Is there somewhere private we can go over a few things?"

Frank nodded, seemingly undeterred by the possible topic of discussion. "Certainly, Dylan. If you think Lydia will be fine for a few minutes, we can take a stroll over to the beach."

With waves crashing to muffle any chance of someone hearing their conversation, Dylan held nothing back. "The baby is not ours, Frank."

Frank steps remained steady. He stared at the sand he pushed with the ends of his boot. He nodded.

Dylan watched him carefully. He needed to trust this man to act in their best interest.

"All right. So, the city is amidst a disaster. I assume she didn't steal the child. She saved his life. I will play along while things get under control. The city cannot burn forever. The list of missing persons is growing by the hour. We won't report the baby as found—rather we will wait for a report that he is missing. Where did you find him?"

"I didn't . . . but she said it was a hotel on Folsom Street."

"My father has connections so don't you worry about a thing. I assume you are interested in keeping the child if nobody reports him missing?"

"Yes, without a doubt."

Moses fell asleep feeding again. Lydia tightened his blanket and set him on her lap while she adjusted her gown. The nurse had brought her an over-sized nightgown for the time being, and a dark blue wool dress to wear as soon as she could get up from the bed.

Knowing Dylan and Frank were discussing matters without her racked her nerves. But the prospect that she could be pregnant in addition to caring for this orphan child overwhelmed her more.

Lord, what are you doing here? Forcing us to depend on you more than ever . . . but why?

She remembered that Frank had also said her grandfather wanted to see her. Feeling completely unworthy of these blessings, she felt she would do whatever he required of her. Despite being in a strange tent, miles from home, with a broken leg, a fever and a newborn to care for, she felt blessed beyond belief.

The world crashing down around them, and God chose her—and Dylan—to fulfill this small, yet significant calling. And to top it off, provided a possible reconciliation with her grandfather.

But they would still face many challenges. What if the Moses had a relative living nearby who wanted to take him back? Her heart sunk at the prospect. If she were indeed pregnant, how would they explain two babies born so close together? What would the people of French Corral think? What would Jaina think?

Lydia's thoughts swirled. She started listened for Dylan and Frank at the tent entrance. She needed answers now more than ever. Beyond curiosity, she needed to know the plan and what her part would be.

How could their lives turn around within only a few days?

The nurse came in, followed by Dylan and Frank and another man rolling a wheelchair.

Dylan came to Lydia's side, kissed her forehead and scooped up Moses. "We will be going now."

Frank explained. "I've arranged for your care in a home on the other side of Van Nuys where fire is not a threat. Father—your grandfather is there as well."

Relief and fear permeated her heart and flesh. She would see her grandfather and she would not need to spend another night away from Dylan. But how would they explain the baby?

THIRTY-SIX

April 20, Friday - late morning

At what vaguely represented morning's light, Frank returned with a baby bassinet and a satchel.

"Dylan, the Post Office is taking limited mail so survivors can contact family outside of the city. Once we get Lydia and the infant settled, I'll arrange for transport if you'd like to contact your family on the mountain."

Dylan nodded. "Thank you, Frank. I doubt my father has even received word about my grandfather's passing, but the sooner he and my mother have all the details, the better."

Afraid any questions would alert the nurses or other ears to the situation, Lydia remained quiet and followed the lead of her uncle and husband. They loaded her and the baby into a motorcar, which soon headed in the opposite direction of the billows of smoke and purple-red sky.

She slept for part of the ride. When the rumble of the car jumped, she woke, startled and disoriented.

"Just a bump in the road. No more earthquakes for now." Dylan laid his hand on her lap. "Your Uncle Frank is a good man. He has provided us with a viable solution. After we get settled in our room, I'll explain."

Upon their arrival, Frank announced the reunion with the grandfather would take place the following morning at breakfast. Everyone needed a good night rest before attacking the challenges tomorrow would bring.

Grateful for the comfort of a real bed and the warmth of her husband at her side, Lydia finally found words. "Only God knows how this will end. I was so frightened—so uncertain of everything. I thought the world was coming to an end and that at any moment, God would take me to the heavens. All I cared about was that you would be there too." Her voice cracked.

Dylan brought her closer and kissed the top of her head. "I am more amazed at you than anything else. Yes, God's hand is in all of this—but you—in a city you hardly know, managed not only to save yourself but the life of a newborn child. I think I may be married to the most incredible woman in the world."

Lydia didn't feel incredible. She'd doubted every moment and every choice she'd made. At more than one time, she'd wanted to die rather than suffer the pain one second longer. Yet, something kept her moving, kept her taking that next, painful step toward hope.

It was what God was working in her that was incredible. She understood that now. There was no other way to explain it. On her own strength, it would have been impossible.

Moses' soft, rhythmic breathing filled the air.

Lydia placed her hand on her stomach, wondering if there was indeed a small life growing there.

Dylan placed his hand over Lydia's. "I guess we will know soon enough. But it would explain your nausea. I was getting concerned."

Lydia kissed his chin, giggling. "God works in mysterious ways, doesn't he? Mama used to say that—" She swallowed the lump in her throat and blinked back tears. "We came down here a few days ago to rekindle the romance and instead, we will go home with two babies attached! Nobody is going to believe it."

They snuggled, talking about wild possibilities for several minutes before Dylan cleared his throat and grew serious.

"There are a few things you need to know before morning."

Her gut filled with dread. *Here we go again.* "I'm beginning to think I will never get you to tell me everything." She sighed and clamped her lips closed.

"To start, I am confessing all. First and foremost, I brought you down here to romance and dazzle you with all the wonders of the city. I intended to sweep you off your feet and meeting your Uncle Moses was a part of the plan."

"But . . ."

He laughed lightly. "But I also had other plans. While you were visiting your uncle, I was going to ask my grandfather for a loan—for more money to run the ranch until summer."

Lydia lay a palm on her husband's chest, knowing he had hoped to have a successful ranch by now.

Dylan sighed. "I can't expect for only four employees to take on the work load all that time. The only way to ensure reliable labor would be to have a way to pay them plus more hired help, regardless of income."

That was why he couldn't hire Dan. "Oh. I guess I would have wanted to know that . . . but I suppose that is your duty as a husband to manage such affairs."

"I thought for sure you'd be angry at me for not divulging every reason I had for coming to the city."

"I probably would have been if not for all that has happened the past couple of days. That seems too futile now. And I need to trust you, even when you choose not to tell me things. I only wish you would have told me so I could help. The sewing machine, the fabric, even this trip, were all expenses that could have waited. I'm sorry if you felt you needed to do those things during such an uncertain time."

"What did I do to deserve you?" Dylan grinned past strained eyes.

"What now?'

"Well, now that we are good, we have to tackle a few more challenges. First, I want to set your mind at ease for the moment regarding the baby. Though there is a chance family would come forward to claim him, Frank has advised—and I agree—to continuing caring for him as if he was our own, and not report him as found. With so many desperate people in the city, only God knows the attempts one would make to claim a child not their own."

How are we any different? But the thought of someone else taking Moses now was unimaginable. He was hers now. "What are we to do in the meantime?

Did you and Frank discuss what to explain to my grandfather?"

"Your grandfather will have the same information as everyone else."

Moses stirred in the bassinet.

Dylan continued in a whisper. "No sense in complicating things further—at least until we can verify your possible pregnancy." He squeezed her reassuringly. "Let's sleep now."

Lydia slept some, but once Moses woke up for a feeding, she had difficulty sleeping again. She could not fathom all the uncertainties they now faced. Were the few months they'd spent starting their new life on the ranch the last of their uneventful life? She thought of the new routine she would need to contrive upon their return. Pregnant or not, she hoped the nausea would subside soon. It came in unexpected waves and she wasn't sure she would have the strength to do much more than nurse Moses, nourish herself, and rest in between.

Oh, God, if this is your will, provide me with the strength I need to sustain two lives in addition to my own.

It was impossible to know what their future held. Perhaps this was common knowledge for everyday people, but she'd held out the belief that once she understood her purpose, the uncertainties of life would vanish, and life would be predictable.

Was this child nursing at her breast a part of God's plan? He was an orphan, like her, and Mama too. She had compassion on him for this, understanding between Mama's attempt to guarantee love after all she'd lost and her own feelings of isolation after her grandfather had rejected her. Without Dylan, Lydia's life would be far different. But she did have him . . . and he was everything she'd ever dreamed up and more. Between his acceptance of her, and belief that God had a plan for them both, her hope soared.

Scooting off the bed and into her wheelchair, she set a sleeping Moses on her lap. Hoping the wheels didn't squeak and wake the baby, she carefully wheeled over the window and drew the curtain back. She looked out the window and saw the stark evidence of how fast things could change.

This city crumbling and burning around them confirmed that the love between her and Dylan could withstand anything thrown their way. Recalling her thoughts of Pete, she became aware that those were only an attempt from the darkness to place doubt in her so she would give in to despair.

And God had protected her, made a way for her to realize that thoughts alone could cause trouble and lead to unknown danger by allowing the thoughts to grow into actions—even if her excuse was curiosity.

With a baby in her arms and one growing within, she'd no longer be captivated by Pete's gaze. Besides, she could help things along even more by suggesting to Dylan they could try to find a wife for Pete soon—to fill the void of his own loss and remove any future temptations that tried to creep in.

More important, orphans and widows needed them. They understood the outcast—the lonely. Hattie needed her too. Instead of a single purpose, she now had a plethora. She smiled at thinking she'd used the word from Jaina's vocabulary lessons correctly.

Lydia's thought of all the people she'd encountered who had experience loss. Deep within, she desired to help them in any way that she could. She wanted to give them hope—provide a place for them to call their own and to find their purpose despite all they'd lost. Dylan had compassion on them as well, she could tell by his willingness to bring Pete and others without a family to the ranch. It was not out of desperation, but of meeting the needs of everyone involved.

By morning, an idea had emerged and excitement and dissolved her fatigue. But before, she would share it with Dylan, she would face her grandfather once again.

THIRTY-SEVEN

April 21 - morning

Dylan woke to Lydia's gentle voice. He opened his eyes, blurry at first, and gradually focused on his wife, sitting in the rocking chair by the window. She held Moses before her and spoke soft words that Dylan could not decipher. She smiled and kissed the babe's cheeks. Hazy, colorless light hovered around their heads as if angels had placed a heavenly cloud of protection over this moment. He could not love her more.

He stayed still and watched them for several minutes. Although the room was only slightly lit in a dark gray hue, he could not deny the connection between his wife and this orphan she'd found in the ashes. How could this child *not* become theirs? Why would God seem to answer her prayer for strength and a reason to press on, only to snatch him away from her?

Dylan had seen Lydia with Brian, and Olive before him. Despite never having been around babies or children her whole life, she had a sense of how to care for them. No doubt, her mama had nurtured her and instilled the importance of caring for the young and helpless. Either that, or God had given her this ability in a supernatural way. An orphan herself, who better than to know what this child needed?

Lydia pulled Moses to her bosom and started to transfer to the wheelchair but stood a moment instead. Swaying back and forth, she drew open the curtain enough for a beam of smoky light to hit Dylan square in the eye. He moved to avoid it, drawing her attention and revealing the fact he was awake.

"Good morning," Lydia whispered.

"Good morning. You really should not be standing, you know?" He leaned on his elbows and scooted into a sitting position. "Do you need me to take him so you can prepare for breakfast?"

Without answering, she hobbled over to the bed, continuing to sway with her steps, and favoring her good leg. She kissed Moses forehead and placed him in Dylan's arms.

Dylan overlapped his hands beneath Moses' head, and lifting his knees, settled the child in his raised lap. Moses eyes grew wide, his little hands pushed out of the blanket as his fingers opened and closed grabbing at the air. Slobber dripped from the bottom of his lip.

"Hi there, little man. How did you sleep?"

Lydia ran her hand over Moses' head, and smiled. "You two get to know each other. I may be awhile." She grabbed a dress from the satchel of clothes collected at the park, sat in the wheelchair, and proceeded to wheel herself into the adjacent bathroom. "And when Miss Gracie gets here, feel free to send her in with a dose of ether."

Dylan chuckled, in awe at how Lydia simply accepted the added challenge of a broken leg. "Would you like help dressing as well?"

Lydia raised her eyebrows while she rolled herself backward enough to give room to close the door. "No, I'm fine. I won't have help once we get back home, and the accommodations here are much easier to manage. But I could use something to ease the throbbing."

The dress was worn, but at least it was clean. Taking a plush towel from the stack near the tub, Lydia soaked it in a shallow tub of warmed water and scrubbed off layers of soot caked under her chin and inside her elbows. She thought she cleaned off more last night, but changing into a clean nightgown was relief enough.

She could hear Dylan talking to Moses through the door. He seemed as enthralled with this child as she was. She closed her eyes, whispering a prayer of thanks. Things could have gone much differently had he denied the child was his and insisted on dropping him off with the police to locate his parents—which he'd had every logical right to do.

Miss Gracie knocked lightly and entered. "I've a clean petticoat for you, Miss Lydia. And new stockings."

Lydia's stomach growled while Miss Gracie tightened the strands. "Wait, Miss Gracie. Not too tight. I've—I hope to make up for two days of not eating." Something about squeezing her waistline did not seem right considering she may be pregnant. But Miss Gracie couldn't know that yet.

Without question, Miss Gracie loosened the strands to a comfortable grip. "Of course, Miss Lydia. You need even more to eat while nursing. But you know that."

It was a slow descent to the dining room from upstairs. Miss Gracie pushed Lydia down a passageway of ramps while Dylan brought Moses to one of the maids to watch over during breakfast. Lydia felt a twinge of nausea, but her appetite was greater. Somehow, she was not nervous about meeting her grandfather again. This reunion would only confirm what she'd suspected all along—that her grandfather was a good man.

She took a deep breath as Miss Gracie pushed her into the dining room. First, she saw Frank and Dylan seated on the long end of the table. They hushed their conversation and stood when she entered.

The window behind her grandfather filled with grayish light, orange-red glowing beyond the garden courtyard. Lydia could not see his face clearly. Then he walked toward her, and his expression became clear. The familiar fleck in his eyes she'd seen that day nearly a year earlier, glimmered instead of glared. No darkness hid in his expression, only sorry and regret within the lines of his frown.

He approached with a steady stride and reached both hands toward Lydia in a gesture to help her to her seat.

"Lydia . . . granddaughter . . . it is a true joy to see you." As he pulled her to stand, he allowed her to lean into his side with her bad leg. He gripped her waist to steady her and kissed her forehead.

Could this be the same man who had pushed her from his home and denied any relation to her? What had happened within that heart of his to cause him to change?

Dylan came to her other side and the two men eased her into her seat.

Once everyone took their seats again, Grandfather spoke. "Let us say a prayer before we begin, not only as thanks for our food, but in recognition of the God of reconciliation and new beginnings."

Tears stung Lydia's eyes. God had intervened here as well. He had softened her grandfather's heart. She bowed her head, agreeing in her spirit with every word her grandfather spoke.

For the first time in weeks, Lydia managed to eat to her heart's content without a hint of nausea. While she nourished her body, her grandfather nourished her soul with words of apology, affection, and understanding.

"My wife, Annie, would have wanted this long ago. To my fault alone, the pain of losing her only grew worse when Charles and your mother, Emelyn, fled to the hills. I allowed bitterness and any reminder of where I'd gone wrong as a husband and father to darken who I'd once been. Then Charles' and Frank's sister . . ." Grandfather Sinclair looked toward a family portrait that sat crooked on the edge of the buffet, glass cracked.

Lydia looked closely at the photograph of Grandfather Sinclair surrounded by Frank, her father Charles, and two women. The older woman stood radiant and confident besides Grandfather Sinclair, each of her hands resting upon Frank and Charles' shoulders. Lydia clutched her heart at seeing a younger woman sitting between brothers. The woman, who must have been their younger sister, looked so much like herself, it took her breath away. They could have been twins.

"Will you forgive me, Lydia? Will you allow me to return the years the locusts have eaten a hundred-fold? I want nothing more than to provide you whatever you need to live a life of abundance, but also, as your husband described, the means to help others."

Lydia sipped her tea while tears filled her eyes. "Thank you . . . I do . . . forgive you." She felt a smile emerge, tears filling in the crevices at the corners of her lips.

Grandfather nodded and then lowered his head. "Of course, considering the earthquake and fires, there is no telling how long it will take to rebuild the estate. But my resources are still abundant enough to help you in any way you desire. First, we must arrange for a grand ball—to welcome, you, your husband, and my great-grandson into the family."

Lydia glanced at Dylan, not realizing word of the baby had gotten to her grandfather. Dylan nodded and smiled. "Thank you, Mr. Sinclair. But that doesn't seem fit considering all the loss and devastation here in the city, even if we do wait."

Mr. Sinclair cleared his throat and nodded. "You'll have to pardon me. The Good Lord has done a heart change in me, but my mind is still set in its ways. Still, I find our reconciliation worth celebrating."

"I agree." Lydia didn't wish to speak out of turn, but at her grandfather's words, she'd felt generations of social stigmas vanish. She fixed a pleading eye on her husband.

Dylan raised his cup of coffee and nodded. "On second thought, I couldn't agree more."

THIRTY-EIGHT

A week later, Dylan and Lydia settled into the Prescot home on Russian Hill. Thankfully, out of the few homes that were spared, Dylan's grandfather house was one of them. Determined neighbors used whatever means they could to ward off the flames caused from explosions that eventually charred the entire northern portion of the city.

Dylan sent a letter to Grass Valley to let his parents know of his grandfather's passing as well as to inform them of he and Lydia's plans to stay in the city for several weeks. He left the details of a possible pregnancy and new baby out of the letter for the time being.

Mr. Sinclair contacted an orphanage in the city to determine the proper steps for Dylan and Lydia to become legal parents of Moses. They had decided hiding things was no longer an option. If God had provided Moses as their own son, He would make a way for them to legitimately and legally adopt him before leaving the city.

San Francisco was blessed with many supplies from neighboring cities not affected by the earthquake or aftermath. Though food supplies were getting low, Dylan received a substantial portion due to his growing family.

Lydia learned that many nursing mothers had been unable to properly feed their infants after the trauma of the quake. This fact enforced her belief that Moses was indeed provided by God and her for him. Once the facts of Moses being found were out in the open, Dylan insisted Lydia see a doctor to confirm her suspected pregnancy. They didn't need the challenge of skirting around the truth to add to their other obstacles.

Having never seen a doctor before, Lydia was frightened of the experience and wanted Dylan with her. He explained it was not normal procedure, but that a nurse would be present during her examination.

All she wanted was confirmation that she was healthy, and if pregnant, that her baby was fine.

She returned to the waiting area at the clinic to await the results.

Moses lay in Dylan's arms, sleeping peacefully. He smiled with closed lips and winked at Lydia.

"He's definitely happier in his *mama's* arms. But he eventually fell asleep after a rather good fight."

Mama's arms?

Looking at her husband and this child warmed deep places in her soul. She could burst with awe at how much things had changed. Yet at how purposeful they seemed. All she could imagine was a life with children at her bosom, wanting and needing her and eager to learn about the world around them.

Using her cane with ease, she sat in the chair beside Dylan and kissed his cheek. "The doctor said my leg will take another six weeks or more to heal. It's a good thing that Miss Gracie agreed to stay with us for as long as we are in the city."

"Yes," Dylan mumbled. "How are you . . . in other areas?" He smiled nervously.

"Well, considering I have begun to produce an ample milk supply as well as a swollen *uterus,* the doctor is pretty positive that I am . . . nearly eight weeks with child."

Dylan shifted Moses to his outside arm and wrapped the other around Lydia. A full smile emerged, and he leaned in to kiss her.

She giggled when he wouldn't stop. "So I guess you're happy about this?"

He shook his head. "All you went through with the earthquake didn't hurt the baby?"

"The doctor admitted the whole situation was and is nothing less than a miracle. Although he said I should be monitored weekly until they confirm a solid heartbeat. I am to rest, eat, and stay hydrated. He doesn't recommend taking the train or the longer journey via stagecoach back to Penn Valley for at least two months."

"Two months! But I've got to—" Dylan stopped and pulled his hand to his mouth. "I guess I should continue to trust God to watch over you. You understand, I will need to check on our ranch and possibly hire more workers right away?"

The doctor walked into the waiting room and stood gazing through eyeglasses rested on the tip of his nose down at a stack of paperwork in his hands. He repeated what Lydia had already explained to Dylan.

"The results confirm pregnancy. However, in this early stage, I can't guarantee that things will continue to go well. You both seem hopeful, and that's a good thing. But you will need to be extra careful to avoid any complications. Considering you are also nursing, normally I would recommend bottle feeding at this point. But with the city's water supply limited, we will have to keep a careful watch that you steadily gain weight instead."

Moses squirmed and squeaked, though his eyes stayed closed. Dylan stood and started to rock from foot to foot.

"Will my . . . nausea continue?"

"It should continue to minimize as you continue to rest and reduce stress factors. The other things you described leading up to the earthquake sound like anxiety, and the pregnancy only amplified your nerves."

That made sense, considering she'd had a similar experience during her last trip to San Francisco, when pregnancy was not a factor.

They left the hospital by late afternoon, doctor's orders in hand for diet, rest, and to report any warning signs. The day was unusually warm, with only a thin layer of fog floating above the lower side of the city—if it could even be called a city.

No longer did buildings and other structure block the view to the shore. Block after block filled with broken remains, burnt bodies, and rubbish Lydia could not begin to describe. The city held a stench like nothing else and the heat only made it worse. Lydia tried to minimize her breathing until the carriage pulled up to the front of the Prescot home.

It seemed to take forever for Dylan and the butler to come around with the wheelchair, gather the baby, and help Lydia onto the street and then up the sidewalk. Miss Gracie took Moses when they entered the kitchen—the easiest path for the wheelchair—and then Dylan started to push her toward the back-hallway ramp.

"Wait," Lydia said. "Can you take me to the parlor instead? I want to be by the window where the garden is."

"You don't want to nap first?"

"No, I'm fine. Moses will need to feed again soon, and I won't be able to sleep if I can smell the dinner cooking down the hall."

"All right then, I will tell Miss Gracie where you are. I need to tend to business matters until dinner." Dylan kissed the top of her head and left her sitting at the parlor window.

Dylan's emotions had not been this conflicted for a while. He was overjoyed with the news of Lydia's pregnancy, and already felt a love for Moses he could not explain—a father's love despite his sudden entrance. Yet, their stability, health and future balanced on Dylan obtaining the proper resources, and considering all options regarding their home and the income they would need to provide for a family of four plus servants and farmhands—it all overwhelmed him.

It felt an impossible endeavor, considering his grandfather's estate would be sold to the highest bidder before the end of the year. He had no choice but to accept Mr. Sinclair's generous offer to finance things. But he was weary about the help continuing if he could not turn a profit soon.

With everything out between Dylan and Lydia, their situation grew more complicated by the day. Lydia wanted to know every detail of how things would work, and Dylan's patience was running thin.

He needed to handle it the way he saw fit. Between him, his father's input, and now Mr. Sinclair's involvement, they did not need another voice in the mix.

Upon entering the office, the trunk from their hotel caught his attention. He could hardly recall what they'd packed in it. Then suddenly, he remembered they'd brought the music box from Lydia's mama—he'd forgotten all about taking it for Lydia to show Uncle Moses during her visit. He hadn't thought of Uncle Moses since he'd climbed down from the pile of remains that had been a tailor shop.

Maybe Lydia would not be so inclined to be involved in the business portion of their affairs if she had something else to occupy her. She could read much better now than she could when they first discovered the box and the letters. He opened the trunk and located the music box. He would give it to her after dinner.

There was a possibility Lydia had learned something from her brief time with Uncle Moses that would shed light on some of the items the music box contained.

THIRTY-NINE

A surge of excitement filled Lydia as she held the music box in her arms. The moment she saw it, she remembered what Uncle Moses said about the box and the key. Without even considering the difficulty of the matter, she immediately began making plans to find her way back to the tailor shop's rubble. Besides, she needed to assist with the proper burial of her Uncle, didn't she? At least she wanted to have a burial service. Dylan appeared filled with regret the moment she shared her plan.

"But the key will open the box, Dylan! I can't believe I would find out where the key went and not have a chance to at least try and find the box. Moses said it was a metal box, so it's probably somewhere under a pile of rubble, waiting for me to find it."

Dylan raked his fingers through his hair. His chest puffed up and his jaw stiffened. "Lydia . . . Sweetheart . . . I know you want to learn more about your mama and her family. But the city is in ruins and you are in no shape to be climbing in piles of debris. I am not saying, yes, but I will send a telegram to someone I think could help."

"Who? I still want to be there...if only in the carriage by the shop. There has to be a reason why Mama had the key with her yet left the box behind."

Moses began to wail and with it, a tingling in Lydia's bosom.

"Uncle Frank, if you must know . . . he had mentioned that Bradford was managing some of the demolition teams."

Oh. Lydia knew Dylan was avoiding mentioning Bradford. Did he think something had happened between them before he found them at the hotel that night?

Funny how the thought of interacting with another man in any fashion aside from the practical, twisted Lydia's insides. How had her mind even considered excitement from attention by anyone besides her husband? She was thankful she had the excuse of an infant and her pregnancy to deter any further advances from men, handsome or not. Her curiosity in that department had vanished the moment the tailor shop had rattled everything from her life she was sure about.

For the next few days, she wouldn't leave the music box from her sight. She read over the letters, for other clues, even skimmed the ledger logs and travel documents. The only item that gave her hope was the key.

Grandfather arranged for the ball to take place at Sutro Baths, still standing in spite of the earthquake. Lydia didn't know that there was an entire floor above the swimming area devised for entertainment and special events.

Mr. Sinclair's on-call ladies' maid, Amanda, came to fit Lydia for her gown the afternoon prior to the ball. As Lydia examined the delicate fabric and embroidery, she considered variations of the gown she could make herself.

"Where did this come from, if I may ask?"

Amanda adjusted the sleeves and wrapped a thin shawl through Lydia's arms. "Paris. This gown came from Paris."

Where was Paris? "I will need to visit there soon. I make dresses myself and would like to find out where they get their patterns from."

Amanda chuckled. "That'd be quiet a journey for you miss. We normally buy our dresses from the tailor's wife, but their shop was destroyed in the quake."

"Actually, my . . . grandmother and mother made their dresses years ago. My mother taught me to sew by hand, but I recently got a sewing machine and took my first department store order."

Amanda stopped cinching Lydia's corset and came around to look at her. "Really? Was that the Hyman Tailor Shop? I think I heard it burnt down and the whole family perished some twenty years ago. Before she passed away Annie Sinclair swore she'd never worn another dress—from Paris or otherwise—as fine as those from the Hyman dressmakers."

A proud smile pressed into her cheeks. She was continuing with the family business. It had never occurred to her before now. "Yes, my mama was Emelyn. But she died just over a year ago."

"I was thinking that story didn't make sense considering the whole family perished, they couldn't have a grandchild," she chuckled. "Too bad you are the only lady left in the household who would desire such dresses. However . . ."

Lydia thought she heard Amanda's thoughts stirring. "Pardon me if this is out of place, but it is my understanding Mr. Sinclair is willing to help you out in various ways. Perhaps he'd be willing to fund you starting your own mail-order dress business."

"Would you like to see one of my dresses?"

"I would love to later. But while you're in the good graces of Mr. Sinclair, you might want to mention it."

Lydia's chest puffed and a lightness swept over her. Sewing dresses had always been something she enjoyed, but knowing she was continuing with something her family had done for years, made the task special.

"And one more thing. There are many people looking to relocate for jobs. If you and your husband are interested in hiring, I know of a husband-wife team who may fit the ticket."

Thinking it strange that such information would come from her grandfather's maid, Lydia was eager to share the suggestion with Dylan while they traveled to the ball. This could answer so many prayers. They would get the workers they needed for the ranch, plus she could arrange for filling more dress orders with someone to help her. In all of it, they would still be helping people while meeting their own basic needs. She never thought her grandfather would be the answer to so many of their needs.

"What's got you beaming?" Dylan greeted her with his usual large, dimple-filled smile.

"God is providing in amazing ways." She whispered in his ear and kissed his cheek while he helped her up into the carriage.

Dylan sat speechless while Lydia explained her ideas and how Mr. Sinclair was providing the means for them to accomplish their goals. He had heard there were people needing to relocate from the city, but he'd been hesitant for safety reasons. Who knows what kind of people he'd get off the street? But a referral—a couple—through Mr. Sinclair's household seemed a viable option. Now all he wanted was to ensure Lydia wouldn't be too ambitious while he took the trip to Penn Valley to get things arranged properly. She needed rest.

Lydia dazzled family and guests alike at the ball. Though she remained in her wheelchair the entire time, she partook in conversations, her smile enchanting everyone through the night. Dylan conversed as well, making his way from group to group, sharing business knowledge and their earthquake story. People treated them like a couple of royals. It was a great feeling.

The hope of a new thing springing forth felt surer than ever before.

FORTY

ydia's heart raced. She clung to the key in her palm, the end of it stabbing her slightly. Bradford approached slowly. Would he stay and watch her open it or get back to his crew?

Lydia moved over to the far edge of the seat so he could place the box next to her. Her hands began to shake and sweat. She wished Dylan was here now.

"Here you go. Yet another miracle in the life of Lydia Sinclair." Bradford shook his head and smiled. "Many of the homes here have been looted, yet this box remained untouched. Someone up there has insured that you were the only one to find it."

As he turned, Lydia ran her hand along the top. Black soot transferred to her fingertips. She took a handkerchief from her waistcoat and rubbed off what she could. It was a copper orange dense metal. No wonder the fire or quake had not damaged it. After cleaning the keyhole as best as she could with the corner of her handkerchief, she placed the edge of the key at the hole.

Hesitating and doubting momentarily that the key would event fit, she pressed in. It resisted at first, make a high-pitched scraping sound, but then the key slid in deep. Lydia's hand continued to shake. She grabbed her wrist to steady it and turned. Nothing. She turned the other way, the lock gave and clicked, and the lid popped up.

Lydia took a deep breath and observed the contents before she touched anything. Fit snuggly into one corner appeared a stack of tattered diaries— maybe six of them. Against those, three small metal boxes with intricate carvings stacked one on the other. Lined along the other end were miniature booklets. Slid in between the neat stacks were a mixture of basic household items, though all looked worn to the point of uselessness. A kitchen spoon, a tea pot, a rolled-up piece of fabric that looked like an apron only because the strings were holding it closed. Three picture frames in the center, only the top edge showing, were wrapped in some type of heavy linen.

Not sure which item she wanted to examine first, Lydia stared for several moments. The diaries could not be Mama's. She'd said the one she had in French Corral was her first. Lydia had no idea what the booklets could be, although they looked like small versions of the ledgers that had been in the music box. The apron, tea pot and kitchen spoon seemed out of place. Were they valuable in some other way?

Lydia reached in and lifted the diary on the top of the stack. It was cold.

The pages crackled despite the care she took to open the book. She slid her finger in to separate them, hoping they would not disintegrate. It took her a moment to realize the words were not in the language she knew—English. She had heard other languages spoken while in the city but had not seen anything written besides English. The odd way language was used in the Bible was hard enough for her to decipher.

Her shoulders dropped. What language was this? How could she tell who wrote it? She proceeded to pull out the remaining diaries—a total of eight. Each one was filled from the first page to the last in the same handwriting. Though she could not make out the words, it looked like the date of the entries was January of 1864. Calculating in her mind, she realized they were written before her mother was even born. The last one, as best as she could order them, was 1884. The closer she looked at the pages, she began to recognize English words in the later entries. Without a way to translate, she wouldn't be able to read them in order. Locating an entry that appeared mostly in English, she read it first.

4 May, 1882

Emelyn came home clearly upset today. She is tired of the school here. She claims she would rather sew with me than to try to make friends with those girls. When will she understand that we must learn to engage with the locals if we will ever fit in? She has no idea what her papa and I went through to get to the Americas. All we sacrificed to provide her with a good life. She often talks of home . . . of the open fields and the freedom she had to play and explore. But that life would not sustain us. How do I convince her that this life is best? We are making good money and as soon as she masters the sewing patterns for the gowns and can take on a project of her own without my supervision, we will double our income. Yet, I worry about her and Papa. They either argue or completely shut me out. I never imagined raising a daughter would be such a challenge. Why do I feel I am in competition with her for her father's affection?

Lydia stopped reading. There were several words she struggled to sound out and she wondered if she was taking the meaning wrong. This must be her grandmother's diary—her mama's mama. She was writing about Mama as a young girl. Lydia questioned why Mama's own diary failed to mention anything about her family life before they'd moved to San Francisco.

"Everything going okay in here?" Bradford leaned into the carriage window, a gleam in his eye.

Lydia shook her head to rid them of thoughts of the possible past and blinked. "Yes . . . yes . . . everything is fine. This box seems to have belonged to my mother's mother—my grandmother."

"Amazing. Looks like you have quite a glimpse into the past. However, I promised your husband I wouldn't keep you longer than necessary and most of my crew are novice workers who require direct supervision. We need to have this block cleared before nightfall."

Lydia nodded. The moment she thought of Moses being due for a feeding, her dress grew tighter at the top—a sign she was filling quickly with the milk Moses would be eager to devour. She stacked the diaries back into the box in the same order shed retrieved them and pulled down the lid. By the time she turned the key to secure the box, Bradford was at the door, ready to move the box to the back and make room for himself to sit beside her.

With no words besides a "thank you" to Bradford, Lydia's thoughts swarmed with the possible reasons that had led to her mama's family to this city. Her mama's life had not simply started the day she arrived in French Corral or the day she started her own diary. She had lived sixteen years before that, and Lydia now had a clue about what that life might have been like.

While Dylan was away, Lydia kept busy caring for Moses, writing to Hattie, and sewing. She asked Amanda about locating some dress patterns, a sewing machine, and fabric. Perhaps the act of sewing would bring her closer to her heritage—closer to the family that had made sacrifices and choices that ultimately led her to a life of isolation in a small valley in the mountains. A life that was now appearing to have a purpose of unlocking the past as well as to revealing a distinct path for the future.

FORTY-ONE

July 1906 - train en route to Grass Valley

Lydia's shoulders burned. Moses had nearly doubled in size while they were staying in the city. He had fussed most of the trip so far, so once she got him to sleep, she dared not move his position. This time, he'd fallen asleep nursing while in a semi-sitting position to relieve him of gas. Her arm was twisted beneath him while the other propped up under his bottom. His chubby little face was so adorable while he slept—long eye lashes and wet full lips complemented his ivory skin tone. He could have easily come from Lydia and Dylan's own flesh and blood.

Dylan sat, straight-faced and intensely focused on the paperwork before him. He didn't seem to notice Lydia was watching him. He had a lot of details to work out upon arriving home on a permanent basis.

Lydia transferred her gaze to the scenery. She tried to take in the rolling hills, jagged mountains and rivers as much as she could while Moses wasn't demanding her attention.

City life had been interesting and exciting for a while. Her grandfather had spoiled her with Amanda's devoted service, elegant rooms, and marvelous food. Yet, she eventually longed for the comfort of home—of the familiar and of doing things for herself once again.

Now, she would also have plenty of help. For they had two more travelers with them this time. Mr. and Mrs. Jones had lost their souvenir shop and their home in the quake and needed employment and shelter. In addition to being close friends with Mr. Sinclair's maid, Amanda, they'd been successful business owners for two decades. After learning a few more details, Lydia knew that this couple was meant to come home with them.

Dylan and Mr. Jones fell into conversation about business and other matters with ease. And Mrs. Jones had several connections in the city she was happy to refer to Lydia for their clothing orders.

Lydia didn't think her love for her husband could increase. But upon his complete trust and agreement to not only hire, but take the Jones' home with them, Lydia's heart swelled. Dylan was determined to succeed in business one way or another. In his excitement, he'd already devised a business plan for Lydia to mass produce custom gowns he was confident would soon be in demand across the nation.

She'd denied the plausibility, feeling incapable of such a feat. She loved sewing, but she couldn't see her talent so far above the rest a that people would request her designs by name.

"But you see things others don't." Dylan had insisted when she protested. "You have a gift. Those patterns you embroider are like nothing I've ever seen. It is like you have the eyes of God and He is instructing you to replicate his creation. Who would think of weaving a vine of flower blossoms through willow leaves? Or border a dress with baby lambs munching on tender shoots of grass?"

Though the designs were unique, she doubted every one of them met the expectations of the world. "Each gown is simply a representation of my own experiences. How can you be sure others will appreciate these—especially since they are so different from modern trends?" Her life had been different—yet by symbolically representing the favorite things from her life in the Valley on a gown, she could share that part of her life with the world.

"Hey." Lydia nudged her foot into Dylan's.

Dylan only moved his eyes from the paper to his foot, then back to the paper. "One moment, Lydia."

The train lurched and then slowed. Attendants began walking the aisles and announcing they had arrived in Sacramento. Lydia moved slightly and Moses instantly whined, though his eyes remained closed. Dylan was too busy organizing his paperwork into his briefcase to notice.

"Here, I'll take him a minute." Mrs. Jones stood from across the aisle and reached for Moses.

"Thank you." Lydia turned and using what felt like all her strength, lifted Moses up to Mrs. Jones. Instantly, she felt the urge to use the restroom.

Mrs. Jones followed her to the train lavatory, where she also helped Lydia change Moses' soiled wraps. Walking about helped Lydia feel a bit better, though she longed to board the stagecoach come morning and climb the mountain to cooler air.

The heat in Sacramento was suffocating. One thing she would miss from the city was the cool summer air. It even got chilly enough for coats some mornings. Anything was better than this heat that smacked her faced as she exited the train. It nearly made her nauseous.

Though summer days could still get hot in Penn Valley, it was more tolerable. The evenings usually grew cool enough to allow for some relief, if only with a slight breeze blowing on dampened bedding.

Moses face grew red and shone with moisture. Unlike Lydia, all he'd known was the cool salty air of the bay. Thus, the entire night, Lydia fought the baby to sleep, and kept him nearly naked to help him stay cool. Nursing alone, made them both miserable.

The hotel was stifling. Not even the slightest breeze blew through the open window. Lydia thought about asking Mrs. Jones to come and wave a board across them, but she hesitated. They were not her servants. She realized she had become accustomed to having someone available to wait on her. She chastised herself for thinking of them in this way.

The slightest breeze wafted into the hotel room at dawn. Dylan had moved to the chaise to sleep, seemingly irritated by the constant up and down of Lydia to retrieve Moses from the cradle, feed him despite constant whining, and attempting to slide back into bed before he awoke again.

Would it be like this back home? Her and her husband unable to sleep in bed together for a full night? She had not realized how much Miss Gracie had assisted her until now.

Sleep deprived and feeling every little inconsiderate thing Dylan did was in protest to losing sleep himself, Lydia kept quiet. Eventually, her eyes grew heavy and she nodded in and out of sleep during the baby's content moments.

The next leg of their journey wasn't any easier. Shortly after they began ascending the hill from Auburn, Dylan began talking as if they'd been conversing all day and he was only changing the subject.

"My mother will be staying with us upon our return."

Jaina had not been a part of their discussions for weeks. And when they had talked about her, it was about how excited she was to have two grandchildren to spoil. "Staying with us? Does she know we've hired Mr. and Mrs. Jones?"

"We will have a houseful, but my mother will be more help than you know. And since she is my mother, we won't have to feel we owe her for anything. She's also looking forward to continuing your reading and writing lessons without your needing to leave home." He winked passed a strained smile. "Her payment will be time with her grandchildren."

"I'm not sure I would feel any privacy with your mother around—" she bit her lip at the words. She didn't mean to cause strife.

Dylan cleared his throat and pursed his lips.

Lydia did not dare to say anything else.

FORTY-TWO

Dylan failed in his attempt to venture into a welcomed subject. He assumed with Lydia's discovery of her grandmother's diary, that she would be elated at starting up lessons with his mother again. Why would Lydia be fine with perfect strangers living among them and still feel privacy, yet with his mother, feel it violated? He had to remind himself again that Lydia did not think like anyone else in this world—a trait he adored, yet one that often irritated him if it meant explaining things most people automatically understood.

He bounced Moses on his lap, the rolls on the child's side a perfect handle to ensure he would not leave his grip.

He knew he had to speak soon, or Lydia would continue her line of reasoning. "One of the projects I will delegate will be to build a lean-to adjacent to the barn. Mother will room downstairs. She will prove to be more help than anything else. Our privacy should not be an issue."

Lydia's shoulders relaxed and she smiled, though coyly. "Of course, it would not be. I'm sorry—I am sure things will be much different now that we have Moses. I imagine her eyes on us all the time. There are moments I would rather she not see."

Dylan flashed to their moment in the living room the evening Pete had arrived. He would not want his mother to see that either. But they were long past things of that nature—weren't they? The earthquake, fires, and becoming a family with children had changed all of that.

Besides, his mother would not dare interject in ways that would cause strife between him and Lydia now. She wanted their marriage to thrive—to become more than what she had with her father, more than Emelyn had had with Charles. More so, she wouldn't do anything to risk endangering Lydia's pregnancy. Dylan believed his mother wanted what was best and nothing more. If anything, her prying was intended to ward off problems, not to create them.

But how could he explain this to Lydia? She would have to see for herself.

A thin veil of clouds created a muggy welcome as they entered Grass Valley. Neil Street was sparse with inhabitants, everyone likely resting before the evenings Independence Day celebrations. Most of the stores had already closed. The carriage rounded the block and turned on South Auburn. The Williams' house was at the bottom of the street.

Windows glowed with electric light coming from lamps and ceiling fixtures. The clank of dishes and the chaos of Olive and Brian's voices overlapping each other hinted at what the not-so-distant future held for Dylan and Lydia.

Hattie yelled and her mother echoed the attempt to gain some control over the little tykes—but to no avail. Their voices only rose an octave.

When the wagon came to a stop, as if on cue, Moses signaled he was ready to eat. He began to squirm and reach for Lydia. She climbed out of the wagon first and hoisting the child onto her hip like an expert, she scurried toward the porch. Dylan stood on the curb, awaiting the reunion between friends he was sure would trump any noise currently coming from the house.

Hattie pulled open the screen and screeched loud enough it rang Dylan's ears. She pulled Lydia and Moses to her and danced back and forth, her screams turning into hysterical laughs. Moses wailed, his face smashed into Lydia's arm while he looked back at Dylan as if to say, "rescue me, Papa!"

Dylan chuckled and turned to unload the wagon.

A short time later, the two women sat knee to knee on the couch, each holding a child on their lap. Brian was enthralled with Moses and tried to play peek-a-boo, not understanding Moses wasn't old enough to participate. But Moses laughed anyway, giggling every time Brain removed his chubby fingers from his face and piped, "boo!"

Dylan stood in the doorway, feeling out of place as Hattie's mom prepared dessert. Her father was nowhere in sight and nobody had bothered to explain why.

"He is simply angelic, Lydia! And to think you found him seconds before that hotel collapsed and flooded." Hattie shook her head, dried tears streaking her cheeks. She let go of Brian with one hand and reached for Lydia's belly. "And you're pregnant too! When I read it in your letter, my mother came rushing into the room thinking I had electric-shocked myself I had screamed so loudly! Oh—I've missed you so much. And I've got some news for you I wanted to share in person." Hattie blushed and pressed her lips together.

"News? You met someone? I knew it. You're too pretty to live the rest of your life as a lonely widow." Lydia beamed, obviously ecstatic for her friend even before she verified the news.

Dylan had a hunch of what Hattie was about to say. He'd kept the detail from Lydia solely to be able to observe this moment between friends. And he was glad he did.

"Well . . . you have been gone for nearly three months. Back in May, I took a trip to French Corral to visit Clara and see how Miss Hastings was doing. She has not been well and moved into the Inn to allow the O'Shea's to tend to her—"

"Oh no . . ." Lydia clamped a hand over her mouth, and Moses nearly wiggled from her hold.

Hattie set Brian down, swatting his behind playfully. "That's another matter I didn't want to worry you with. But first, let me tell you what happened."

Lydia nodded and repositioned Moses to give him a view of Brian and Olive playing with blocks beneath the window.

"So . . . I was at the Inn, and Mrs. O'Shea was telling me that Miss Hastings was adjusting and guess who walks in?"

"Who?" Lydia mimicked Hattie bouncing on the couch. She raised her eyebrows.

"Pete." Hattie smiled and winked, then bit her lip.

Lydia turned a dark shade of red, then took in a deep breath, letting out with a huge smile. "Pete? What was he doing there?" Her voice squeaked a little, as if trying to hide disappointment.

Dylan felt a frown emerge but kept watching.

"He was ordering pies and slid up beside me at the counter, almost as if I wasn't there. I looked at him, not realizing it was Pete at first, and cleared my throat, nearly choking back what was about to leave my mouth."

"What were you going to say?"

Dylan shook his head, snickering to himself. It had not taken Lydia long to learn the ways of gossip. Of course, Hattie was talking about herself, so it wasn't technically gossip. But she sure soaked in the details like a dry rag dipped in fresh water on a hot summer day.

"I was going to say for him to take his business somewhere else, there was no vacancy. But when I turned, my fingers brushed the side of his arm and our eyes locked."

"What did he say?"

"He said, 'pardon me miss, my eyes were adjusting to the light and I didn't notice you were that close.'"

"Eyes adjusting to the light? That is absurd. He nudged you on purpose, he—" Lydia's eyes dashed to Dylan. She lifted Moses up off her lap and crossed her legs. "Dylan, can you take Moses for a while?"

"Sure thing." Dylan walked over and scooped up the baby. "I'll take him to the room while I sort out our luggage."

The women's voices seemed to grow softer, and not only because he went down the hall. He was sure Lydia had more to tell Hattie about Pete than she thought Dylan knew. But no matter, he felt satisfied that once she heard of their engagement, he would not have to worry about chance encounters or finding Lydia and Pete alone. He knew most of what transpired before their trip were invisible roadblocks intended to discourage and frustrate them. The forces at work were determined to deter them from fighting for the marriage God had planned for them from the start.

Watching Hattie glow warmed Lydia's heart. Her friend was back in every way—and in love and engaged to Pete! The news brought relief to Lydia in many ways. Yet, the trip had exhausted her to the point she could only listen. All she needed to do was listen since Hattie was not short of words this evening.

"With Dylan gone, I can tell you more details." Hattie winked and smiled.

Should Lydia tell her about the times Pete seemed to be okay with standing or sitting so close to her? This was one of those times when she probably did not need to say something. Finally, she was realizing why others kept things from her. The information would only hurt or bring doubt about their true intentions. She didn't need her friend knowing that Lydia had been attracted to Pete, regardless of how short-lived.

"We ended up talking at the back table at the Inn for hours. I never did end up visiting Miss Hastings upstairs. Pete and I found our pain about losing our spouses made it hard for either of us to feel right about being happy. He said he was feeling better since living at your ranch and not surrounded by drunken, womanizing miners day and night. He told me your presence alone made him feel like he had a home again."

Lydia felt her eyebrows raise and heat creep up her neck. "He told you that?" She whispered loudly. "Did he say why?"

"You're embarrassed by that?" He went on to say despite your age, he felt comforted by you as a son would with his mother."

Lydia questioned if he'd been fully honest with Hattie. Memories of his hand lingering on her waist and how he kept winding up near here during moments nobody else was around told Lydia there'd been more going in his own heart and mind at the time.

Hattie kept her enthusiasm as she finished her story. "Although he admitted you were beautiful, he wouldn't entertain anything except a professional relationship given you were married, and your husband was his employer. He saw you both as a godsend and he'd finally realized why."

"Why?"

"He only gazed at me for his answer. My belly did a flip and I felt my breathing grow rapid." Hattie smiled and pretended to fan her face with her hand. "And I was positive in that moment that God had brought us together. I only needed to wait for Pete to say he felt the same."

FORTY-THREE

August 1906 - Rolling Oaks Ranch, Penn Valley

Lydia rubbed her lower back and rolled her shoulders. Her pregnant belly bulged out like an over-sized ball now, and she could not see her feet when she stood up straight. Her hip pain had grown considerably worse the past few weeks, making it difficult to sit or stand for long periods.

The doctor said that due to how her leg had healed, it was now a bit shorter than the other and was possibly causing strain to her back. But she pressed through the discomfort, determined to finish the bridesmaid dress she was sewing before dinner. It was her second try in creating one with a panel that would hold her belly, yet still fit the normal parts of her body in an appropriate manner.

She couldn't do much about her growing bosom either, it would escape the top of her gown unless she added a neck piece. But that would make her too hot. A summer wedding in any formal wear would be torture.

However, it was worth it to see her friend in such happiness once again. At times, Lydia thought Pete was much more attentive than Dan had ever been. But she would not mention this to Hattie. She was grateful that Hattie was willing to marrying again so soon. They'd even talked about trying to become pregnant again at the same time.

"Lilia . . . Lilia . . . Moses stuck!" Brian shrieked as he ran into the sewing room.

Lydia jumped up, catching her fingertip on the needle.

She followed Brian through the kitchen and into the living room. Her heart raced and her breath quickened as her mind ran through all the possible ways Moses could be stuck. Where had Olive and Hattie gone? They'd all been in the living room moments earlier.

Brain would not walk fast enough. She grabbed his hand and led him through the doorway while sucking the blood from her pricked fingertip.

"There he is!" Brian pointed toward the wood box next to the fireplace.

At first, Lydia couldn't tell Moses was there, then she saw a black shoe bob up from the box.

She ran over—there wasn't any wood in the box since it was in the hottest part of summer. Moses lay on his back, purple, his face contorted in a wail, yet he wasn't crying.

Without thinking Lydia bent down and scooped him up, holding him fast to her chest and patting his back. Was he choking on something?

"Hattie!" She screamed, hoping her friend was within earshot.

Hattie came through the other door after the thumping of feet on the stairs. "What is it . . . I was taking Olive to the bathroom."

"Is Moses hurt, Mama?" Olive asked. Lydia could barely make out the child's worried eyes through her blurry ones.

"He can't breathe!" Lydia patted Moses back, but nothing happened.

Hattie seemed calm—amused even. She grabbed Moses from Lydia's grasp and flung him face down over her arm. In a hard swat, she pounded once on his back. A sliver of wood chip flew forth to the floor and Moses sucked in, coughed, then started to cry.

Lydia breathed, a sharp stab ran up her leg and into her hip, forcing her to sit in the armchair at her knee.

Hattie brought Moses over and Lydia lurched toward him, pulling him in between her bulging belly and bosom. He clung to her, his arms slightly scraped from the insides of the wood box. Snot and tears covered his face, but Lydia kissed it all anyway.

"I'm sorry, Lydia. Brian was playing so well with him over there, I didn't think . . . well . . . I didn't think." Hattie shook her head and ran her hand through Olives curls.

"It's okay, Hattie. Brian came to the rescue . . . didn't you, Brian?" Lydia was grateful for the little guardian angel. She could not be angry at Hattie. She would have thought they were fine too.

"He did?" Hattie crouched down and reached for Brian. Come here, my little hero."

She pulled her two children close and kissed each on the head, and then on their mouths. "You want to go help Pete water the horses?"

Squeals substituted a "yes" from each of them.

A moment later, Moses pulled at the top of Lydia's apron. His crying had calmed, though he was still breathing hard.

Lydia proceeded to nurse him and rested her head back on the chair. Through the corner of the window, she watched Hattie, holding onto the hands of Olive and Brian, making their way through the yard and over to the corral.

She couldn't allow her mind to wander to the "what if" of the previous moment. She could only feel gratitude. Here she sat, a babe at her breast, another growing inside her, her best friend and her two children she adored only yards away. Dylan was in town, picking up his mother along with an order of fabric bolts.

From isolation in a valley separated from the world to a life of defeating and overcoming one obstacle after another. She was living the life of adventure she only dreamed of as a girl.

Though the coming months would no doubt bring challenges, she had learned enough earlier in the year to understand that nothing in this life was guaranteed. But she was ready to embrace it all. She refused to feed into fears of losing anyone she loved and even if she did allow her thoughts turn to worry, she was confident that no matter what, God would be with her in every moment.

FORTY-FOUR

A thunderstorm hit Penn Valley on the day of Pete and Hattie's wedding. They ended up stating their vows with close family and friends on the covered porch. Additional guests gladly held umbrellas or whatever else they could find to keep the rain from dousing their heads in support of the couple. The babies screamed in protest, though Olive thought it a joy and hopped down into the soggy grass to dance in the rain.

Once the vows were complete, Pete and Hattie joined Olive in a celebration dance in the grass. Before long, the entire wedding party and all the guests were dancing and sloshing around the yard in their formal attire, hair in sopping strands and not a frown in sight.

Once evening set in, Hattie and Pete went upstairs to their "honeymoon suite" and the party transferred to the barn. Lydia didn't think she'd had as much fun at her own wedding, but she didn't care. She sat Moses on her belly, and rocked to the sounds of banjos, drums, and harmonicas. The heat still lingered long enough after the storm for everyone to dry off by the end of the party.

Dylan and Lydia waved good-bye to Mr. and Mrs. Williams as they left with Brian and Olive in tow. Moses slept soundly beneath a blanket over Dylan's shoulder. Evening creatures chirped, rustled, and croaked.

"Do you want to go for a walk?" Dylan said as he gently adjusted Moses into a cradled position. "Mother can keep a watch on him inside while we're gone."

Lydia smiled. A midnight summer walk was a sensational idea. She still hadn't started a daily walking routine since they'd returned from San Francisco. Maybe tonight, Dylan could help her determine the path that would make a new ritual for her and her own children. The half-moon sat high in the clear sky—only thin sheets of steel-blue clouds remained as evidence of the storm. She knew it might be a muddy venture, but one glance at her shoes told her they were already a mess.

"That sounds wonderful. I'll wait here on the porch for you."

A few minutes later, Dylan escaped through the screen without Lydia hearing him. She'd been focused on the sounds outside and the memories that surfaced from her childhood. Crickets, bats, a moon that shed a path of cool-white beams across the valley.

Dylan entwined his fingers with hers and they stepped into the yard and walked past the chicken house and toward the horse pasture. Without either of them talking about which direction to go, they walked in one accord through the field and to the grove of oak trees surrounded by large, mossy boulders.

Lydia's toes squished with each step, but the coolness made the nighttime heat bearable. When they got to the rocks, Dylan removed his hat and set it on one boulder before leaning on the other one and pulling Lydia toward him.

Her belly bumped his belt before he could lean in far enough to kiss her.

Lydia giggled and moved her belly to the side, nesting her hip into his waistline. She nuzzled his neck until his breathing quickened.

Dylan wrapped his arms around her, one beneath her belly and the other above. "My sweet Lydia, how much our life has changed since the last time we were here."

Lydia felt her face grow warm. She smiled at the memory of their romantic interlude behind the rocks. "How much it has . . . far beyond my dreams no doubt. I had many doubts that day you know. Doubts about everything, including you."

Dylan loosened his grasp. "Really? I felt the same way. I felt like a failure and that I didn't deserve you after all. You had trusted me, and I was losing our farm without hope."

"No, I was doubting myself worthy as your wife. I had not gotten pregnant yet, I couldn't learn to keep quiet. My curiosity alone could have ruined everything." Lydia was grateful that she didn't have to elaborate. Even though Dylan had forgiven her, she still felt guilt gnaw at her at the thoughts of what could have been and how it could have ruined all they'd worked toward.

But now, her love for Dylan was more secure today than it had ever been. She turned her face and gazed into his eyes—filled with the reflection of tree branches bordered in moonlight.

He pulled her closer, leaning his forehead onto hers. A layer of mud sloshed below their feet as they did their best to mold themselves together.

The baby turned, and a body part protruded from her belly and into Dylan's hip. He smiled, verifying he had felt it.

Then he brought his lips to hers, slowly at first. As if taking her into the only space remaining between them, he kissed her deeply. She leaned into him even more and considered the consequences of them joining here and now, beneath the moonlight and in the muddy grass.

As if reading her thoughts, he unclasped the back of her dress.

Dylan draped his jacket over Lydia as a makeshift blanket. The top of her bare belly poked through the side, a radiant smooth evidence of their love shining in the moonlight. She snuggled beside him, undeterred by the parts revealed to the sky above.

Dylan knew Lydia did not realize how unconventional their relationship was. Of course, most gentlemen never revealed the details of their love life. But he had a hard time imagining many proper pioneer women willing to engage in such activities in the wide-open field. He would not make it a habit of course but would cherish this rare time as an opportunity to realize the amazing and unique gift Lydia was to him.

In a way, he felt like Adam with Eve. In the garden, long before sin entered the world. Her innocence to the world's ways could make her vulnerable to evil. But with him, he only desired a true nature, that which he believed was God's original plan. She was not tainted by the world—only curious about it.

They did their best to cloth themselves with their now soaked and muddy attire. Detouring behind the house, they pulled dried garments from the laundry line and snuck back through the pasture and to an empty stable in the barn. Dylan dried off the parts Lydia could no longer reach and they both changed into dry clothing.

"Won't your mother notice we changed our clothes?" Lydia looked worried.

"If she does, she won't say anything about it. I've already set up our evening needs in the stable closest to the outhouse. I'll be back with them in a moment."

In the barn, Dylan and Lydia made their bed on pile of hay—horse blankets dividing them from the prickly dry blades. Jaina hummed a lullaby to Moses in the next stall, where they had arranged his cradle and a mattress.

Still warm from the summer air, they only used a light blanket. Dylan lie on his back and Lydia on her side facing away from him.

The rooster crowed long before sunrise. Dylan left their makeshift bed with care, hoping Lydia would remain in her slumber. The morning air was refreshing and sweet for the time being. He checked in the other stall to see how his mother and Moses were doing, but they weren't there.

Leaving the barn, he spotted Jaina with the bundle of blanket, seated on a tree stump beyond the horse corral. She faced the horizon where the sun was about to rise. As Dylan approached, his mother rocked slightly back and forth. Not wanting to startle her or wake the baby if he was asleep, he came around at a wide angle so that she'd spot him with the corner of her eye.

"Good morning, Mother," Dylan whispered, kissing his mother on the head and observing a very content, yet wide-awake Moses.

"Good morning. We were about to watch the sunrise. Would you like to join us?"

"Of course."

A motionless mist rested above the meadow between them and groups of oak trees and boulders at the end of the property. Birds twittered from far away branches. A frog croak echoed from somewhere along the forest line.

Only their breaths and an occasional gurgle from Moses interrupted the natural sounds of a summer morning about to envelop the ranch.

Dylan was surprised at how at ease his mother appeared despite sitting in her nightgown on a tree stump. She seemed as enthralled with baby Moses as everyone else.

A silver glow emerged in a thin line along the horizon. With it, deep blues and star light faded into pale purple. When oranges and pinks began to flow into the violet and lavender hues, Dylan broke the silence.

"While we have this moment alone, there is something I have been meaning to ask you."

Jaina kept her eyes on the horizon and sat Moses up against her middle so he could look out as well. He kicked his feet, stuffed a fist in his mouth and started sucking on it and cooing.

Jaina laughed lightly. "What is it, my boy?"

The sunrise reflected on her cheeks, nose, and chin. Her beauty shone despite tousled hair and plain clothing. Dylan adored his mother and wanted to make sure he had finally met the expectations she'd had for her son.

"Are you happy with me? With us . . . Lydia and me? We know marriage and life is a long journey and we are not naïve to the fact we will still face challenges. But it is important to me, to us, that you approve."

"The only approval you need to seek is God's. From what I can tell, you cherish your wife as Christ did the church and she respects and honors you the best way she can. I have never not approved of either of you—separate or together. I only wanted what was best and was concerned Lydia's lack of experience would cause problems. But I see now that she is the purest of souls. Not without faults, but so willing to learn and do good. I could not ask for more for my son—or our heritage."

Tears pricked at Dylan's eyes. His mother had changed in many ways. Had Lydia been a part of it? "Thank you, Mother. I know serving God is the priority. But with you staying with us for now . . . I wanted to know if there was anything—"

"Do not change a thing because me. I'm here to help and support you—not get in the way. In a couple of months you'll be counting the days between my stays—looking forward to a few lone minutes with your wife while I visit my grandchildren. I do not need to remind you how fortunate you both are to have never experienced the loss of a child." Her gaze drifted down to Moses' head. "And for this little one to choose the most loving parents to be his replacements."

Her words spoke volumes. Yet, he didn't risk asking her to explain the shadows in her gaze.

"Enjoying a beautiful sunrise without me?" Lydia's voice penetrated Dylan's quaking heart.

He spun to see her standing behind them, a blanket wrapped around her, though a shoulder peeked out from one side. "I was letting you sleep."

"And I was telling your husband what great parents you have turned out to be." Dylan's mother smiled—more genuine than he'd ever seen.

"This child seems ready for farm life," Lydia rubbed her belly. "Waking up with the cows and ready to roll."

They all chuckled.

"Do you think the newlywed couple is ready for breakfast?" Lydia winked.

"Probably not," said Dylan. "But Mother and I will do our best to keep Moses happy out here if you'd like to get started."

FORTY-FIVE

Wanting to shed the sweat and dried rain clad garments, Lydia stopped at the clothing line to grab yet another replacement garment before heading into the kitchen. The warm night had easily dried the clothing hung there and she removed a basic sun dress and apron to change into.

She hurried to change in the corner of the sewing room, staying far away from the other side of the house and the stairs in hopes not to disturb Hattie and Pete. She pondered her own wedding night with Dylan. How much different had it been for Hattie with a second husband? Lydia shook her head before her thoughts got too detailed.

One thing she did recall the morning after was that her and Dylan had to get up right away to work and prepare their own breakfast. She was determined to ensure Hattie and Pete could spend all day upstairs if they wished.

Lydia plucked a half-dozen eggs from beneath warm chickens, then released the hens to peruse the yard. The air still clung to her, the heat overwhelming her more than any summer she could recall. Maybe pregnancy made it less bearable.

Omelets, sausage, strawberries and blackberries filled two china plates a short time later. A fresh pot of coffee steamed. Lydia had not heard a sound above her. Could they still be asleep? They had to be hungry by now. She had not fully thought through the moment she would need to carry their breakfast upstairs.

The faraway cry of Moses broke her thoughts. Dylan jumped up on the porch, a fussy, red-faced baby in his arms. He swung the kitchen door open, shook his head and laughed. "I held him off as long as I could."

Lydia wiped her hands on a towel and nodded at the plates. "Actually, you came to the rescue. I was wondering how I would make an entrance with their breakfast and not . . . well . . . interrupt anything." She felt heat creep up her neck at the suggestion.

Dylan let out a hearty laugh. He took the tray of breakfast plates and coffee cups and made his way to the stairs.

September 1906

Four bedrooms, two couples, a mother-in-law, and three children made for chaos and then some. Jaina did her best to help, but often took it upon herself to decide when the children needed fed, napped, and even bathed. Pete and Dylan stayed out in the field and barn most days, by the time September and cooler morning and evenings began,

Hattie and Lydia had started their own early evening walk routine—leaving Jaina with the children while they made an excuse to collect berries or wildflowers before dinner.

"It has been really nice having you close by day after day, Hattie." Lydia gathered pale violet lilies, and bright yellow black-eyed Susans. "With Jaina going back to Grass Valley tomorrow, I was hoping we could have a nice evening with us four adults after the children are sleeping."

"I am looking forward to that as well. She has been wonderful—so much different than I expected. Still, I can't help but feel her gaze, her thoughts that my children are out of control." Hattie only swept her hands along the tops of grass and petals. She let Lydia choose the flowers.

"I think the same thing at times. She has suggested letting Moses take bottles of goat milk and says I'll never put on the weight I need for this child if I keep nursing him. But I can't bring myself to do it. My milk saved his life. Until he is ready, or this child is born, I am in no hurry to wean him."

"I still regret weaning Brian. But my milk was gone. You are fortunate God has blessed you with the ability to nourish two children at once."

Lydia fell silent for several minutes, thoughts of the past gnawing at her again. But she needed to make sure all was well between them first.

"Everything . . . between you and Pete . . . it's good, right? Even though you aren't living alone."

Hattie giggled. "Things are more than good," Hattie beamed. "I almost feel guilty about it. Dan slips my mind at times, until Brian makes that smile that reminds me of him again. I can't believe how things transpired—how God brought us together after all we lost. I have nothing to complain about. Why? Are you and Dylan doing okay?"

Lydia nodded and pressed her lips together. "Yes, we are. Although accounting for the size of this current household has had us in a quandary at times. But really, he's glad to help. We have a plan for after the baby comes. But a few things must work out first." Seeing her and Dylan's rendezvous point of oaks and boulders, Lydia smiled and then guided Hattie in the opposite direction.

"But?" Hattie nudged Lydia, smiling coyly.

Lydia's stomach roiled in a way she knew had nothing to do with the child inside her. "I wish I knew how to handle these things better . . ."

"What things?" Hattie stopped, her long brown curls swaying.

"When to speak and when no to. Just when I think I have it figured out; I begin to doubt myself."

Hattie tilted her head to the side and raised her eyebrows. "Oh, Lydia. You know you can tell me anything! Even the things most ladies shouldn't speak." She winked.

Lydia took a deep breath. "Okay . . . but Dylan does not know I'm going to share this with you and I'm sure he'd rather forget all about it. But I feel like you should know."

Hattie smile faded and her forehead wrinkled. "Now you have me curious. What is it?"

"It's Pete," Lydia blurted and looked down at her shoes, a layer of dried dirt and grass seeds dulling the shiny black leather.

"Pete?" Hattie brushed her fingers across Lydia's cheeks and held them there until Lydia looked her in the eye. "Did something happen . . . between the two of you?"

Lydia sighed, relieved at her friend's perception, but terrified of admitting it. "Not exactly. I thought you would catch on the first time I told you about him coming to work here."

"What happened?" Hattie laughed lightly though her forehead creased in contrast.

"There were a few moments where I thought he might . . . get too close. I didn't know what was happening since the only other man who had stirred such feelings in me was Dylan. When you said he made your heart flutter, I figured it was normal. But it kept troubling me."

Hattie put her hand to Lydia's mouth and smiled. "You are a silly woman sometimes and your imagination can get the best of you. I could tell you thought Pete was attractive. But I also knew that your devotion to Dylan was greater."

"You're not angry with me?"

"Of course not. But I have noticed how you sometimes seem to avoid him."

Lydia could say nothing more. She felt a huge weight lift and reached out to hug her friend. "This is why I'm so glad to have you as my friend! However, there is a second half to my confession."

Hattie squeezed hard, then kept a hold of Lydia's shoulders and made a weak attempt at a scolding expression. "Second half?"

"Dylan has arranged for a business loan to open a dress shop in Grass Valley, complete with a large upstairs apartment to accommodate our growing family." Lydia caressed her swollen belly with both palms. "We planned to tell both you and Pete together. But he has decided it's best for everyone to deed you both this house and the ranch."

Hattie clapped her hands and squealed. "The whole ranch? Pete was just telling me last night that one day he would love to run a ranch like this . . . to provide work for those who need it."

Lydia smiled. "Pete has proven himself a hard worker and according to Dylan, expresses a desire to work the land and horses indefinitely. With more dislocated workers coming from the city, distributing tasks and chores will become easier. The lean-to attached to the barn will be completed before winter and should accommodate all the male workers. And the two bedrooms not used by you or the children should be sufficient to accommodate the female staff—widows and unmarried young woman from the city will be offered short-term residence for training and jobs in Penn Valley, Grass Valley or Nevada City."

Hattie nodded, her curls bobbing with every one of Lydia's words. "That still gives us plenty of room for more children too. Brian and Olive really love it here. Lydia—I can't believe it. Thank you from the bottom of my heart! But then you will be further away."

They continued discussing the details as they walked back to the house. The friendship and bond her and Hattie had formed over two short years amazed Lydia. She had never dreamed of a life with a friendship such as this but had long learned that God's plans for those he loves are often much higher, longer, wider and deeper than humans can comprehend.

Blessing her with a friendship was a small glimpse into that love.

FORTY-SIX

November 1906

The pains started in the early hours of the morning. At first, Lydia thought she needed to use the restroom, but the urge was more intense. Dylan was already outside working. Moses whined and reached for her from his crib when she returned from the restroom.

Lydia's belly relaxed and although her back ached slightly, she managed to dress herself, change and feed Moses and almost make it to the bottom of the stairs before another cramp began.

Though the tightening stopped Lydia for a moment, the pain was bearable. She succeeded in occupying Moses in the kitchen, collecting eggs with him wrapped to her back, and milking Megan before feeling a need to rest and breathe. Sitting on the porch edge, she set Moses on the grass to crawl around. It was a crisp fall morning. Clusters of orange, red, and brown leaves covered the yellowed lawn. Moses grabbed a soggy leaf, and looked back to Lydia, as if for approval to stuff it in his mouth.

"No, Moses. Those are not for eating." She stood quickly to grab the leaf from his hand, only to be folded over with a stronger pain that radiated from her back and around her middle.

"Come on Moses, let's go see what Papa is up to." Bending cautiously, she lifted Moses with a squat and wrapped his legs around her hip and belly.

His arms flapped and his feet wiggled around as soon as he saw they were going to the barn. He loved petting the horses and "helping" Dylan work. He observed every movement his papa made as if he was making them a permanent memory for the day he could copy every task.

Twice on the way to the barn, Lydia had to stop and let the cramp pass before she could continue. Moses protested as she gripped him to keep him from squirming out of her arms. A brisk breeze flung leaves around at her feet, but her mind was nowhere near the weather.

Miss Hastings! She needed to get word to Miss Hastings.

"Dylan!" Lydia yelled, hoping he was in the barn and not far off in the pasture.

"Eya!" Moses mimicked Lydia and yelled at the barn as well.

Dylan ran out, a rake clutched in his hand. His face paled and the rake fell at his feet.

He rushed over and grabbed Moses, yet his eyes remained on Lydia. "It's time? Why didn't you ring the bell on the porch? Wait for one second while I lock the barn stall. Don't move!"

With Moses slung on his hip, Dylan raced into the barn. A clank and a slam later, he was back at Lydia's side.

"Can you make it back up to the house?"

Lydia laughed, feeling another wave of cramps begin. "Yes, but let this one pass first . . . they aren't—too bad . . . yet . . ." She bent her knees and leaned into Dylan.

His breathing quickened and Moses babbled on as if to tell his papa all about their morning.

"Okay . . . I'm okay," whispered Lydia.

They succeeded in getting to the house without another contraction slowing them down. Going upstairs was not an option. Dylan laid Lydia down on the couch and placed Moses in the living room playpen they'd bought after his choking accident. Moses whined, but Dylan seemed more concerned with Lydia.

He placed pillows behind her and covered her with a quilt. "Should I start a fire? Just to have it going?"

"Okay." Lydia knew labor could last a long while the first time.

Dylan paced and rubbed his forehead. "What was I doing?"

"Fire . . . you were going to make a fire." Lydia closed her eyes as the cramps became more intense. She rolled to her side and gripped the arm of the couch.

Dylan fell to his knees at her side and rubbed her back. "Does this help?"

Lydia nodded—her only able response until her belly began to soften and allow her to breathe. "Miss Hastings . . . you need to get . . . Miss Hastings."

Dylan stood and raked his fingers through his brown curls. "Of course! I was thinking there was something else we needed. Is there time for me to make a fire first? I will need to take Moses with me.

But first, I need to leave him here so I can go out and alert Pete."

Once Dylan left, Lydia sat up. She couldn't lie down when she felt capable of sitting or walking. She went to the kitchen and plucked a dried biscuit from the basket on the table. Then, she started a full kettle of water and whipped up a batch of eggs. Moses continued to belt out a blend of wails and unintelligible words from the living room.

When Lydia returned to him, a plate of scrambled eggs and a biscuit in hand, he giggled and reached for the food. Lydia pulled a chair to the play pen and shared the breakfast with Moses. He gnawed each bite with his gums, groaning and drooling and making an awful mess. But he was happy and seemed satisfied not being held for the moment.

The waves of cramps eased for a short while and Lydia felt relaxed. The water kettle screamed. She made sure Moses was finished with the food in his mouth, then went to steep some tea.

Dylan burst into the kitchen door. "What are you doing?"

"I'm fine. I can't simply lie there like that. I am sure it will get much worse, but until it does, let me move about the house . . . please?" She giggled and reached for his arm. "Women have babies every day, my dear. We will be fine." She kissed his cheek, lingering long enough to feel the tension in his jaw ease.

He smiled with only one side of his face and pressed his lips together. "I know . . . I know. But this time it is my child and my wife having the baby."

Moses screeched.

Lydia called to Dylan as he exited the kitchen. "I gave him some eggs and a biscuit. But he is probably ready to nurse and nap now."

He waved his hand to indicate he heard her.

Another wave of cramps radiated from her lower back and around the front of her abdomen. It grew tighter and tighter, until it felt as hard as the table she leaned on. She tried to breathe but had not inhaled enough when the cramps began. That one felt like the most intense one yet. When it was over, she took several deep breaths before clinging to the walls and making her way into the living room.

"That one was a little stronger than the others, though they seem to be coming further apart. What is Pete going to do?"

"I sent him to get Miss Hastings and to telephone my parents and Hattie in Grass Valley—or would you rather Hattie stay in town—"

"No, I need Hattie here . . . I want her with me. I know we will have a houseful, but I'd rather have that than be alone . . ." When the words escaped, she felt they came out wrong. With Dylan at her side, she wouldn't be alone, but what she meant was having her friend with her who had already given birth twice.

Dylan's forehead wrinkled briefly. Then he sighed and nodded.

By the time Lydia nursed Moses and Dylan laid him down to sleep, the contractions were closer and stronger.

Dylan had to leave Lydia on her own to bring in the horses from pasture. When he returned, she asked for him to take her upstairs—even if it took time. She needed the comfort of bed and to be nearer to the bathroom. Recalling some of the items Miss Hastings required for Hattie's birth, she asked Dylan to gather them, if for nothing else than to give him something to do. He seemed lost but his constant attention to her was causing more tension than she dared to verbalize.

After ensuring Lydia was as comfortable as possible, Dylan dashed downstairs to gather the items Miss Hastings would need.

What was taking Pete so long to get her?

Although he knew labor was imminent, he didn't realize he'd be this nervous. Was everything Lydia experiencing up to this point normal? She seemed relaxed about it despite the pain she must be enduring.

Lord, please keep your hand on her and our child.

A stream of panic entered Dylan's mind. Pete had lost his wife and child in childbirth. Would God allow such a thing to happen to him as well?

He shook his head. There was no reason to go down that path of thoughts. Miss Hastings was on the way and once she arrived, everything would be fine.

It had to be.

Clouds streaked across the sky. The sun was higher now, a silver-gold glow between the clouds and the deep-blue autumn sky. The morning was over and time for Megan and the other cows to be milked. But he could not leave Lydia alone again.

A low sound Dylan could not place came from upstairs. As it grew louder, he realized it was Lydia moaning. There had to be something else he could do for her. But all he could do was pray. Then his eye caught the banjo in the corner. Would playing it wake Moses? Not if he kept it low.

A pitcher of water in one hand, a glass in the crook of his arm, and the banjo in the other, he strode up the stairs. Then back down again to gather the other items. He saw the dust before he heard the wagon enter the driveway. Pete and Miss Hastings were finally here.

Skipping stairs, Dylan bound back up to the room.

"Lydia, sweetheart. Miss Hastings is here."

Lying on her back, but propped up to a near-sitting position, Lydia smiled sleepily. "Okay." She reached a limp arm toward Dylan.

He approached.

She clutched his hand. "I love you. Our baby will be here . . . before we know it . . ." She closed her eyes then. The blanket over her belly rose, indicating another contraction. Her gentle grasp tightened around his hand. He stayed, setting his hand gently on her belly and breathing along with his wife until it softened.

The front door creaked, followed by a clamor of footsteps. Moses whimpered from the crib, then pulled himself to stand, rubbing his eyes with chubby fists.

Dylan kissed Lydia on the forehead. "I love you."

He scooped up Moses from the playpen. But the infant dove toward Lydia, not even acknowledging Dylan.

"Mama is resting now, Moses. Come, let's go see Megan? You want to help me milk her?"

At the word Megan, Moses spun his head around and pointed to the window. Dylan felt proud that although Moses was a long way from speaking, he understood their words.

"Let me kiss him quick," Lydia whispered, eyes still closed.

Dylan obliged, then descended the stairs.

The afternoon blurred from one contraction to another. Before Lydia realized the time, she wondered why the room was so dark. Was it a rainstorm? She opened her eyes. It was sunset already. Miss Hastings sat in the corner, rocking gently and humming a hymn. Lydia heard the faint sounds of Olive and Brian echoing from downstairs.

"Where is Hattie?" Lydia rolled from her side to her back to get a better look around the room. But the motion triggered another contraction. She gripped the bed side and allowed the moans to increase along with her pain.

Miss Hastings kept humming and stayed seated. All Lydia could do was breathe slowly and wait for the pain to pass.

Then the sheets behind her warmed suddenly.

When her back and belly relaxed, she found her voice. "I'm wet . . . I think."

Miss Hastings stood, scooted over to the bed and flung the quilt back. The profile of her head nodded before the setting sky in the window behind her.

"Hattie was feeding the children dinner. I will get her, and a clean set of bedding. The sack has ruptured now. Prepare yourself . . ."

She scooted away from the soaked part of the bed and tried to turn again, only to be hit with a searing pain across her middle. She shrieked.

Miss Hastings didn't appear alarmed and continued to exit the room, leaving Lydia alone for seconds before Hattie flew through the doorway.

"Hey, little Mama." Her voice was soft, yet firm.

Lydia heard Hattie cross the room and felt the warmth of her sitting on the edge of the bed. "I've got a fresh cup of tea for you, when you think you can sip on it."

Lydia nodded and moaned, feeling lightheaded.

"You need to breathe." Hattie reminded her.

A few seconds later, Lydia could speak. It was then she took a deep breath. "I know . . . I keep trying . . . to roll over but when I do another contraction starts."

"Do you think you can make it to the bathroom? I can help you change and then we will swap out the bedding and you can lay on your other side once we're done."

"I can try. I feel like I've been lying here in the same place for hours. I need to move . . . even if it hurts."

Hattie nodded. Lydia had four contractions in the process but managed to make it to the bathroom, which provided some relief, even though it was temporary.

By the time Hattie and Miss Hastings had Lydia back in the bed, the pains felt as if they overlapped with little relief in between. The pressure built below until Lydia felt no choice but to bear down hard for relief. When she did, Hattie pushed back the quilt and Miss Hastings pulled Lydia to the end of the bed. Lydia screamed, not ready to be moved.

"I won't move you again, but now you are ready."

Lydia thought it was almost over. The room grew darker and Hattie left her side for a few moments and lit the lanterns and candles. Lydia set her head back, anticipating the next wave of pain. But nothing happened.

She closed her eyes and breathed long and slow, savoring the break. Miss Hastings took her stethoscope to the lower part of Lydia's belly. The room was strangely silent for several moments.

"Is everything okay?" Lydia asked when Miss Hastings only pursed her lips.

"Fine." Her cold fingertips pressed around the top and sides of Lydia's belly. "Get ready to bear down again, even if you don't feel the urge."

Lydia was confused and frightened. What did that mean? Would Miss Hastings tell her if something was wrong?

Her heart raced and despite the cool room, she began to sweat. Then her belly tightened rapidly— so much that she couldn't take in the air she needed to push hard. Hattie pulled Lydia's knees to her side, but to no avail. The pressure below did not change.

Hattie left for a moment and returned with more pillows. She placed them behind Lydia and then moved Lydia's hands behind her own knees. "I am going to help you from behind. If this does not work, there are other ways to deliver."

Confused again, Lydia felt tears sting her eyes. It seemed both ladies were holding back information, but all Lydia could do was follow her body's lead. The next urge was far greater, and she sucked in as soon as she felt it arrive. She pushed down hard, feeling her forehead strain and her eyes bulge.

When it was over, her teeth ached. She tried to look down and saw a dark spot on the bed. Her eyes met Miss Hastings with alarm.

"Just a little blood, Lydia. It's normal for some births. But Hattie is right. We should try to move you. The baby is not quite in position yet."

"Move, how?"

"Hands and knees."

She had to trust them both. It made little sense and she was afraid that moving would increase the pain. But she was ready for this to be over with—whatever it took.

"You sure you don't want a drink?" Pete tried to hand Dylan a shot glass of whiskey.

Dylan added another log to the fire and turned away from Pete and toward his mother. "No, thank you. I want a clear head when I greet my wife and child for the first time."

Jaina nodded with approval and tightened the blanket wrapped around a dozing Moses. "You will both have opportunity to celebrate soon."

Olive and Brian were deep into playing with the miniature doll house. Brian held a cowboy figure atop a wooden horse, making braying sounds. Olive tucked tiny children figurines into their bed and whispered prayers to them.

Then they both shot their heads up to face the doorway leading to upstairs. A long, loud scream echoed into the entryway.

Dylan's heart lurched into his throat.

Everyone in the living room grew silent. The crackling fire popped.

Another scream that sounded more like a grunt from one of the farm animals seemed to vibrate the room.

Brian started to cry.

Pete lifted him from the floor and sat him on his lap on the couch. "What's this cowboy doing, Brian?"

Brian smiled as tears dripped down his cheeks. "He chasi'n the ingins."

"Is that so? What did the Indians do to him?"

"They stole his cow, a' corse."

Jaina chuckled and glanced toward the doorway, then made eye contact with Dylan.

A second later, a sound like a mewing kitten floated through into the room.

It was music to Dylan's ears.

He wanted to bound up the stairs but waited for Hattie or Miss Hastings to come down instead.

Footsteps creaked above, then grew louder onto the stairs.

Hattie walked in, her cheeks wet with tears reflecting firelight. Her large eyes accompanied a soft smile. "Dylan, you have a daughter."

"Mama!" Brian and Olive dropped their toys. Brian leapt from Pete's lap and Olive raced to Hattie's knees, clinging tightly.

Dylan exhaled, his hands suddenly clammy. "C-can I see her . . . them?"

"Just a few more minutes. Lydia wanted me to tell you right away that they were both fine."

Lydia held her daughter close. Fat purple lips, a button nose, and long-brown eyelashes sat among a porcelain-white complexion. Her round face was smaller than a melon in early fall. Orange moonlight glowed from the window—the harvest moon had risen along with the waves of pain and welcomed this little darling into the world.

Miss Hastings left the room, soiled linens in a wicker basket. As she exited, Dylan met her in the doorway. Lydia only saw from the corner of her eye, unable to loosen her gaze on the infant in her arms.

Dylan sighed and approached gingerly. When at her side, Lydia shifted her gaze. Tears welled in her husband's eyes and they sat speechless for several seconds.

"How are you, my bride?"

"It is so hard to explain." Lydia spoke softly. "I am exhausted, yet exhilarated. Full of hope, yet full of fear. We have a daughter . . . a child of our own . . . fully dependent on us for years to come." She pressed her lips together and looked again on the face of her daughter.

"She is beautiful . . . just like her mother." Dylan set his hand on the sleeping infant's head.

"She is perfect . . . she has known nothing but the beat of my heart and the warmth of my womb. My heart breaks knowing one day she will know of pain and loss and the awful things in this world she will need to avoid. Suddenly, I know exactly why Mama kept me in the Valley all those years. She did not want this moment, this experience . . . to end."

Dylan winked. "Yet, this child would not be here had she had her way."

Lydia nodded. There was no way to completely shelter her daughter from the world. "But there is a way to keep her dream alive . . . to do whatever we can to love and protect our daughter for as long as possible."

"What is that?"

"I would like to name her Emelyn Ruth. For my mother and for the Bible story that represents so much of our own story."

"I think it is perfect." Dylan leaned in and kissed Lydia on the lips. Then he grazed his daughter's forehead with a father's kiss.

EPILOGUE

P ete and Hattie Evan took over Rolling Oaks Ranch later that winter. In time, they had made it a refuge for orphans and widows from the mines, the earthquake, or any other catastrophe that led to the need of a temporary home and work skills. Hattie taught the women to sew, who in turn became seamstresses for Lydia's shop in Grass Valley. Pete taught the men the ways of ranch life. The affection they had for each other remained as if they were newlyweds for all their years together.

The loss of their first loves had made this second chance that much more precious. And they were not about to waste it on petty arguments or filling their time with idleness.

Lydia and Dylan made Grass Valley their permanent home on December 24, 1906. As they celebrated Christmas and the coming year with their newborn daughter, Emelyn and adopted son, Moses, they had plenty of reasons to give thanks and praise to the Lord. He had given them the greatest gift aside from their salvation—a family to love and cherish and the chance to use their talents to help others.

Dylan's business plan allowed a percentage of sewing shop profits to be dispersed to fund the ranch, which reduced stress for Hattie and Pete to turn a profit while they sought to provide a valuable service to the community more than anything else.

Grandfather Sinclair and Uncle Frank visited often and took dress orders back to the city—already on the mend with rebuilding and new business ventures budding at every vacant lot. He'd sold the property of the Valley to the state park for the extension of the Bridgeport area. He then gave every dollar to the Rolling Oaks Ranch fund for orphans and widows. Hattie and Pete also came into town at least once per month.

During a dinner celebration on Valentine's Day 1907, Hattie announced she and Pete were expecting their first child together. Lydia gulped back a laugh, then revealed her own pregnancy—and a late October due date.

Amazed at all God had provided for them, yet consistently relying on Him for strength during the times of uncertainty, they knew that living by faith was an act of living daily for an unknown future.

No eye could have seen, nor ear heard, or heart have known the future that God had planned for this young and naïve couple. When their love alone was not enough, God's love sustained them. This is the legacy they would pass on to their children and grandchildren.

One evening in early spring, Lydia sat in their backyard garden. Emelyn Ruth lay in the cradle sleeping while Dylan took Moses on a walk to the hardware store—a favorite pastime for father and son.

In her hands, she held a brand-new diary and a pen. She had not had a diary before but had long desired the skill to pen her own story as it began in the Valley so many years ago. Facing the prospect of caring for a newborn, one-year-old and two-year old thrilled and frightened her all at once. If she did not get this story down soon, it may never be written.

She took in a deep breath and began . . .

The valley in which Mama and I lived seemed to have been cut off from the passage of time. At least it seemed that way to me, for it was all I had ever known . . .

Author's Note and Reference Section

To start, a note to the readers of my original *Beyond the Valley*—I apologize for not getting you Book 2 sooner! If 2020 taught me anything, it's that my writing goals can no longer be put off.

This story was so much fun to research and write. And it was a joy to dust it off, polish up the details and finally put it to print! I hope you enjoyed reading it even more. Lydia and Dylan's journey, though fictional, contains many truths that young couples come to discover if they are willing to stick things out.

The last line of the Epilogue is also a paraphrase of the writing prompt I received in my tenth-grade creative writing class at Nevada Union High School in 1992. At the time, my mom, my sisters and I were boarders at Oak Tree Farms horse ranch and boarding house in Penn Valley, California. Pete Brennan (represented in name only as a fictional character in this book) had and has since taken in exchange students and others over the past thirty years. The house shown on the cover of this book is the exact house where we lived on his ranch and is now recognized as a historical location in Nevada County, California.

The evening after I received the writing prompt, I was sitting in my room upstairs and looking out at the valley surrounding the house. It is there the story of *Beyond the Valley* was born, though it would take near thirty years for it to realize its full potential.

The area of Penn Valley, including the narrow, twisting road that leads from Oak Tree Farms down to Bridgeport and up to what remains of French Corral will always be a place of inspiration to me. During the unpredictable and unstable years I lived in Nevada County as a teenager, and then as a naïve newlywed and young mother, this place always reminds me of where I came from and of God's plan over my life—even long before I knew Him or how to call Him by name in my times of trouble.

I will always be grateful for His grace in new beginnings and how the Yuba River and its natural surroundings bring healing and peace to my soul.

References:

Writing *Below the Mountain* took detailed research, given the setting and events surrounding the 1906 earthquake in San Francisco, California. There are enough facts and stories out there to create one thousand novels! For the history buffs and San Francisco experts, I used and applied the most thorough research available to me as it related to this specific story.

The following is the list of resources I referenced to create authentic (though fictional) scenes, especially the ones that took place right before, during, and after the earthquake and fires.

- *Historic San Francisco: A Concise History and Guide* by Rand Richards. Published 2011 by Heritage House Publishers.
- *Disaster! The Great San Francisco Earthquake and Fire of 1906* by Dan Kurzman. Published 2001 by Harper Collins.
- *The Great Earthquake and Firestorms of 1906* by Philip L Fradkin. Published 2005 by University of California Press, Ltd.
- California Historical Society Research Library on site at 678 Mission Street, San Francisco, California 94105. (Multiple historical documents, journals, etc.)

www.ingramcontent.com/pod-product-compliance
Lightning Source LLC
Chambersburg PA
CBHW030833110726
47900CB00006B/1866